**She would have to be very clever
with Marcus Sergius Peregrinus.**

"So tell me," Annia said, sheathing her dagger, "where is this place you have my baby?"

He looked into her eyes, gauging them for sincerity, she suspected. "If you will come with me, I will show you. I don't have much time. I have to get back to my men soon."

"Aah," she said. "Well, don't let me keep you."

He cocked his head, a question. "You are coming with me?" he said.

"Certainly," she said, trying to keep the sarcasm out of her voice. "How else could I get to my baby? Only you know where she is."

They walked civilly, side by side down the dark street. The only light came from the uncertain moon.

She didn't trust this man. She knew better than he where her baby was. He had taken her daughter to the place of exposure, where the slave traders circled like hawks. Annia meant to get there.

She had to get away from him first.

When he turned, she took her chance. She ran.

MILINDA JAY

When she's not writing—or reading—books, Milinda Jay designs fun sewing projects for www.janome.com, and *Sew News* and *Creative Machine Embroidery* magazines. She also teaches college students how to write. She lives with her husband, five wonderful children and two dogs near the beautiful beaches of Panama City, Florida.

Her Roman Protector

MILINDA JAY

⟨H⟩ **HARLEQUIN**® LOVE INSPIRED® HISTORICAL

Recycling programs for this product may not exist in your area.

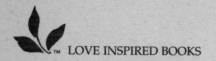 LOVE INSPIRED BOOKS

ISBN-13: 978-0-373-28253-1

HER ROMAN PROTECTOR

www.Harlequin.com

Printed in U.S.A.

If I go up to the heavens, you are there;
if I make my bed in the depths, you are there.
If I rise on the wings of the dawn,
if I settle on the far side of the sea,
even there your hand will guide me,
your right hand will hold me fast.
—*Psalms* 139:8–10

To my husband, Hal, my real-life hero,
who made this book possible.

Acknowledgments

It takes a community to write a book,
and I am so grateful for my writing community, without
whom this book would have never made it to print.
Thank you to Jill Berquist, Tanya Brooks, Mark Boss
and Janice Lucas for reading this book in draft form
and giving me wise suggestions for editing.

Thank you, Stephanie Newton and Kathy Holzapfel,
for teaching me how to write romance.
I'm still learning. Thank you, Michael Morris,
for sharing your writing wisdom.

Thank you to Dr. Sarah Clemmons and her amazing
assistant, Jan Cummings, for allowing me to teach
humanities at Chipola College, where my students
helped me learn all about the Roman Empire.

Thank you to the Cheshires, a group of fabulous writers
who gave me courage during the harrowing process of
getting a first book published: Carole Lapensohn,
Ruth Corley, Marty Sirmons and Mark Boss.

And thank you to my brilliant editor, Emily Rodmell,
who believes in me enough
to help make me a better writer.

Rome, 49 AD

Chapter One

Moonlight shone through the tiny window, casting a gentle glow on the face of Annia's beautiful newborn baby girl. The tiny gold bear charm on the baby's necklace sparkled for just a moment before the moon took refuge behind the clouds.

"If I could only tell you how much you are loved, and have you understand," Annia murmured.

She laid the baby down on the prickly straw-filled mattress and pulled the urine-soaked cloth from beneath the swaddling, deftly replacing it with a clean one. She picked up the newborn and kissed her tiny head, then cradled her in her arms.

"My sweet baby girl," she murmured into the soft newborn hair, "I will love you as much as a mother *and* a father."

Annia herself was not feeling particularly loved. Nine days ago, she had given birth alone except for the midwife and Annia's slave, Virginia.

Annia's husband, Galerius Janius, had divorced her on false charges of adultery. He had separated her from her two small sons and exiled her to this small villa at the outermost edge of Rome.

But he didn't take her baby. Not even he could be that cruel.

Or perhaps he had forgotten the baby in his rush to marry the wealthy cousin of the emperor.

Annia placed the baby in her wooden cradle, and the scent of rosemary filled the air. The mattress, stuffed with carefully chosen herbs, kept the infant safe from the chills brought by the heavy Roman mists.

The baby slept, and Annia considered calling Virginia for a taper. Perhaps if she read for a while, her heart would stop hurting so badly. She looked at the scrolls stowed neatly in the racks she had built on her wall. Maybe a Psalm would remind her she was not alone in her pain.

"Lord, keep my children safe," she whispered.

The ache of losing her boys hurt far worse than having her husband discard her.

Annia could only hope that Janius's new wife would find the boys tiresome and send them away. And then Annia could have them back.

Janius had made it clear for many years that he did not love her. Shortly before he accused her of adultery, he revealed that he had *never* loved her.

Perhaps her boys would remind Janius of Annia. Or he would want them out of his sight. Possibly she would get them back even sooner than she expected.

She lay down and covered herself with a light wool blanket. She might be able to sleep on this happy thought.

Before she could drift into blissful forgetfulness, the rhythmic crunch of hobnailed sandals echoed on the basalt-paved streets below.

It was the footsteps of soldiers. She sat up in her bed. Their torches lit the street below, reflections casting ghastly shadows on the frescoes covering her tiny bedroom walls.

The banging of bronze against wood told her they had come to her villa.

Why? What could they possibly want with her?

She heard Virginia shuffle down the stairs in her soft house sandals.

"Who's there?" Virginia asked.

"Marcus Sergius Peregrinus, commander of the *Vigiles*," a gravelly voice answered. "By order of the emperor Claudius, we are here to retrieve the stolen property of Galerius Janius."

"What stolen property?" Virginia asked pertly. "The only thing here is the wife he divorced, and she is no longer his property."

"It is not the woman we are here for," the gravelly voice continued. "It is the baby."

"The baby?" Virginia asked. "What does he want with her?"

"She is to be exposed before sunrise," the man said. "To die or be taken by the slave traders as the gods decree."

Exposed? The barbaric custom of leaving an infant out at the specifically designated place of exposure to die or be picked up by slave traders was something Annia had never expected to have happen to one of her own children. *Dear heavenly Father,* she prayed, *please, not that.* But the Roman father—the *paterfamilia*—had the power of life or death over any of his children. And he was not required to be merciful like her heavenly father.

Annia had always considered the ceremony shortly after birth whereby the midwife placed the newborn at the father's feet to be picked up and named or left on the floor, indicating it was to be exposed, merely a formality.

Surely, no father in his right mind would order his own healthy child exposed.

Annia tried to remember what her midwife had said when she brought the baby back to Annia. But the memory was a blur.

"Leave us alone," Virginia said to the gravelly voiced commander. "What possible harm can a baby do such a gallant as Galerius Janius? Does he fear a child?"

"That is not for me to determine," Marcus Sergius replied. "Now open the door, or we will be forced to open it for you."

The door opened. "Wait here," Virginia said. "I will get the child."

"Annia," Virginia called, running up the stairs, "Annia. The *Vigiles* are here."

"Is there a fire?" Annia asked, her humor masking the raw panic in her heart.

"No," Virginia said. "They've come to take Maelia. Galerius Janius wants her exposed. Do something, Annia."

Annia loosely belted her *stola*, the tunic-like dress— allowing it to fall easily over the coarse slave's tunic she wore beneath. She donned a blue silk *palla*. Rather than pinning the long oblong covering with the traditional bronze pin, she threw it casually over her shoulder and wrapped the baby in a matching blue silk blanket. She walked down the stairs, her footsteps certain, though her heart quaked.

"How can you be so calm?" Virginia asked. "They want to take her away."

"Be quiet," Annia hissed. "I will make certain they do not."

She walked beside the small pool that formed the center of her modest villa and into the atrium where her guests waited.

"You wish to see me?" Annia said to the commander,

demanding an accounting of his presence with her question. She handed Maelia to Virginia.

Marcus Sergius transfixed her with dark eyes under a leather helmet. His build was strong and hard, his chiseled features matched his gravelly voice. He was younger than he sounded, perhaps midthirties. And even in the uneven light cast by the lantern he held, she could see he was a handsome man.

She felt certain she had seen him before. Had she walked by him on the street as he led his men? That wasn't it. A dinner? That was it. He had been invited to one of Galerius Janius's dinners. It seemed a lifetime ago.

"May I see the emperor's order?" Annia asked.

He took a scroll from beneath his leather breastplate and handed it to her.

Annia examined the purple wax seal. She read the scroll. It was genuine. She looked up at the man. Marcus Sergius avoided her eyes.

"If you must go through with this barbaric practice on my child," Annia said, her voice steely, "then I will go with you. I will carry her to that place of death and lay her on a pile of rubbish myself." She handed Virginia the scroll and took Maelia from her arms.

The fierce commander raised his chin. "That is unheard of," he said.

"Just because it is unheard of does not make it impossible," Annia returned. She stood tall, but her height was nothing compared to his.

"Hand me the baby, *domina*," Marcus Sergius said, holding out his arms.

"I said I will take my baby to that place of horror." Annia pushed her way through the eight soldiers and out the large wooden door. She stepped out onto the sidewalk in front of her villa and began walking down the street, her silk *stola* swishing behind her.

The *Vigiles* stared, their mouths agape.

"What are you waiting for?" Marcus Sergius demanded. "Follow her."

She was soon forced off the street by a merchant's wagon, the metallic clamor of iron wagon wheels turning on stone pavement filling the air.

But she feinted to the opposite side of the street from the surprised soldiers. She looked behind her to make certain she had lost them.

She had.

The night police—*Vigiles*—were heading in the opposite direction.

The moon was her friend and ducked behind a cloud just as she melted into a narrow alleyway.

Sheltered by the darkness, she shed her silk *palla* and *stola* and dropped the baby's blanket. Beneath all of it she wore the rough homespun of a slave, and her baby was wrapped in slave's swaddling. Annia wore soft leather *calcei,* as well. The moccasins were comfortable and perfect for running.

She had no time to take off the baby's golden *crepundia* necklace, its tiny toys jingling on their string, nor her own gold necklace with its matching bear charm. She prayed no one would notice the expensive jewelry marking her as anything but a slave. She wrapped the baby tightly in the rough wool blanket she'd hidden beneath the silk and fashioned a sling from her long wool belt.

She secured the sling around her and tucked the baby beneath her breasts.

And then she ran.

The streets of Rome at night were dark and noisy, filled with merchants carrying their wares in the carts that were forbidden on the Roman streets by day. As long as she stayed close to the swiftly moving traffic, she was safe.

She looked like a slave, as her former husband had often reminded her. She was small and dark like her mother's people in Britain. Her eyes were large and brown, and her hair was dark and so curly that she had to keep it cut short like a boy's. Otherwise, it grew in a wild tangle around her face that even the patient Virginia was hard-pressed to comb out.

In the darkness she could not see to avoid the street trash and nearly slid on a pile of smelly kitchen offal, scattering a group of howling street cats dining on their supper.

Fueled by anger and fear, Annia ran. She was quick and she was strong. She listened for the telltale sign of hobnailed sandals following her, but heard none.

Had she escaped so easily?

She had never been so grateful for her athletic training in Britain as she was now. She had been the laughing-stock of other Roman matrons when she was married to Janius because she insisted on training like a man. She ran. She exercised. She even sparred with anyone willing to take her on.

In Britain it had been necessary. Even after Claudius had come and secured the island for Rome, you never knew who or what might jump the stone fence of your outpost farm and try to seize your cattle and rob your stores.

In Rome, the exercise allowed her to live within the stifling social order with a measure of contentment.

She paused, hiding behind an erect wooden board inserted into the pavement. The board and weighted bronze bolt safeguarded the jewelry shop behind it. Maelia slept, tied snugly against her.

It was completely dark. She heard movement at the

end of the street. When the moon peeped from behind the cloud, she could see a human figure stop, walk forward a little, then stagger against a wall.

She breathed a sigh of relief. It was only a drunk.

She crept from behind the sheltering board, looked right and left and dashed down the now dangerously moonlit street. She prayed the moon would hide itself again, but it did not.

Annia felt she was running in glaring daylight, so bright did the moon shine. She could see the cracks in the basalt squares of the road. She could almost make out the lettering on the walls above the closed shops.

She grasped the baby nestled safely in the makeshift sling. Fear propelled her forward once again. But when she turned down the next alley, she ran directly into a hard-chested Roman soldier who grasped her tight.

Marcus Sergius hadn't expected to find her so quickly, but he thanked the one God that he did.

Only Marcus could keep this baby safe, but he hadn't the time to explain that to her.

The woman struggled like a bear. He held her tightly against him, careful not to crush the infant. He felt Annia's warmth through his thin leather chest-plate. The baby nestled beneath Annia's protective arm, her other arm pinned safely beneath his.

She kicked his shins, her legs surprisingly strong, though her moccasins were too soft to cause any real damage. She tried to bite through his leather breastplate.

She was nearly successful.

"Give me the baby," he said to her. "I won't hurt her." He tried to keep his voice level and calm, but he found himself jumping with each vicious little kick.

"You won't hurt her?" she said, jeering. "No, you probably won't. She wouldn't be worth much on the slave market if you damaged her."

This was not going as he intended.

He had managed to successfully separate himself from the eight new recruits, but at any moment one could appear. They were young and stupid. None had seen battle. Each thought soldiering glamorous.

Young fools. He hoped they would never see the horrors he had seen in Britain against Caratacus and his guerrilla warriors.

Could she understand if he tried to explain that he had a safe place for her baby? The fury in her voice and the steely anger in her eyes told him what he needed to know.

Perhaps he could take her with him. No, that would be too dangerous. She was beautiful.

And that very beauty would be noticed. Someone would see him accompanied by such a lovely slave carrying a baby.

No, he had to take the baby and leave her here. He would come back for her later.

It should have been easy. He thought back over his plan. It usually worked. It had worked many times before. He went into the house in the dark of night. He took the baby. He sent his young recruits to rest at the local eating place under the auspices of needing to be alone while he exposed the baby at the vegetable market.

But what really happened, that is, what really happened on every night except for tonight, was that instead of taking the baby to the vegetable market to be picked up by slave traders, he took the baby to his mother.

His mother took the teachings of the Master very seriously when He said to care for widows and orphans. She left the widows up to someone else, but she set it as her life's mission to care for orphans, specifically the babies that would most certainly become slaves or die if left on the rubbish pile.

And her strong, handsome son, home from the war and conveniently placed as the commander in charge of the *Vigiles,* was the perfect accomplice.

But Annia was different. He had never come in contact with a mother who fought so immediately for her baby. Usually, the husband ordered the wife drugged with poppy juice so that she was unaware of exactly what was taking place.

Of course, this was the first baby he had taken from a divorced woman. It was also the first he had taken so long after birth. Usually, the marriage was intact, and the husband simply did not want to divide his wealth with another child. The child was taken at birth, and the wife complied because she feared losing her marriage.

A stomp on his toe brought him back to the very real woman in front of him. He was going to have to render her unconscious. He knew this, but he did not want to follow through. It was the only way he was going to be able to get her baby to a safe place without attracting any further notice.

He would have to act quickly. He placed his fingers on her jugular and pressed. He held her other arm down, and kept the arm on the baby.

He caught her when she fell, untied the baby and left the woman there. He knew she would awaken very quickly, and he had to be gone when she did.

The baby slept, but Marcus took no chances. He sprinted through the dark back streets of Rome as if he were going to the market. But, instead of turning at the road leading to the forum, he doubled back around the baths and ran as quickly as he could to his mother's house.

He had no time to explain why he was dumping the

baby unceremoniously in the *ostiarius's* arms. The elderly man who watched the door was accustomed to such wriggling bundles.

Marcus couldn't let the woman stay on these streets alone at night. She could be captured or worse. Anger filled him at the thought of the things that could happen to her.

He had to reunite her with her baby.

He turned as quickly as he could and sprinted back to where he had left her.

She was gone.

Dear God, he prayed, *please let her be safe.*

He passed street after street with no sign of her. He tripped over a family sleeping outside in one alley and scattered a group of young street urchins in another.

Where could she have gone?

He retraced his steps, this time more slowly. Had someone taken her? Had he gone past her? Did she know a different way to the place where babies were exposed? Was she thinking of another place of exposure?

And then he realized that she had probably already reached the forum and was searching in the offal for her child.

How could he be so stupid? He had seen how quickly she ran. Why hadn't he gone there first?

Now it was he who was sprinting as if his life depended on it. What made this woman so important? He tried to convince himself he would have done the same for anyone, but he knew differently. Something about her haunted eyes, her quick-thinking ruse. Here was a woman who gave it all, held nothing back.

When he heard a group of men laughing and heard her scream, he moved swiftly in.

The men were circled, one holding her by the hair, another holding a lantern up to her face.

"What have we here?" the man holding her asked. He was large, probably a blacksmith or shipbuilder, someone accustomed to using his body for hard work. His muscles glinted in the firelight, and the group of men surrounding him waited.

But they waited like hyenas who watch prey caught by a lion. They would take their turn only after he had his fill.

Marcus knew he would have to be very careful.

"So there you are, you little minx," Marcus said, striding into the center of the circle, his voice as deep and loud as he could make it.

It had the intended effect, startling the men with its volume.

Even the blacksmith, or whatever he was, jumped a little, but he maintained his grasp on her hair.

"Running from me once again. You thought you could get away this time, did you?" Marcus strode into the group of men breaking through them as if he were the emperor himself.

"Thank you, sir," he said to the blacksmith.

Marcus grabbed Annia roughly and jerked her away. Fortunately, in his surprise, the blacksmith let go of her.

Marcus pulled her away, berating her all the way, "You curly-haired vixen, what did you think? Were you thinking I wouldn't catch you? You wait until I get you home…."

Annia let out a small yelp when he pretended to slap her face, and the men circled around them and laughed.

"Thank you, sirs," Marcus said, putting a hand over Annia's mouth. "This little one has run away one too many times. I may have to sell her at market."

"I'll buy her," the blacksmith said. "How much will you take?"

"Well," Marcus said, "she actually belongs to my father. But give me your name and where you conduct your business, and you will be the first one to know when we put her up for sale." Marcus shot the man a charming smile. "I would shake your hand, but as you can see, mine are quite full."

The men parted to let him through.

"Suetonius Rufus," the blacksmith called. "My shop is three streets over near the baths. I'm a blacksmith," he continued.

"Thank you, sir," Marcus said. "I will remember you by your red hair."

The man touched his hair, and Marcus pulled Annia safely away around the corner, out of the man's line of vision.

When they reached the safety of the baths, Marcus took his hand off her mouth.

"You did me no favors," she spat. "I would have escaped on my own." And she unsheathed a tiny dagger to prove it.

"Really?" he said, pulling her into the dark recess of the inner fountain. "Well, *domina,* next time, I will let you defend yourself."

She was shaking and held the dagger to his stomach. "Where is she?" she hissed. "Where did you take my baby?"

"Put the dagger down, and I will tell you," he said.

Chapter Two

He must take her for a fool. How many other women had this handsome man lured into believing he was saving their babies, when in truth, he was selling them into slavery?

She had to be very careful with this one. He was strong, he was smart and he seemed determined.

Well, she had fought fierce warriors in Britain, hadn't she? Surprising them with her strength?

He would not be surprised. He had already gauged her strength. She would have to be very clever with Marcus Sergius Peregrinus. Very clever indeed.

"So tell me," she said, sheathing her dagger, "where is this place you have my baby?"

He looked into her eyes, gauging them for sincerity, she suspected. "If you will come with me, I will show you. I don't have much time. I have to get back to my men soon."

"Ah," she said. "Well, don't let me keep you."

He cocked his head, a question. "You are coming with me, yes?" he said.

"Certainly," she said, trying to keep the sarcasm out of her voice. "How else could I get to my baby? Only you know where she is."

They walked civilly, side by side, down the dark street. It was a few hours before dawn, and the streets were now quiet. Even the merchants' carts had stopped, having already delivered their wares.

The only light came from the uncertain moon and the pitch-smeared torches illuminating sacred images at a few street corners and crossroads.

She didn't trust this man. She knew better than he where her baby was. He had taken her to the place of exposure where the slave traders circled like hawks. Annia meant to get there.

She had to get away from him first.

The silence was broken by the cascading water of a neighborhood fountain. When they reached the fountain, the statue of a small boy—his arms reaching out in supplication, a stream of water flowing from his mouth—was illuminated by a single flame placed strategically at the water's edge.

During the day, this same fountain was busy with women, children and slaves taking turns filling their wash buckets and water jars to carry back to their homes.

But tonight, it was eerily silent, the only sound the soft rush and gurgling of the water.

"Are you thirsty?" Marcus Sergius asked.

Annia was thirsty, incredibly thirsty. She ignored his offer of help and reached up to the trickling water, cupping her hands and drinking deeply.

Marcus waited for her to drink her fill and then reached up to drink.

When he did, she took her chance. She ran.

Apparently, he had expected her to run and he caught her before she even reached the pavement at the edge of the fountain.

They both went down on the hard stone, he on his back and she atop.

He grasped her arms, and she kneed him in the stomach. She pulled away and unsheathed her knife.

Both on their feet, they circled each other. His breathing was heavy, as was hers.

She jabbed, but he pulled back and then reached for her knife.

But she was quicker.

His eyes widened. She was used to it. He hadn't expected her to be this good with a weapon. What proper Roman matron could wield a knife with such dexterity?

The look on his face now was one of respect. What had he recognized? Before she could move again, he had countered. He seemed to know exactly what she was going to do before she did it, and now he was holding her wrist, tightening his grip until she was forced to drop the knife.

"Trained in the wilds of Britain, as well?" he said, his voice ragged.

Now it was her turn to stare wide-eyed at him.

Fury strengthened her. She poised to run as soon as she had the chance.

"I would rather not do this," he said, "but you leave me no choice."

With the dexterity of a battle-trained legionary, he caught her wrists in a leather thong and pulled it securely. Her wrists bound, she was forced to walk humbly behind him.

"Where are you taking me?" she asked. "I know your type," she said. "Ready to make a gold coin off anything possible."

She could tell from the set of his shoulders that she had angered him. He said nothing.

"I have money," she said. "I can buy my child from you. I can get you all you need."

"I don't want your money," he said.

"I've yet to meet a soldier who didn't want money, who wasn't willing to buy his way to the top so that he could stop fighting and send other men in to do the bloody work."

At this, he turned on her, yanked the leather cord down, savagely squeezing her wrists so tightly that tears smarted in her eyes. He pulled her close.

"You, *domina,* have no knowledge of what you speak. Close your mouth, and let me take you to your baby before I change my mind."

The struggle in his face was palpable. She had struck a chord in this man. A deep one. The pain in his face spoke of unspeakable horrors. She was embarrassed and ashamed, but she was not certain why.

He was her enemy. He had her tied with a leather thong. Why did she feel such compassion for a man who had sold her baby and was now leading her to be sold?

She almost apologized but held her tongue.

She had no choice but to allow him to lead her to the place of enslavement. Perhaps, if she was blessed, she would at least be enslaved with her baby.

They stopped in front of a row of shops separated by a high wooden double door replete with bronze doorknobs.

Annia recognized the front door of a grand villa.

In the center of each door was a giant bear's head holding a large ring in its mouth to be used as a knocker.

A bear's head on a Roman door? Odd. Usually, the door carried a wolf, or even a lion, but rarely a bear.

Was it a sign? In Britain, bears meant strength and survival.

Characteristic of very wealthy Romans, this villa

rented its street-front rooms to various shop owners, their signs barely visible in the darkness. There were four shops on either side of the door. Annia leaned back to see how many floors this villa held.

Three stories high. She guessed that the shop owners lived directly above the shop, and perhaps the floor above that was rented out to other tenants.

She had been the mistress of just such a villa.

Marcus lifted and dropped the knocker.

It sounded her doom.

Immediately, the door opened.

Annia felt her fate closing in on her. Why? Why had Janius been so determined to get rid of her baby girl? Did he fear having to provide a dowry for her? Did he fear he would have to divide all his new wealth with his youngest daughter?

And if he was so quick to get rid of this newborn, what would keep him from getting rid of their two young sons?

Surely Janius would not harm his own flesh and blood.

And yet he knew this newborn child to be his, and he had no qualms about exposing her.

Annia closed her eyes and whispered a prayer. *Protect me, Lord. Protect my child.*

"Mother," Marcus said, his voice registering warm surprise. "Why are you up?"

"I had a bad feeling about this one," a woman's voice responded, "but you have brought her home safely?"

Home? Annia wondered. *Home for whom?* But she had no more time to ponder this question.

"Annia," Marcus said, "I would like for you to meet my mother, Scribonia."

Annia felt slightly off-kilter. Such a formal greeting for a would-be slave?

And Scribonia? Wasn't that the name of her midwife? Surely not the same woman.

When Marcus moved out of her way, the lanterns lighting the atrium were directly behind the woman, blinding Annia and reducing the woman before her to dark, shadowy outlines. Annia could not make out the woman's face or even the color of her clothing. She seemed tall, taller than Annia, and very thin.

Annia couldn't tell if this woman was her midwife or not.

The woman seemed to be reaching for her.

Annia was frightened. What did the woman want of her? She wished that she could see better. She glanced at Marcus, but he had already moved forward, into the atrium behind his mother. He brushed past her.

"I must go now, Mother," he said, and kissed her on the cheek. "Already, I fear the men may have left their duty and gone home."

"Be careful, son," his mother said, and then turned her attention to Annia.

Annia recognized the voice now. It was the midwife. She held something in her arms, and she was reaching to hand it to Annia.

When Annia held her hands out in response, the soft bundle placed there was none other than her baby girl.

Marcus gave a satisfied nod before closing the door behind him.

The night was black, the black that happened just before dawn. Marcus knew he'd better hurry if he was going to catch his men at the eating place before it closed.

Why had she been so stubborn? Why hadn't she believed him? In spite of himself, Marcus was confused. He liked to be trusted. She hadn't trusted him.

But then again, why should she have trusted him? He came into her house in the dead of night demanding to take her baby to be exposed.

How was she to know that he really didn't mean to do it?

Could she learn to trust him?

Why did he care? What did it matter? His brain felt twisted in knots.

He couldn't stop thinking of her.

He was back in Rome and looking for a wife, not the divorced mother of three children.

But there was something about the woman, something fierce, something beautiful, something that made him yearn to protect her.

It was late, and he was tired. Otherwise, he wouldn't be thinking such thoughts.

When he arrived, his men were waiting as instructed. They were the last customers.

Trained to be as faithful as Roman soldiers in the field, the *Vigiles* sat around a long table, their mead cups before them. When one nodded, his neighbor clouted him awake.

The penalty for sleeping on guard in the field was death by stoning. The men were loyal to one another as well as to their sergeant.

"Sir," one of his men said, "we feared for you."

"We thought to come after you," another broke in.

"But the order," a third said, "was to stay here until you returned."

They looked up at him hopeful, fearful.

The Roman army was built on fear, and these young men longed to be a part of the army.

Marcus felt for them. He remembered the same longing for adventure, the taste for discipline, the desire to be a part of something that would allow him to prove himself.

And get away from his family.

Wasn't that the dream of all sixteen-year-old boys?

"You've done well, men," Marcus said. They tried not to smile, but the boy in each of them couldn't help being pleased. "Let's go."

They gathered their leather coin purses and strapped them to their belts.

Marcus paid Gamus the merchant, and his close friend. "Thank you, Gamus. I apologize for the long night."

"Ah, Marcus. I am happy to help you. But before you go, step back here. There is something I'd like to show you." The merchant waved him into a back room, and Marcus sent the men outside, where they lined up in close formation.

Marcus nodded and waited for him to speak. He knew Gamus had something important to say.

"What I've heard is not good for us, Marcus," Gamus said, his voice hushed so that Marcus had to lean close to hear. "There is talk that the emperor wants the Jews out of Rome."

"We are not Jews," Marcus replied. "We are followers of the Christ."

"Ah, but Claudius doesn't know that. He sees us all as one big group of rabble-rousers. When the Jews go, I fear, so must we."

Gamus straightened another amphora, pulling his cleaning cloth from beneath his belt.

"But where? Where is it safe? The empire stretches past knowing," Marcus said. He had heard this rumor himself, but had thought it just that.

Gamus's words frightened him. What about his mother? What about her villa full of rescued babies? How could they possibly be moved?

"It seems he merely wants us out of Rome," Gamus replied.

"I see," Marcus said, somewhat relieved. At least they would not be banned from the empire. "Do you have a place to go?"

"Yes, I have a country estate in Britain," Gamus said, "a gift granted by Claudius for my long years of service in the army. My wife and I would like to retire there one day. Perhaps sooner rather than later. And you? Where would you go?"

The thought of leaving Rome was something he did not want to consider. He had just returned to the city of his birth after having been gone for twenty long years of service. He had a dream to stay here, to gain enough power to bring peace to his city.

"I don't know," Marcus said. "My father would love to move back to Britain, as well. He was happiest there, I believe. I would rather stay here. I believe I can be of the most use right here."

"That may be so. Well, lad, perhaps the emperor will leave us alone. We are a peaceable people."

Marcus agreed. It was the very peace of his faith that made him long to become a prefect.

"Well, my friend, thank you for entertaining my men."

"Is the baby safe?" a female voice boomed, startling both men.

Gamus's wife appeared in the stairwell next to the storage room. She was wrapped in a white linen robe, her hair mussed from sleep. Her warm smile, round, rosy cheeks and jolly disposition seemed at odds with her booming voice.

"Yes, Nona, the baby is safe." Marcus smiled up at the kind woman.

"Good, good, then," she said, clapping her hands together. "Now see your men home and come back here. I have dough rising, and by the time you get back the bread will be baked." Her eyes sparkled and Marcus had to say yes, and pray that her voice didn't wake everyone on the street.

"Thank you, Nona. You always take care of my stomach."

"Well, child, you need your strength to traverse this wicked city. You must walk many miles each night."

"Not so many," Marcus said.

Nona smiled and retreated up the stairs. "See you in the morning light," she said.

"How are the rescues going?" Gamus asked. "I worry about you, lad."

"My mother's villa is full to bursting," Marcus said. "I'm not sure she can take any more babies. Tonight might have been my last rescue."

"Good," Gamus said. "I don't like the danger for you. Too easy to be seen. Your mother has done a good thing all these years rescuing those poor, abandoned infants and trying to reunite them with those mothers who did not want them exposed. But she is only one woman, and Rome is a large city with many abandoned babies every day."

"She only rescues the ones she delivers and knows the mother's heart to be broken when the father orders exposure for lack of dowry money or some perceived weakness," Marcus said.

"I know, lad, but it is becoming dangerous for you."

"I do worry that my men are growing suspicious," Marcus said.

"Not to worry. I give them as much mead as they want."

Marcus laughed. "Thank you, my friend."

"Good night, then," Gamus said.

The night was spent and the gray dawn of morning rose around them as Marcus led the men down the street and back to their garrison.

The hobbed nails of their boots pinged against the stone as they marched into the early light.

The men were good, but what was he doing here leading a group of eight firefighters on a mission to keep the city safe, night after night?

He had a plan. He just prayed it worked. He had distinguished himself in Claudius's wars in Britain. Serving under General Vespasian in the II Augusta Legion, he had fought to secure the southern and midland territories, but the north and west were yet to be subdued. He had been offered land in Camulodunum, which he accepted, but chose to continue his service in Rome rather than retiring after the requisite twenty years of service in Britain. Aside from despising the cold, damp climate of Britain, he had ambitions. Ambitions that could only be fulfilled in Rome. Ambitions that he hoped this Galerius Janius could help him fulfill.

"Sir," one of the young men said, snapping Marcus out of his deep rumination.

They had reached the wealthier section of the city. Here the doorways were wider and the walls marble. The shops hid grand villas behind their walls whose owners rented the street front of their villas to merchants. This served a dual purpose. Besides bringing in a tidy sum in rents, the shops buffered the noise of the streets away from the living quarters. The villas were veritable oases in the heart of the city.

The sun's rays dappled pink upon the neatly swept street and sidewalks, quiet but for the sound of iron bolts being opened and boards being stowed away, marking a new day for the shopkeepers.

As it was too late for shop carts and too early for chariot traffic, the street itself was deserted.

Except for Galerius Janius, who stood in the middle of the street before his massive villa, waiting.

"Marcus Sergius?" Janius said, stopping the *Vigiles* with an upraised hand. "My friend," he said. "And how goes it with you this fine morning?"

His well-fed belly hung over the edge of his tightly belted tunic, and he balanced his carefully wrapped toga imperiously over his arm.

"Well, sir, and you?" A prickle of doubt ran through Marcus. Perhaps he should not have trusted this man. Had he been followed? Had someone seen that the baby was safe in her mother's arms rather than in the place of exposure?

Marcus couldn't imagine what had made Annia marry the man standing before him. Perhaps she had little choice. Perhaps it was a marriage arranged by her father.

Perhaps she had reason for the adultery of which she was accused.

"Yes, yes," Janius said, measuring Marcus and then his men. "A fine crew you've assembled here."

Marcus nodded. "Yes," he said, "the emperor has very clear guidelines for the *Vigiles*. They must be able to fight fires as well as keep order in the streets. For this reason, the requirements of service are the same as for a legionary." Why did he feel the need to defend his men against Galerius Janius?

"Really? How quaint," Janius said. "Well, if you would like to come inside, I can pay you for your troubles."

Janius headed into his house, confident that Marcus would follow.

When Marcus didn't move, Janius turned. "You did follow my orders, did you not, soldier?" His eyes narrowed, and he looked more carefully at Marcus.

"I did," Marcus said. Something in the window above caught his attention. But whatever it was moved away as soon as Marcus looked up.

"And was your little mission successful?" Janius asked.

"It was," Marcus said, though the words were bitter in his mouth. To give this man satisfaction was more difficult than he imagined. He wanted to paint the true picture in painful detail for this man.

The baby Janius had ordered exposed, the baby Janius wished dead or enslaved, was safely ensconced in a villa even more lovely than this, being nursed, no doubt at this very moment by Annia herself.

What he had done was dangerous. If Janius discovered the truth, Marcus's hopes of becoming prefect, or even an important member of the Praetorian Guard, would be destroyed.

"And was the little beauty snatched up by slave traders or eaten by dogs?" Janius snorted and laughed.

"I didn't stay to see," Marcus said affably, clutching his sword.

"Well, good, then," Janius said. "The less offal on the streets of Rome, the better. I have no intentions of supporting an unfaithful woman's spawn."

Marcus's hold on the *gladius* tightened. Janius noticed.

"Armed for warfare, are we?" he asked.

"Just habit, sir," Marcus said, his voice affable still. "As you said, the less offal on the streets of Rome, the better."

Janius's eyes narrowed.

"Well then," Janius said. "Good day."

"Good day to you, sir," Marcus said.

"Oh," Janius said, turning around. "Here is a coin for your troubles."

"No, thank you, sir. It was my duty. The baby had been ordered exposed at birth and was not. The law was broken. My men and I went in to correct a wrong. It is my job to be sure that the law is upheld."

Janius looked at him, his head cocked to one side, as if he was gauging the truth of his answer.

"What a fine man of the law you are, then," Janius said, the words dripping with sarcasm. "I will still keep my end of the bargain and recommend you for a promotion in rank." His smile was wide, his eyes narrow.

Marcus's expression was impassive.

The men waited as Janius turned again and walked into his house. As soon as the door closed, however, Marcus looked up and caught sight of two little brown eyes peering at him from the open window above the shops.

Clearly, this was Annia's son. He had the same small features, the dark eyes, curly hair. He looked nothing like his father.

And based on the look of horror on his face, the little boy, who could be no more than ten years old, had heard the entire conversation.

Marcus wanted to tell the boy his baby sister was fine and his mother, too. But he had no way of doing so.

And the boy had clearly marked him as the enemy. The one responsible for taking his baby sister to her death.

Chapter Three

The woman, Scribonia, led Annia to her room. They climbed two flights of narrow wooden stairs, above the shops, above the shopkeepers' quarters, into the very top floor of the villa.

Both Annia and Scribonia wore soft leather indoor sandals. So silent were their footsteps that Annia could hear the gentle breathing of babies as she walked by the rooms leading to hers.

Scribonia held her lantern high, parting the curtain that formed the door of the small room so that Annia could see her way in.

The room was bare but for a cradle, a small bed and a table.

Scribonia lit the candles in the bronze wall sconces and one on the small table beside the narrow wooden bed. Candlelight flickered on the mother-of-pearl shells inlaid in the wood, and played on the rich red damask bedcover.

It smelled pleasantly of rosemary, and brightly painted murals covered the walls. Annia would have to wait for the morning light to make out the images.

"We'll talk in the morning," Scribonia said. "You and

your little one have been through quite the ordeal. I hope you find peace and rest here."

She kissed Annia on the forehead, and Annia felt the tears well in her eyes. Scribonia kissed her as her mother might have.

The midwife disappeared down the hall, the curtain door fluttering behind her before Annia could think to express her gratitude.

And thank her son, Marcus.

How terribly embarrassing for her that she had not done so.

When Annia allowed herself to relax on the bed, she could not stop thinking of the look on Marcus's face as he left the villa.

It was the look of a job well done. It satisfied him that she was here safe and sound with her baby.

Annia longed for someone who made her feel safe and protected. But she was afraid to hope for such a thing. To hope meant letting her guard down, and then who would protect her?

Her life for the past few months had been anything but safe and protected. Nothing was as it seemed. Could she really trust these seemingly kind people?

What did they want from her? Was it money? Power? Position? Annia was hardened by the excesses of those who had surrounded her since she came to Rome as a young bride.

Rome was vile. She had learned early to trust no one. Here, status and power ruled supreme. She would leave it as soon as she possibly could. She longed for friends and family that she could trust, those she had left behind in Britain. Here, Virginia had been her only true friend. Yet Virginia was also her slave.

As soon as she was able to do so, she would draw up papers for Virginia's freedom.

Her baby girl nuzzled her breast, reminding her what *was* important.

She slept only a few hours before Maelia woke her with tiny snuffling sounds. The early morning sun shone a pale orange through the tiny window.

Scribonia knocked lightly, and Annia called her in.

"Good morning," Annia said. "What would you like for me to do?"

Scribonia smiled wryly. "What can you do?"

"I can grow flax, I can take it from flax to linen, or I can harvest it for linseed oil or flaxseed. I can spin the yarn and weave it into cloth, and embellish it with embroidery." The words tumbled from Annia's mouth, and Scribonia's smiling and nodding kept her talking.

"I can raise sheep and shear them. I can card wool and spin it, I can weave it and sew it. But the best thing I can do with wool is to make it repel water and to sew a *birrus*."

"Do you mean you know how to make the hooded capes that soldiers treasure for their ability to insulate against the cold and rain?" Scribonia's smile was joyous.

"Yes," Annia said, "I can."

"You are a child of many talents," Scribonia said.

Annia blushed with pleasure at being called thus.

"I can also grow herbs, herbs that cure and herbs that make food taste good," Annia said.

"But you are only one person," Scribonia said. "You can't do all of this here. Which is your favorite? Which do you prefer doing?"

Annia thought long and hard. "It's a very difficult choice," she said.

Scribonia laughed again. "Yes," she said, "I'm guessing it must be. Most of the women here I must teach how to do the simplest things, but you, you could teach us all how to do many things."

Annia smiled, and the warmth in her heart grew. It had been a very long time since she had been praised by someone who wasn't her servant or her slave. It felt good.

She looked up at Scribonia and thought about how much she had smiled when she mentioned the *birrus*. "I think my favorite thing must be working with wool," she said.

Her comment was met with a wide grin from Scribonia. "I was hoping you would say that. I would love for us to be able to make water-shedding capes for our people and maybe even sell some in the market. Why, that would give us enough money to add on to the villa and save more babies."

"How did Janius discover Maelia lived?" Annia asked.

Scribonia was silent.

Annia filled in the silence. "I suspect it is because Rome is small, and the tongues of the gossips busy," she said bitterly. "Someone told someone who then told Janius that my baby girl was alive. He couldn't stand it, could he? His great fear was that his fortune would be divided among too many children. Once he ran through all of my money, he had to get rid of me and find another woman, one whose money and family connections could buy him the position he wanted."

"Ah, yes, but don't be bitter," Scribonia said. "Because those very gossips who revealed the secret of your baby also revealed the secret of Janius ordering the baby to be exposed. And because of those gossips, I was able to make certain that Marcus was the man sent to do the deed."

Annia blushed at the thought of Marcus and the trouble she had caused him.

Scribonia looked at her as if she read her mind. "Don't worry. I knew you would fight for your baby. But I didn't know you were trained as a fighter. I didn't realize I was sending my son on a mission that might endanger his life—not from the slave traders, but from the baby's mother."

Her blue eyes danced, and Annia knew Scribonia liked her spirit.

"I am so sorry," Annia said. "I had no idea."

"Of course you didn't, you poor child. You simply wanted to protect your baby. Now, let's get started with your morning work."

Scribonia called to a woman old in years, but the woman's movement made her seem much younger than she was. "Basso, could you take Annia out back? She knows something about sheep."

They walked through the villa past the *lararium,* the family altar that, in most Roman homes, was dedicated to the household gods. But in this home, Annia now knew, the altar was dedicated to the one God. They reached the inner garden surrounded by the marble-columned peristyle. The porch formed a shady area around the inner garden, protecting the rooms surrounding the garden from the harsh July sun.

In the outer garden, past the living quarters of the villa, was a second pool, this one much deeper and clearly meant for bathing or swimming.

She loved swimming. There was a river close to her home in Britain fed by a warm spring. She and her mother had loved bathing and swimming along its banks when the weather warmed. She hadn't been swimming outside since she was a young girl. The possibility filled her with joy.

They walked through to the rear entrance of the villa. It opened out onto a large field.

Basso pointed to her right. There was a small pasture with a nice-size herd of sheep. Just below it was a round pen with three sad-looking sheep.

"We aren't very good with sheep, it seems," Basso said wryly, pointing to the three penned sheep. "I'm pretty sure these are badly in need of shearing."

Annia laughed. "I'll see what I can do."

Beyond the sheep pen was a stream, fairly swiftly running. It eddied and swirled, and there were places where it grew large and then narrowed again.

"The stream is perfect for washing the wool," Annia said.

"Really?" Basso said. "So far, it has been good for nothing but overflowing its banks during storms and giving us all a lot of extra backbreaking work."

Annia could hardly wait to get started.

A young woman trailing a toddler walked up to her as she headed for the sheep pen. Annia stopped to greet her.

"I was hoping I would get to meet you soon," the young woman said, her green eyes sparkling, her hands out to welcome Annia. She was a little taller than Annia, with bright red hair and a sprinkling of freckles. "You're new. I'm so glad you are here. My name is Lucia. And yours?" Her words tumbled one on top of the other.

"Annia," she said. "And this is Maelia." Annia opened the sling, revealing the sleeping infant.

"Oh, she is lovely. I know you must be so proud."

"I am," Annia said. She looked around, surveying the walled garden, the vast fields, the stone fence.

"You are worried you were followed?" Lucia asked.

"Yes," Annia said, "aren't you?"

Lucia laughed. "No, not really," she said. "This is Julius."

Julius was a sturdy tot, well into his second year. He darted away from Lucia and ran as fast as his chubby legs would carry him to the sheep.

"You can't imagine the trouble he's gotten into," Lucia confessed. "He'll make a great soldier, though. He fears nothing. I named him Julius after the great conqueror and emperor."

"He is wonderful," Annia said, and meant it. Julius reminded Annia of her own two boys, and her heart pulled so hard that tears rose to her eyes.

Lucia didn't notice. She had a watchful eye on Julius.

"Are you going to help with the sheep?" Lucia asked.

Annia nodded and smiled. "Yes, I'm eager to see them." She arranged a soft bed for Maelia beneath the shade of an olive tree, using the baby sling for both cushion and cover.

Lucia led Annia to the pen. She opened the rickety gate and waited while Annia inspected their coats. They were well past shearing time.

"I wasn't sure when to shear them," Lucia said apologetically.

"Do not worry," Annia said. "We will just need to take our time combing the wool."

Lucia nodded solemnly.

The sound of dogs barking sent shivers down Annia's spine. The sound continued. She looked at Lucia.

"They bark every time there is a visitor," Lucia said. "You would be surprised at how good their hearing is. Why, I've been way back out in the olive grove, surrounded by the dogs, and the next thing I know, their ears are pricked up and they are bolting to the front entrance, barking the entire way."

It hadn't taken Janius long to find her, was all Annia could think. Maybe not. Maybe it was just a street vendor. Why would Janius want to find her anyway? Hadn't he ordered her away and the baby disposed? Annia looked over at Maelia and then looked around for a safe hiding place.

But just then Annia heard a splash, then a plop. She recognized the sound, and then she heard thrashing. "Where's Julius?" Annia yelled, torn between saving her own child from Janius and Julius from drowning.

Annia ran for the stream, looking for Julius. She thought she saw a tiny hand and ran for it. She yanked off her *stola* and stripped down to her linen shift.

She ran into the water and swam for the child, who had now disappeared under the water and was only visible by his thrashing.

The current had dragged him to the center.

Annia swam hard, then dove underwater where she thought he might be. The spring was clear, and the baby was struggling, his eyes open. He was paddling like a tiny dog trying to make his way to the top.

Annia snagged him and pulled him up, laughing with relief at the surprised look on his face.

He coughed a little, then tried to head back into the water. The little fish.

"You saved him," Lucia said, snatching him up and hugging his sopping body to her chest, soaking her *stola* and nearly suffocating the child in the process. "I can't swim," she said to Annia. "He would have drowned if you hadn't been here." She began sobbing, and the little boy cried with her.

Even through the cacophony of the wailing sobs, Annia could hear the dogs barking. It was Galerius Janius after her. She was sure. She snatched up her clothes, wrapped Maelia in her sling and ran.

Chapter Four

The dogs signaled his arrival at his home. He heard them start their clamor when he was at the front of the villa.

His mother cleverly drugged the dogs on the nights he planned to bring home an exposed baby.

But at all other times, the dogs were loud and seemingly aggressive, though not really. They barked but then almost broke their backs wagging their tails and licking whoever walked through the front entrance.

Marcus looked over the tiled rectangular pool with its myriad fountains straight through to the *tablinium*, his father's formal office and reception room. Framed on either side by marble columns, the peristyle garden formed its background. The impressive office was built by his grandfather during the reign of Augustus and was the place where clients came to speak with his father each morning.

Some came to borrow money, others came to lend, and some simply came to socialize. They sat in the long marble benches on either side of the *impluvium*, often lulled to sleep by the tinkling of the water as it trickled from the roof and flowed through the many fountains.

Marcus strode over the blue-and-white floor mosaic tiles and straight in to see his father.

"Ah, Marcus," his father said, beaming when he saw him, rising from his massive ebony desk with its mother-of-pearl inlays and coming forward to embrace his son. "I will be glad when you can allow yourself to fully retire from the service," he said.

"I would hardly consider being the head guard of the night watchmen service," Marcus said.

"But you chose this profession," his father responded.

"If there is ever anything I can help you with here…" Marcus started to say.

But his father held his hand up to stop his words. "No, no, my son. All of this I have under control. You choose your own life. Do not feel burdened by the obligations here. As of yet, there are none. I am hale and hearty and easily manage."

And it was true. His father, Petronius Sergius, at fifty-seven years, managed very well on his own. His hair was white, but his body was in perfect shape. He exercised daily at the baths and was proud of his physique.

"Here," his father said, "sit." He pointed to one of the folding stools, and Marcus unfolded it and placed it in front of his father's massive desk.

He sat and enjoyed the view of the brightly colored painting on the wall beside his father. The painting reached across the entire wall and featured a woman playing a lyre with her little boy looking over her shoulder.

"Your mother would like to have you home more, but I say build your own life. Any word of the new position?"

"I've heard nothing yet," Marcus answered. "I'm starting to ask for favors from a few men who I think might be able to put in a good word with the emperor."

"Be wary of those from whom you ask help," his father said. "Remember, you will be in their debt."

Marcus studied his father. Had word traveled back so quickly, then?

"I've enlisted the help of one Galerius Janius."

"I've heard of the man," his father said. "Cousin to the emperor through his new wife. Divorced his first wife on charges of adultery. What did he ask of you in return?"

Marcus looked down. How could he tell his father the truth? What had sounded like an easy deal at the time now seemed somehow corrupt.

"He asked that I take the baby born to his first wife to be exposed."

His father tried to mask his shock. "And you agreed?" he asked, gripping the sides of his desk.

"I brought her here. It seemed harmless," Marcus said. "If I exposed the baby, I knew the baby would live. If someone else did it, the baby would die." He felt the blood rise to his face.

"And indeed, in a sense, it was harmless. But do you understand that your harmless idea may have endangered every woman and child in this house? Do you understand that a man like Galerius Janius trusts no one, as he himself is not trustworthy?"

"I'm sorry, Father. I had not considered the risk," Marcus said. How could he have been so thoughtless?

"Were you followed?"

"No, not home," he said. Had he been followed? He was certain he had not. Possibly to Gamus's shop, but nowhere else.

"You are an experienced soldier. I trust that you know when you are being followed. I trust you to protect this house."

"Yes, Father. I am sorry," Marcus said.

"We will hope that there will be no repercussions on this particular escapade," his father said. "We will speak of it no more."

"Thank you, Father." His father was the *paterfamilias* and was owed respect. Marcus had no trouble showing that respect. He felt it deeply.

"Eventually, this place will be yours," his father said, his tone no longer chastising.

Marcus was relieved. "Yes, I know that, Father, but you and Mother have many, many good years left."

His father laughed at this. "Your mother would like nothing more than to spend the rest of her days here saving babies. I can't say that I blame her. Her work is good."

Marcus raised his eyebrows at this. His father noticed.

"Father, I don't mean any disrespect, but I'm not sure that saving a few babies is going to make a dent in the thousands of babies that are taken into slavery." The words that had been swirling around in his brain had finally found a voice. Marcus felt uncertain about his thoughts.

"You may be right," his father said, without judgment. "But we are called to help those within our reach. If everyone could just help those that are put in front of them, think of what a wonderful world we would live in."

Marcus considered his father's words. Was he right?

"When I was a young man," his father continued, "I felt the same way you do, son."

Marcus's eyes widened in surprise. It made him feel better that even his father had doubted.

"But as I get older," his father said, "I understand God's call on our lives to be less grand and, instead, very personal. We are called to minister to the ones God puts right in front of us. And we are wrong to give up because we can't save the entire world. We may not end infant exposure in the Roman Empire, but each life we save is precious."

"I hadn't thought about it like that," Marcus said.

His father nodded. "I hope one day to retire to the estate in Britain. I wouldn't mind going home to finish out my days."

His father had been born in Britain, where his father's grandfather had arrived with Julius Caesar and decided to stay. His grandfather had established a thriving trade between Rome and Britain, and maintained a villa in both places. Marcus's father brought his mother to Britain to help manage the estate built on land that had been bought with olive oil. He liked the simplicity of life in Britain.

"How was our villa in Britain when you saw it last?" his father asked.

"Prospering," Marcus said. "The crops were thriving, the sheep reproducing and making enough wool to make an army of capes."

"If only we had someone who knew the secret of making those capes," his father said. "We could make a fortune."

They strode out the back garden and into the field beyond. Marcus wanted no listening ears around when he spoke with his father about Annia.

But his father was called back by a client and was forced to return to his office.

Marcus would have to wait.

He looked out over the fields, hoping to catch a glimpse of Annia. He wasn't certain, but he had a feeling she would be drawn to the fields, and not to the work inside the house.

"Are you looking for something, master?" It was Basso. Her wise old eyes missed nothing.

"The young woman I brought in last night. Is she well?"

"Yes, your mother set her to work with the sheep." Basso smiled.

"The sheep?" Marcus asked. It seemed an odd assignment.

"Yes, at her request. It seems she was raised in Britain and knows something about sheep."

Marcus remembered the street skirmish. She had fought like one of the blue-skinned warriors, though minus the poisoned darts. He scanned the field but didn't see her.

"Thank you, Basso," he said. "Your flowers are, as usual, the pride of the family garden."

She smiled appreciatively. "It's a tricky business," she said, "tending medicinal herbs. Some must flower to unleash their healing powers, and some must not. I have to be aware of each individual plant, and watch them as if they were a yard of two-year-olds."

Marcus laughed, and Basso turned back to tend the flowering medicinal herbs in the inner garden.

He was glad she turned. Marcus didn't want Basso to see his fast gait and guess how much he wanted to see the girl again.

But nothing escaped the notice of Basso. "Why so eager?" she called out to him.

Marcus had to smile.

"I like sheep," he said, laughing.

"Is that it?" she said, and chuckled. "Go along with you, then."

He walked to the sheep pen, but the only one there was young Lucia and her waterlogged toddler, Julius.

"Well, little Julius," Marcus said, bending down to talk

to the little boy who seemed not the least bit disturbed by his sodden state. "What happened?"

The boy stuck his thumb in his mouth and gazed solemnly back at Marcus.

"He fell in our spring-fed stream, and thank God, Annia can swim. She saved him."

Julius sucked his thumb and nodded, waving his fingers for emphasis.

Marcus laughed, but was immediately sober. "How frightening that must have been for you," he said to Lucia.

"Not really," Lucia said. "The truth is, I didn't even realize what had happened until Annia fished him out."

"Where is Annia?" Marcus asked as casually as he could muster.

"I don't know. She gave Julius back to me, said something about dogs barking and then snatched up her baby and sprinted for the olive groves. The woman is like no one I've ever met. She swims like a fish and runs like the wind. Who is she, really, and where is she from?"

"That, my friend, is a very good question," Marcus said. The less the women knew about one another, the safer they all were.

"Well, when you find her, let me know," Lucia said. "I need her to teach me how to take care of the sheep."

"It looks as though you've got your hands full looking after your own little lamb," Marcus said, indicating Julius. "Are you sure you don't want to find something inside the inner garden to do? Might it be safer there for your little one?"

"Perhaps I should consider harvesting the flax. That field is the farthest away from the water," Lucia said, shaking her head.

Marcus laughed and headed toward the olive grove. The silvery-green leaves and gnarled trunks comforted

Marcus. He had spent many happy boyhood days in the shady grove, imagining himself a soldier.

"Annia?" he called, but there was no answer. He walked among the trees. Where could she be, and why would she be hiding?

The olives would not be ready to harvest for another two months. What could she be doing out here?

He thought again about what Lucia had said about Annia hearing dogs barking and understood her fear.

Just then he heard the baby cry, a tiny mew, followed immediately by Annia. "Shh," she whispered, "it's all right."

She was very close.

"Annia," he said, and heard her sharp intake of breath. "I am alone. No one else is here. The dogs bark at everyone who comes to the front gate for my father. No one knows who you are but my mother and me. Please don't be afraid."

Annia crept out from behind an olive tree, her infant in her arms. He wanted to comfort her.

"And how do I know I can trust you?" she asked, her eyes dark and serious.

"I don't know how to prove myself to you," he said, calmly, evenly, looking deeply into her soft brown eyes. "All I can say is you must try to trust me."

His encounter with Janius gave him some insight into her fear. Most of the women felt safe and secure behind the thick concrete-covered stone walls of the villa. He wondered if Annia would ever feel safe.

She looked at him warily. Then glanced beyond him—it seemed she needed to verify the truth of his words.

Her gaze returned to study him. Finally, after what seemed like an eternity, she nodded. "All right," she said. "I think I can do that."

He relaxed a bit and was suddenly overcome with a very uncharacteristic lack of assurance as to what he should say next.

But she spoke for him. "Now," she said, "why don't you come help me shear some sheep?"

Just like that, she shifted from a frightened deer to a cheerful companion. He admired her verve.

He laughed, and tired though he was, he followed her to the sheep. There would be plenty of time for sleeping in the afternoon. For now, he was going to enjoy her company and maybe learn something about shearing sheep.

And he was going to think of a way to put Janius off the trail of this woman and her baby. Permanently.

Chapter Five

The presence of Marcus calmed her, and she was able to focus on the task at hand. Shearing sheep.

The shears were dull. Annia sent Lucia to the kitchen with them and a request to have the cook sharpen the shears with her stone.

Lucia was happy to get Julius as far away from the stream as possible.

Meanwhile, Annia directed Marcus in the fine art of sheep bathing.

"We have to bathe them before we shear them," she said. "We need to get rid of all the excess matter in their coats that might dull the shears."

Apparently, whoever had been in charge of the sheep had not paid attention to this nicety.

"That sounds reasonable," Marcus said, nodding agreeably and awaiting further instructions. She liked that he was willing to learn from her. Most men resisted instruction from a female.

"Where is your sheepdog?" Annia asked.

Marcus seemed surprised by the question. "I think all the dogs are in the atrium," he said.

"Not those dogs," Annia said, "your sheepdog. The one that is trained to herd sheep."

"I don't think we have an actual sheepdog," Marcus said. "Our coin comes from olive oil, not sheep. I think all of our sheepdogs are in Britain."

She raised a quizzical eyebrow but didn't have time to question him further about her homeland. Instead, she had a challenge in front of her. One that was proving to be more difficult than she expected. She tried to remember if she had ever bathed sheep in a stream without a sheepdog helping her.

She hadn't.

"Well, it looks as though you're chosen," she said to Marcus.

"Chosen for what?" he asked.

"To be the sheepdog," she said.

She hoped he was as affable as he pretended to be. If not, this was going to get very interesting very quickly.

"You are going to run behind those bedraggled creatures you call sheep and drive them, one at a time, into the stream."

He looked at her for a moment and then burst out laughing. "You want me to play the sheepdog?"

"Yes," she said, smiling.

Marcus shook his head. "I've done many things for women. But never this. Pretending to be a sheepdog to these bedraggled sheep?" he said, cocking his head to one side and grinning.

"Yes," she said, then continued her instructions. "When I finish giving the beast a quick dunk in the spring, you are going to need to drive her right back into the pen."

Marcus grinned. "Are you trying to make a fool out of me, or is this what must happen?"

Annia smiled. He really had never worked with sheep.

"Well, you may look a little foolish," she said, "but the sheep will be washed and ready for shearing."

Annia was quick to fashion a hanging cradle for baby Maelia.

First, she removed the bronze pin that secured the long, blanketlike *palla* to the shoulder of her short-sleeved shift, her *stola*.

Scribonia's gift, the *palla,* was long and octagonal, made of a finely woven lightweight wool. It was perfect for fashioning into a makeshift cradle on the lowest branch of an ancient olive tree that grew alone a few yards from the stream.

She felt Marcus's admiring eyes on her makeshift cradle, and had to laugh.

"Is there anything you can't do?" he asked.

"You are very easily impressed," she said, "that or you haven't been around many mothers with babies. Though when I think about it that seems odd since your mother has a house full of them."

"I haven't been here long," Marcus said.

"Really?" Annia said. "I thought you were born and raised here."

"Off and on," Marcus said. "But I joined the service as soon as I could, a bit before my seventeenth year. I finished my twentieth year in the service this year and came home to plan what I will do next."

"And what will that be?" Annia asked, hoping in spite of herself that it would be something close by.

Ironically, this man—who had come to her private abode with an armed guard to take her baby—made her feel safe.

"I don't know yet," he said. "Now, tell me which sheep you want to start with."

Annia turned her attention back to the sheep. It was clear he did not want to talk about his future plans.

Was it because there was a woman involved? Was he promised in marriage to someone?

It made sense. He was young and handsome enough to land any woman he wanted. His parents probably had the perfect young woman picked out for him.

Why should she care? She shouldn't. But she did. She would like to know that this man, whose company she was beginning to enjoy, was not thinking about another woman.

Stop this foolishness. You will never remarry. You don't want to. You aren't interested in men. Marriage was the most miserable state you've ever experienced. You were forced to be with a man who didn't love you, who said you looked like an elf, not a woman, who kept you only for your dowry.

She shook off that downhill spiral of thoughts, shed her *stola* and marched down to the stream clothed only in her tunic.

She found a sandbar and positioned herself on it.

"All right," she said, "send in the first victim."

Marcus walked into the pen and chose the closest sheep.

He positioned himself behind the dirty sheep and pushed her forward.

She circled back around behind him.

He tried it again.

The sheep circled around behind him.

He looked up to see Annia laughing at him.

"You think this amusing?" he yelled, positioning himself behind the sheep once again.

His yelling had an unintended effect. The startled

sheep surged forward. He bolted with her, and all the other sheep followed.

The sheep lopped along wildly in the opposite direction from the stream.

"You make a poor sheepdog," Annia said, laughing until tears streamed down her cheeks.

He ran to catch up with the sheep and tried herding them as if he *were* a sheepdog, barking orders behind them, "Move, go, go." Finally steering them all back into the pen so he could start all over again and perhaps get it right.

Once inside the pen, he looked over at Annia, who was still laughing. "I think I can do it now," he said, laughing with her.

This time, he was careful to position himself behind one sheep and slam the gate quickly behind himself before the other two escaped.

When the sheep made it into the stream, Annia wrestled her down into the deeper water, careful to hold her shaggy fleece so that she didn't float away. Annia scrubbed the filthy coat as best she could, then guided the flailing sheep safely to the shore. She watched Marcus try to herd the sheep into her pen.

He ran like a crazy man, whooping and clapping to herd her.

When the sheep was safely fastened in her pen, he looked up at Annia.

"How did I do?" he asked.

"Very well," she said. "I'll make a sheep farmer out of you yet." He really seemed to care what she thought. It made her happy.

"Just what I've always wanted to do," Marcus sa d, "grow up and be a sheep farmer."

She laughed, and he brought the next sheep out.

When all three sheep were washed and ready, Lucia, trailed by Julius, arrived at the pen with newly sharpened shears.

"I hate to send you back in again, but I forgot something. Can I get you to go back and get some old cloths to pat them dry?" Annia asked.

"I'm happy to," Lucia said. "Going back and forth keeps Julius busy. He likes going on errands. It keeps him from straying."

Lucia's happy smile brought yet another pang to Annia's heart.

She missed her boys.

Would she ever see them again?

Before she was divorced and sent away, the boys, at ten and six, were jolly, joyful things, always getting into scrapes in the back garden, trying to catch some bird or small animal for their make-believe wild jungle.

They'd heard of the wild jungle from some of the slaves. The boys had worked hard to make their own.

Tears smarted in Annia's eyes.

Marcus noticed. "Is something wrong?" he asked.

"Nothing," she said, wiping the stray tear from her cheek. "Just missing my boys."

"Your boys," Marcus said, "they mean a lot to you."

"The world," Annia said.

Marcus thought of the brown-eyed child peering at him from the window at the top floor of the villa of Galerius Janius earlier this morning.

The child was loyal to his mother, that was clear.

There was nothing Marcus would love more than reuniting Annia with her two boys. His father might be right. Perhaps God called His people to help others, but only one at a time.

Right now he had to make a plan to get Janius off their trail. As soon as they finished shearing the sheep.

"You start with three shears down the belly," Annia said after she had wrestled the first sheep to her back and wedged the sheep's head securely between her legs.

Quickly and expertly, she sheared. "See?" she said. "First, you hold the skin taut with your left hand, and three quick shears, and you are finished with the belly."

She held up the wool for him to examine, then tossed it beside her.

"This is the tricky part," she said, and gingerly sheared between the sheep's legs.

"Next, you roll her over a bit, and three more shears gets the back leg, then the tail, the neck and the shoulder."

She cut expertly, and very soon there was a pile of wool beside her. After she laid the sheep down one more time and sheared up the back, she checked the sheep's face for leftover hair, and the task was complete.

She made it look so easy and even fun that he wanted to try it. He wasn't certain why, but suddenly it seemed important to him to please her.

She helped him out, but it wasn't as easy as it looked.

"Look," she said, flipping the sheep to its back, "now you stand over her, and secure her head between your legs, like this."

She placed her hands on Marcus's legs, parting them just enough for the sheep's head, and then pulled the sheep between them, and with her sure hands squeezed his knees back together around the sheep's head.

"See," she said, looking up at him, "it's easy."

He tried to focus on the sheep. It wasn't easy.

When she looked up at him to see that he understood how to hold the sheep, he opened his eyes wide and nodded. "Yes," he said, a little too eagerly, "I get it."

He could smell the sweet scent of her hair. Was that lavender?

He had forgotten the fragrant pleasure of women who smelled good. In Rome, the custom was a daily bath. Sadly, this was not true in the rest of the empire, and the smells of dirty human bodies had sickened him time and again as he traveled through crowded conquered cities.

But this sweet smell, sweet touch… This might be what he had returned to Rome for.

But no, he thought. *She has three children, she is divorced—she is not what I planned.*

Perhaps planning was not the answer.

He couldn't remember the last time he had so enjoyed a morning. Watching Annia shear the sheep was something he would never forget.

She was a small woman, but she was strong and agile, made obvious by the way she was able to hold the sheep down to shear them.

The sound of barking dogs cut through his ruminations.

He checked Annia and was relieved to see that she was so busy with her shearing that she had heard nothing.

"I'll be back," he said. "We need bags for the wool."

She nodded her approval without looking up, and he left.

The hair on the back of his neck was raised. The barking of the dogs did not sound normal.

Usually, they barked and were silenced by the slave as soon as the visitor entered the house.

But this time, he heard the dogs chasing someone through the villa, barking madly. The sound was coming closer. Marcus pulled out his *gladius* and ran.

He ran inside the walled garden and slammed the outer door securely behind him. He stood guarding it.

The only entrance to the back fields was through this wooden door. A stone wall surrounded all of their fields, built by his great-great-grandfather during a time when the empire was not yet an empire and fields were not secure from foreign invaders.

No one would get past him and through to Annia and her baby. No one.

A clatter of footsteps on the stone-and-marble floors, then soft padding as the intruders, followed by the slaves and barking dogs, hit the grassy garden.

"Stop. Stop, I say." Marcus could hear two of the house slaves yelling at the top of their lungs, in hot pursuit of someone.

The first thing in his line of vision was a young boy, no older than ten, chased by barking, slathering hounds, followed close behind by a group of panting house slaves.

The boy feinted to the right and left and lost them around a curve of rosemary hedge. Marcus had to admire the boy's skill.

Who was he? He looked so familiar.

No. It couldn't be.

The boy caught sight of him, and ran at him, teeth bared, fists raised, ready for the kill.

Marcus dropped his *gladius* and held his hands out to catch the boy.

But the boy was more clever than that.

He pulled a knife from his belt, and now Marcus had to somehow wrestle the knife away from the boy without cutting himself or the boy in the process.

The slave that grabbed the boy from behind was unprepared for the blade, but the boy did not wish to waste it on the slave.

He aimed and threw, and had Marcus not looked up

from the slave's hands to the boy's arm, he might have been hit squarely between the eyes.

The boy's skill was undeniable.

Marcus ducked, and the knife pinged into the wooden door, quivering.

The slaves had the boy on the ground now, and would have made short work of him.

"Stop," Marcus said. "Let him go."

"Let him go?"

"Yes," he said.

"But he tried to kill you."

"Yes," Marcus said, "I know. He believes himself to have good reason to do so."

The boy struggled on the ground. "Murderer," he shouted when his face was no longer buried in the dirt. "Kidnapper. May your skin be blighted and your children die in their mother's womb. May your days be full of pain, may your death be horrible and your afterlife worse."

"A mouthful for such a small boy," Marcus said, whistling admiringly.

"I'm not small," the boy said.

When Marcus signaled once again for the slaves to let the boy go, he ran straight for Marcus and would have gouged out his eyes had Marcus not been prepared for the assault.

"Go get Annia," Marcus ordered one of the slaves.

"Who is Annia?" the slave asked.

The boy grew still.

"My mother?" he asked, his voice quavering.

"The new woman we brought in last night with her baby."

The slave moved through the door behind Marcus.

"So you are the slave trader," the boy said through clenched teeth.

Marcus held him securely, his arms crossed behind him. The boy was stronger than he looked, just like his mother, and just as quick and lithe.

"You look very much like your mother," Marcus said.

"No," the boy said.

The moment Marcus relaxed his grip, the boy slipped from Marcus's grasp and bolted for the open door.

Marcus watched him run past the slave and into his mother's arms, knocking her to the ground with the force of his crazed embrace.

Marcus knew they were both crying, and he called the slave off.

"Leave them be," Marcus said. "They have much to talk about."

Marcus walked into the villa, trying to remember what it was that had brought him in.

The bags. That was it. He needed bags for the sheep's wool.

His father met him halfway down the villa walkway.

"I think we need to talk," his father said, and pulled Marcus into his study.

"Who was the child?" his father asked.

"The son of Annia, the woman we brought in last night."

His father looked past him into the atrium where water flowed peacefully into the *impluvium* from the open-mouthed cherubs.

"I fear this child spells trouble for us all," he said.

"Yes," Marcus said, "but the trouble began before the child came, though he has certainly multiplied it. One of my men reported to me this morning that Galerius Janius—the man who ordered the baby exposed—does not believe she was actually exposed."

"Do you think he will come looking for you?" his father asked.

"He already has," Marcus said. "In the barracks. There is no danger of him following me home. The men don't know where I live," he added.

"And the boy?" his father queried. "How did he find you?"

"I think he must have followed me from his father's house. I saw him watching us from the window when I reported to the father that the deed was done." Marcus squirmed uncomfortably on the small wooden folding bench that sat in front of his father's massive ivory-inlaid ebony desk.

"Do you think anyone followed him?" his father said.

"I don't think so," Marcus said, "though I can't be sure."

"Well," his father said, "we must do what we can to protect the other women and children we have housed here. We can't risk the lives of so many."

"What do you propose, Father?" Marcus asked.

"They must go."

"Go?" Marcus repeated. "But where?"

"Far from here," his father said.

"Give me two days, Father. I think I might be able to come up with another solution."

His father studied him. "You are an experienced soldier. Battle-hardened and wise. But something about this woman… Otherwise, why would you risk so many lives?"

Marcus felt his stomach tighten. "I know what it must seem like to you, Father, but I think that a better plan can be found. And you needn't worry. She is not the right woman for me. But it is a matter of honor to protect her."

He believed his own words. She was not the right woman for him. But she was lovely.

"Make it fast, son," his father said. "You have no time to lose."

Chapter Six

"I thought you had died, Mama," Annia's son Cato said, lapsing into his baby name for her, "and I thought the baby was eaten by dogs."

"We are both here, safe and sound," she said. She hugged him hard, so hard that he pulled away.

"Mother," he said, reverting to the formal address, "you are suffocating me."

Annia laughed. "I am sorry. I am just so happy to see you."

"And you say the soldier, Marcus, saved you? Brought you here to this safe place?"

Annia nodded and smiled. Out of the corner of her eye she saw Marcus slip through the gate again and come out in the green pasture. He sat with them beneath the gnarled olive tree.

Cato turned to Marcus. "I owe you an apology. You've saved my mother and my baby sister. For that, I am eternally grateful. Accept my apology?"

Marcus stood and shook Cato's hand as if he were a grown man.

"I accept," Marcus said.

Annia tried not to smile overmuch.

Cato dropped Marcus's hand and offered him a stiff salute.

Marcus nodded. "Very good, son, very good. You will make a Roman soldier yet."

Cato's smile covered his entire face.

Annia wondered when the last time Galerius Janius had paid attention to his son, as Marcus had just done, or offered the boy hope for the future.

"How do you like my home?" Marcus motioned for the boy to sit down and then sat down beside him.

"Very much. It is quite lovely." Cato turned to his mother. "There are so many babies here, Mother. More than I've ever seen in one place in my life. I had to dodge them running through the villa to find you."

Annia nodded. "Scribonia is the mother at this house. She has been saving babies whose mothers want to keep them, but whose fathers have ordered to be exposed."

"And my job," Marcus added, "is to help make certain the babies make it here safely. And the mothers, too, if that is their heart's desire."

Annia caught him stealing a glance. She looked away but blushed. She was half embarrassed and half proud of the fight she had put up against him.

Cato nodded solemnly. "When I'm a father," he said, "I'm going to keep all of my babies."

Annia laughed.

Marcus patted his back, and Cato pointed to the baby. "She is lovely, Mother, sweet and pink. I'm so glad I could see her. She looks so comfortable there." His voice was wistful as if he longed to be the baby in the front pack.

Growing up was hard. Harder when your family fell apart when you were ten. How awful this had to be for him. Divorce was common in Rome. But that it was common certainly made it no easier on the children.

Annia unwrapped baby Maelia. "Would you like to hold your new sister?" she asked.

He smiled in answer and held his arms out for the babe. Annia eased Maelia onto his lap.

Annia looked at her two beautiful children. She had not expected to be allowed this joy, this pleasure, ever again. Annia smiled over his head at Marcus. She hoped he understood how very much she appreciated all he had done for her.

He smiled back.

But she needed her third child, Flavius, now more than ever.

Cato held his baby sister and kissed her head. "I will never leave her," Cato said solemnly. "I'll protect her. Father doesn't want her, but I do. Why doesn't Father want her, Mother? Why doesn't he want you?"

Marcus's instant scowl told her all she needed to know about his feelings for Galerius Janius.

"I don't know why your father doesn't want us, Cato. I think he believes that money and power give him happiness. You must remember that true joy comes from God alone. If you read your scripture and pray, if you find good friends who believe in the one God as you do, and live a life of love, you can find happiness."

"I know all of that, Mother," he said, exasperated. "You've taught us that since I was a baby."

Annia smiled and took his hand and squeezed it. "You are a good student, Cato."

He smiled, but she could tell there was something on his mind that he needed to say.

"Father's new wife doesn't know the Christ. And Father has changed the altar. It's to Hera now," he said, "and some other gods and goddesses that I don't know."

Annia's heart beat hard in her chest. This was not good

news. This was very frightening. The lives of her boys were in grave danger.

She exchanged a glance with Marcus.

"Has she said anything to you about your worship?" Marcus said.

"No," Cato said, "but Father doesn't answer our questions, so I'm not sure what to do."

Emperor Claudius cast a blind eye on Jewish believers, but for the Romans who were not Jewish, and who had accepted the one God, he was not so forgiving.

"You must be very careful," Annia said.

"Oh, we are," Cato said. "One morning, she saw us worshipping. We do our scripture reading and singing and prayer every morning, just like you taught us."

"And what did she say to you?" Annia asked, trying to keep the panic from her voice.

"She asked what we were doing, and we shared the good news of the Christ with her," he said, smiling broadly.

Annia's mouth was a grim line.

Marcus stood.

"You aren't pleased, Mother?" he asked, his face falling.

"Oh, my child, I am so pleased," she said. "It's what the Christ called us to do. It's just that you must be very, very careful."

"Should we stop our morning prayers?" he asked, his face scrunched as if he were trying to absorb words he didn't understand.

She took his hand and said, "Never stop your morning prayers. The peace you receive will help you throughout the day."

He nodded solemnly.

Annia smiled. "There are many things in this world I

don't understand. But what I do know is that I love you and want you, and am so happy you are here I can hardly stand it."

"I must take my leave of you," Marcus said. He took Annia's hand in parting. "I will do what I can," he whispered to Annia. "Your other son. He needs to be here, safe with you. I will make it so."

Tears rose in her eyes. "Thank you," she said.

Cato and Annia watched Marcus walk away.

"He seems a nice man now, not at all what I thought when I was chasing after him," Cato said.

"Why were you chasing him?" she asked Cato. "How did it happen that you were able to come here?"

"I overheard Father talking to this Marcus, again," he said. "I went to the window and saw the soldiers, and they frightened me. Then I heard what they were saying, how the baby had been taken care of—eaten by wild dogs—and that man Marcus just stood there. He denied nothing. And Father was glad."

Cato squeezed his eyes together angrily and swatted away tears.

"I hated Father, and I hated Marcus for getting my baby sister and taking her away, so I determined to find the man who took my sister. I followed him through the streets."

"Were you scared?" Annia asked.

"No, I wasn't scared. It was daytime. I would have been scared if it had been night, but I would have done it all the same."

"I'm sure you would have. You are a brave boy," his mother said. If only Flavius had been able to sneak away with him.

"Can we get Flavius here soon?" he asked, as if reading her thoughts. "He will be scared without me to sleep with."

"I'm not sure how we can get Flavius, my son," she said, "though there is nothing I want more."

"I'll think of something. Why, I'll go back and get him and bring him here just as I came. It wasn't so hard."

His face was serious, and he handed her the baby and stood as if he were going to get his brother at that very moment.

"I don't think that is a very good idea just yet. Someone may follow you back here and take all of us. Then your baby sister and I, we may both die."

Annia hated speaking such harsh words to the boy, but they were true, and she knew she had to paint a very clear picture. Otherwise, this son, so very much like Annia, would be off—convinced he could get his little brother all alone, using only his wit and his wiles.

The boy's face was pained, and he was silent for a few moments, thinking. "I can't leave him there all by himself. Now that I know you and my sister are safe, I can go back and care for him. Don't worry, Mother, I will be back."

Cato hugged his mother.

"No, son. You need to stay here. I don't want to lose you again." Annia held him tight. "You are my precious child. I don't think I could bear being separated from you again."

"Don't cry, Mother," Cato said. "I will make it so that we can all be together again, and so that Father loves you and the baby and Flavius and me just as he used to."

She took Cato's face in her hands and looked into his eyes. "What makes you think he doesn't love you and Flavius the way he used to?" she said.

He looked away. "I didn't say that," he said evasively.

"But you did," she said. "That's exactly what you said.

Why? Has your father done something to make you think he doesn't love you?"

"No, Mother. It's just that…" The boy paused and looked down at his feet. He scrubbed the sandy soil with his leather sandal and gazed out at the newly shorn sheep.

"What?" Annia asked, holding the boy in her arms and rubbing his sturdy back gently.

"It's just that since Father's new baby with his new wife was born, he doesn't call us in to dinner. He doesn't ask us to go places with him. He won't come and do things with us when we ask him. He looks at us as if he doesn't know us."

The boy's chin trembled, and tears welled in his eyes. "I don't think he loves us anymore, Mother. That's why I must go be with Flavius. He will be frightened without me."

"I understand, son," she said. "I understand that you want to protect your brother. But the best way to protect him may be staying away right now. Sometimes waiting is the brave thing to do."

Annia uttered these words with conviction. But she wondered if they were true.

Wait for what? What was she waiting for?

For Marcus to get her boy for her?

Did he care enough to do that?

There was only one person who really cared for her boys, and that was Annia herself.

Was she alone in this world?

Lord, she prayed, *please give me the strength to do whatever it is that I need to do to keep my boys safe.*

She had one in her arms right now. How precious he felt. What if she lost him again? What if she lost him and never got to see either of them again? It was more than her heart could bear to think of such things.

"Mother?" Cato asked. "Do you have any food? I'm a little hungry."

He broke away from her tight grip, and she had to laugh.

"Oh, my sweet child. I am so sorry. Of course you are hungry. Please forgive me for not offering you something to eat and drink right away. Let's go eat. I'm hungry, and I feel certain there is food in the kitchen."

She wondered when he had last had a decent meal. Was he being fed? Surely the slaves were caring for him as they had done before she was exiled.

She wrapped Maelia in her baby sling and tied her to her chest, and they made their way back to the villa garden.

Cato squared his shoulders as he walked.

"I smell something cooking, Mother. Do you smell it?" he said.

"Yes," she said, "it smells like fresh bread and some kind of stew. I'm hungry, too. Shearing sheep is hard work."

"After we eat, we can think a little more clearly," Cato said.

Annia tried not to laugh at his very serious observation. He was such a little man.

But she feared for the boy. She feared that once he was determined to go back to his little brother, nothing would be able to stop him.

In the kitchen around a large wooden table, several of the women Annia had seen singing this morning were gathered. They looked tired but happy. The women sat talking with one another, feeding their babies and eating the fare before them.

It made Annia miss Virginia. If Janius found she was alone in Annia's villa, he would find her and sell her at the slave market. He knew how much Annia loved her. Annia must find her before then. But how could she do that?

Annia looked around her and found comfort in the familiar sounds of women laughing and babies babbling.

Cato's eyes lit up when he saw another little boy about his age across the table eating bread.

"Would you like some?" the boy asked, offering Cato half of his loaf.

"Yes," Cato said, and took the soft, warm bread the boy offered him.

Annia's heart sang. A friend for her son. Maybe that would keep him here?

But what if he stayed? Would that endanger them all? Would Galerius Janius come looking for him? Even now, were her husband's spies just beyond the safety of the villa walls?

Chapter Seven

Marcus had assured Annia that he would get her son. But how? Was Galerius Janius a man he wanted as his enemy? What had changed? Three days ago, all Marcus wanted was a position in the Praetorian Guard. Rescuing Annia and her baby two nights ago had changed him. He now wanted something else. But what was that something else? Was it real? Was he fooling himself?

What he did know was that if he wished to continue his plan for promotion, he would need to find another supporter. One who was still in favor with the emperor.

He made his way to the home of his friend, Gamus, for the after-duty breakfast Nona had promised him.

As he walked down the quiet streets, he felt eyes on the back of his head.

He sensed he was being followed.

He stopped, and listened.

All was silent.

Perhaps he was unreasonable in his fear. Twenty years fighting one ambush after another in Britain would do it to anyone.

But there was more to this than unreasonable fear, and he knew it. Someone was following him.

Marcus seated himself on one of the wooden stools surrounding the round tables in Gamus's shop. Gamus was there, along with a fellow believer, Callus, who had served as a centurion, but was long retired.

"You need a wife," Callus said to Marcus, "and some healthy baby boys," he laughed.

"Yes, I agree," Nona said. "A good-looking boy like you must have someone in mind."

Marcus had no one in mind, no one at all, but the picture that seemed to draw itself in his mind's eye was a woman, small, dark, with brown eyes, curly hair and a temper to match a tiger's.

Nona caught his eye. "You have someone, don't you." She shook her finger at him. "I recognize that look. Who is she?" she asked, piling his plate with fresh bread, goat cheese mixed with garlic and rue and fresh olives.

Marcus filled his mouth full of the fresh, warm bread and grinned mischievously.

Nona shook her head knowing very well Marcus had stuffed his mouth so he would not have to talk.

"Take care that you marry a woman who has never been married before," Callus said.

"And why would you say that, Callus? Why would you think that necessary?" Gamus asked.

"Purity. Family purity," Callus said solemnly. "Why I'm quite certain old Petronius Sergius, the boy's father, would find it an offense to the family honor for Marcus here to bring home a woman sullied from a previous husband."

"Bosh," said Nona. "I would take a seasoned wife with knowledge and experience in child rearing and running a home over the pasty-faced girls I see riding around in their fine litters carried about like well-dressed dolls. Honestly, I would trade ten of those doll wives for one solid woman who knows an honest day's work, loves her husband, manages a household and cares for her children." Nona walked away shaking her head.

"How do you stand on the wife question, Gamus?" Marcus couldn't help asking. Nona's words had soothed his soul, but Callus had unsettled his mind.

What if his father felt the same as Callus? Did he believe a woman previously married would sully the family name? He looked up at Nona.

Nona stood still, watching and listening. Something was at stake here, Marcus could see that clearly enough.

"Well," said Gamus, twirling the mead in the clay cup before him. "I do not know."

"Not sure, huh?" Nona asked. "Was it the fault of a young bride that her husband divorced her simply because she had no fortune?" Nona's eyes blazed, and her voice boomed. "And did I sully the honor of your family, having been twice a bride?"

"Certainly not," Gamus responded. "My dear, you are the love of my life, and my family, while they lived, adored you."

Nona was soothed.

The sun's rays lighted the cracks beneath the closed door, illuminating the blue leaves and swirls of the floor mosaic. Marcus helped Gamus open the doors while Callus fussily finished his meal, picking up the breadcrumbs with a wetted forefinger.

Marcus knew it was time to take his leave.

"Thank you, Nona. It was filling and good, as always." Marcus kissed her on the cheek.

"Any time, my boy. I love having you at our table. We miss our boys. One in Britain, another off in Corinth. I can only hope to see them again before this life is over."

"Don't be so dramatic, wife," Gamus said. "Of course

you will see them. They are young lads, not yet thirty summers, and you and I have barely seen fifty. We have many, many good years left to us. If they don't travel to us, we will travel to them." Gamus caught Nona's hand and kissed it.

She laughed, and kissed him on his head, cleared the table and began wiping it down with a damp linen cloth.

She lifted Callus's plate just as he made a last swipe at the breadcrumbs, and snatched it away. She then wiped the table down, pointedly, in front of him.

Clearly, Nona was ready for Callus to be gone.

"I best be off, as well," Callus said.

After Callus made his way down the early morning street, Gamus pulled Marcus aside.

"If you are blessed enough to find a woman like my Nona," Gamus said, "You will be a happy man indeed."

But the truth was, Marcus was not so certain. It wasn't that he didn't agree with Gamus. Nona was wonderful. But, really, what Callus said was what Marcus had hoped and dreamed. A wife of his own, his first, and he her first husband. That had always been his ideal.

He watched Callus make his lonely way down the road. He looked back at the warmth of Nona's smile shining down on Gamus.

Surely he could have the bride he'd dreamed of and the happiness of Gamus and Nona.

Marcus headed back to the barracks for some much-needed sleep.

His watch began when the sun set and lasted until the sun rose. The summer watches were much shorter than the long winter ones, and for that he was grateful. It gave him more time to make a plan and prepare.

He felt like he was going into battle.

He was.

A battle unlike any he had been in before.

He was accustomed to facing fierce warriors, slashing swords, spears and arrows.

What he was not accustomed to facing was this feeling in his heart that made him want to do something that was completely foolish.

Why did he have such a fierce desire to protect this woman and her children?

He told himself he would do it for any woman who found herself in such a position, but he knew that was a lie.

There were women all over Rome whose husbands had divorced them and kept their children away.

It was the law for the *paterfamilia*. The children were the husband's property, even in divorce.

Was it the fierce love she had for her child?

Annia's face rose before him, the liquid brown eyes, the strong, lithe body.

Enough. He had a mission, and it was essential—a matter of life or death to Annia and her children—that he be successful.

His father thought him foolish.

But he believed himself correct. The woman needed protecting, her children needed rescuing. It had nothing to do with any feelings he had for this woman. He was a soldier, and his goal was to protect. That was it.

If Galerius Janius would expose his daughter when he had plenty of money to support her and pay her dowry, what might he be tempted to do with his other son?

Just a few blocks from Gamus and Nona's abode, Marcus was stopped by one of his young soldiers. "Why aren't you asleep, soldier? Tonight will be a long night if you spend the day on the streets," Marcus said, his gravelly voice breaking the early morning silence of the street.

The young man paused, clearly winded. He put his hands on his hips and breathed deeply. He had been running. Obviously looking for Marcus.

"Galerius Janius is looking for you, sir," the young man said between ragged breaths.

"Why is he looking for me?" Marcus asked, though he had an idea.

"He doesn't believe you took the baby to the place of exposure. We assured him you did, but when he asked who of us saw you actually expose the baby, none of us could answer."

It was true, then. He had been followed. How much did Janius know, and why had it taken him three days to question Marcus's handling of the baby? Had the boy been followed?

The soldier looked at Marcus expectantly.

His question was one Marcus would not answer. He paused and looked the young soldier in the eyes. "The place of exposure is not a sight fit for eyes to see."

The young man seemed satisfied.

"I will take care of Galerius Janius," Marcus said. "You go get some sleep."

"Thank you." The young man turned and headed back in the direction of the barracks.

Oh, to be a soldier young enough to believe that the man in charge could take care of everything, could keep you and your company safe.

Marcus knew Galerius Janius would not be satisfied with the words of a mere night watchman like the young man with whom he had just spoken.

To be hunted down by Galerius Janius would be dangerous indeed.

He could not allow that shell of a man to destroy the mission his mother had worked so hard to build.

Nor could Marcus allow Janius to get anywhere near Annia and her baby.

Marcus turned from the road leading to his father's villa and walked beside the odiferous Tiber River. He would sleep in the barracks today.

Marcus looked down into the river, then back up again quickly. Had he been a younger man, or one with a weaker stomach, he would have gagged. The river was dotted with dead bodies, thrown from the gladiatorial ring and tossed from the Cloaca Maxima, the dreadful underground prison. The bodies were stopped by the mud and silt at the bend of the river. Eventually, the current would catch the bodies and carry them past Ostia and out to sea.

In a city with a population close to a million in an area only ten square miles, such horrors were common.

He had forgotten about this particular macabre view while he was in Britain.

There, in that faraway misty isle, it came in the shape of enemy warriors painted in blue descending upon them in the night, shooting poisoned darts at them in their sleep.

In spite of the river, Marcus was glad to be in Rome where the horrors were at least predictable.

He was also glad he had talked to his father. His father knew Rome and had the added experience of shielding his mother's secret mission for many years.

Though he had wanted to earn the office of Praetorian prefect on his own, Marcus was not too proud to ask for his help. His father was only too happy to help. His friends could help Marcus reach his desired position.

When Galerius Janius had hired him, Marcus thought

he might be able to help him in his goal of obtaining the rank of prefect for the *Vigiles*.

If he found favor with the emperor in that capacity, he might be appointed prefect in charge of the emperor's personal armed guard, the Praetorians.

Janius was a cousin of the emperor. He had promised to speak to Emperor Claudius about appointing Marcus a commanding position in the Guard and considering his noble service in Britain as a recommendation for the coveted prefect position. If Marcus exposed the baby.

Now, it seemed, Janius was no longer in favor with the emperor.

His only other option if he did not achieve his lifelong dream was to manage one of his father's villas, either here or in Britain.

He preferred to become prefect.

As prefect, Marcus could build a life of his own here in Rome. He could buy his own estate—he had much coin saved from his years of service—and raise a family.

But the thought of loving a wife and children frightened him.

The horror of twenty years of battle made his fear of losing what was dearest to him a living, breathing entity.

In Gaul and in Britain, he had seen women pulled from their husbands, babies slaughtered, whole families pulled asunder and sold into slavery.

Rome was far from safe, but the horrible nightmares replayed themselves in his memory. They woke him at night, and tormented him by day.

To love meant to risk losing everything.

Was he ready for that?

Regardless of his own fears, he must come up with a plan to keep Janius away from Annia.

* * *

Sleep came easily to him once he was bunked down in the barracks.

He awoke to the sun casting long shadows beneath the door of his officer's cubby.

He washed his face and rinsed his mouth.

No time for a proper bath before he went on duty. He would have to wait until morning.

He and his men began their casual watch march through the city. Their area was easy to patrol—primarily the wealthiest neighborhoods and a few *insulae*. The crowded apartments were four stories high and prone to fires.

Tonight was quiet. A light rain blanketed the city making fires possible but far less likely.

It was in the hot, dry conditions of early August that fires were most common. Still, it was necessary to inspect the *insulae* and make certain cooking fires were being prepared safely and buildings were safe for their inhabitants.

"Uff," one of his men grunted when a resident of the *insulae* above them dumped her evening garbage on his head.

The soldier did not break formation.

"Halt," Marcus commanded. The men halted in perfect lines. "Wipe yourselves clean. It is difficult to see with cinders in your eyes," he chuckled good-naturedly, and the men smiled, relieved for the break.

They broke rank, and dusted themselves off. There was a neighborhood fountain nearby, as well as a public toilet. These conveniences were built to keep the poor happy so there would be no need for uprisings. Whatever the reason for the marble fountain with its adjoining three-story water tower and commodious public facility, Marcus was glad for it.

Marcus gave the men a break to relieve and refresh themselves. He did the same.

When they returned to their positions, a young slave boy stood waiting for Marcus.

"A message for you, sir, from Galerius Janius." The boy handed Marcus a small, carefully rolled paper.

Marcus unrolled and read it.

It was better than he could have planned.

The scribbled message was the solution to all of his worries.

The cruelty of the man who wrote the message was beyond Marcus's imagining, but there it was. A clear message of salvation.

Arrest the child, Flavius Janius, who refuses to bow
to the emperor's gods.

"Line up, men," Marcus said. "We have another mission for Galerius Janius."

He heard discord in the rear and stopped.

"Does someone have something to say?" he asked.

A soldier stepped from the ranks and said, "Yes, sir. Sorry, sir."

It was the same young man who had brought him the message yesterday.

"What is your name, soldier?" Marcus asked. "You are either very brave, very foolish, or a little of both."

"Arrius Pollio," the young man said, "begging your pardon, sir."

"Speak, soldier," Marcus said.

"Well, sir," the soldier said, and then seemed to lose his courage.

"What is it?" Marcus said. "Speak, man."

"Well, sir," Arrius said, "are you quite certain we can trust a message from Galerius Janius?"

A shadow of doubt faded Marcus's exuberance over an easy solution to his problem. What if the young man's doubt was well-grounded? What if this was a trick?

"Have you any evidence that this might be a trick?" Marcus asked, though he guessed the man hadn't any, probably just a hunch. But as a seasoned soldier, Marcus knew to respect hunches.

Not that they were always accurate. Simply that they might sometimes save your life. Marcus stalled, waiting for the soldier to answer.

Arrius Pollio was silent.

Marcus needed more time to think through this warning, but that time was not available to him.

He would simply have to move forward on the order, realizing that it could very well be a trick. And if it was a trick, well, he would have to find his way out.

He had gotten himself out of many tight positions before.

Marcus looked at Arrius. "Well?" he said.

"Nothing more, sir," the man said, lowering his head.

"Thank you, soldier. Line up." Arrius Pollio obediently returned to his place.

He appreciated the young man's wisdom and concern. He marked him as one he would be wise to promote.

However, he had no time to do anything other than follow the orders on the message.

Marcus remembered what Gamus the merchant had overheard. He hoped the information was accurate.

It seemed that Janius was not in favor with the emperor and was attempting, at all costs, to find favor.

According to the order in Marcus's hand, in order to

win favor with the emperor, Galerius Janius was willing to sacrifice his own child.

It would be a hard-hearted emperor who would allow such a sacrifice. Claudius did not have that reputation. Addle-minded, but not hard-hearted.

Claudius had been the only one of his family to not be murdered by his grandmother, Livia. She had the habit of killing whoever she felt might get in the way of her son, Tiberius, becoming emperor. She had thought the stuttering, physically misshapen Claudius to be no threat. When Livia's dreams came true, and Tiberius became the unwilling emperor, he was a complete disappointment.

Tiberius shirked his responsibilities as ruler and left control of the empire in the hands of Sejanus, the head of his Praetorian Guard. Chaos ensued. When Tiberius and Sejanus eventually died, Claudius was crowned emperor. He proved himself a decent emperor whose mind was quite clear in spite of it all.

The man Tiberius had trusted to help him rule had, instead, wrested power away from him. Worse, Sejanus's anti-Semitic policies had created panic and bloodshed in the Jewish population. It was these wrongs that Marcus wanted to right by becoming part of the leadership of the Guard.

"Forward, march," Marcus ordered his men, and prayed that his hunch was correct, and that he would be able to free Annia's youngest son this very evening.

He was met at the front entrance to the villa by none other than Janius himself.

A small child stood whimpering beside him, held securely by a large slave.

The child could only have been five or six years old. His hair brown and curly, his physique tiny, this must be the youngest son of Annia.

"Take this heretic," Janius said. "Deliver him as I have requested. If you don't, it will not go well for you. I have eyes all over the city."

Galerius Janius pushed the child forward. Marcus caught him, resisted the temptation to comfort him and grabbed the boy's tiny bound wrists.

Galerius Janius stood, his face flickering in the torchlight.

With his free hand, Marcus clutched his sword. It seemed to be his natural reaction each time he came into contact with Galerius Janius. How he would love to use it on the portly oaf standing before him.

The gold about Janius's loose neck flashed in the firelight, and his narrow shoulders sagged. His arms were flaccid. The man couldn't defend his villa, much less his country.

Marcus doubted Galerius Janius would find any sympathy with the emperor. He heartily regretted the deal he had made with this man.

The little boy stood trembling beside him.

"Take him," Marcus said to Arrius Pollio. He pointed to the trembling child. "He is your charge. You will be certain the heretic doesn't leave our guard." He spat out the word *heretic* with such conviction that Galerius Janius looked at him with widened eyes.

"Perhaps I have misjudged you, soldier," Galerius Janius said to Marcus. "It seems that we share a similar hatred for those who refuse to bow down to the emperor."

"Render unto Caesar what is Caesar's, and to the God what is God's," Marcus said, his face impassive.

"Well said, my good man, well said," Galerius Janius said. "Though the Caesars are gone, the sentiment is the same. You are wiser than I guessed."

Janius would be surprised to know Marcus was quoting the Christ.

Galerius Janius offered Marcus a gold coin, and he took it, further sealing Janius's trust.

"Well, then," Galerius Janius said, "good evening."

When Marcus looked to the window above, he saw a beautiful woman, dressed in a red silk *palla,* her arms jangling with bracelets, the gold glinting in the light of the single candle glowing before her in the window sconce.

She smiled when she saw the child pushed roughly from Janius to Arrius Pollio.

"Father!" the child screamed. "Please. Don't let them take me."

Janius did not even look back at the child but turned and walked through the door.

The woman at the window laughed and blew out her candle.

Chapter Eight

As was their custom, Marcus led the *Vigiles* to Gamus's shop for late-night refreshment.

Usually, Marcus made this the last stop of the evening, after the men had fulfilled all of their duties, inspecting their entire quadrant for fires or misdeeds.

Nona, Gamus's wife, was usually in bed by the time the men came in, and Gamus usually served them.

They arrived early tonight. Marcus needed Nona's help with the boy.

The child had been brave after Arrius had calmed the boy enough to hoist him onto his shoulders. Another *Vigile*, with a boy just his age, reached for the boy when he nodded and was in danger of tumbling from Arrius's shoulders.

"Ah," Nona said when she caught sight of the child, "a little soldier. Where did you pick him up?" She engulfed him in her arms and took him with her to the kitchen, where she sat him on a mat on the floor. Marcus guessed she planned to feed him.

But he also guessed the child would fall asleep the minute he was placed on the floor.

"Why, the little lamb." Nona came out of the kitchen,

balancing a tray of cups. "He fell asleep before I could even fill the cups. Whose is he?"

Her question was lost in the clatter of Marcus's men seating themselves on the rough benches on either side of the long table

The night had been hot and their duty required them to march up and down narrow streets, and hundreds of *insulae* stairs.

They had marched past rows of closed shops—food shops serving meals on the spot, servicing the street vendors and craftsmen—and checked the public bathrooms and fountains for safety.

And now they were hungry and thirsty.

"Any fires tonight, lads?" Gamus asked.

"No, sir, none that we saw anyway," Arrius responded.

Gamus smiled.

"A good night, then."

"Yes, sir, a good night."

There was a familiarity between the two that Marcus had never noticed.

He followed Gamus to the cellar.

"What happened?" Gamus asked.

"Galerius Janius again," Marcus said. "This time, he sent for us to arrest his son for being a 'flesh eater.'"

"Is that what they are calling us now?" Gamus asked, laughing.

He busied himself about the cellar, pulling out more cups, and filling them.

"Yes," Marcus said. "It's not the first I've heard of it. They hear about the communion practice. They see it as a secret ritual, and they hear that we share the body and blood of Christ. Thus, we are flesh eaters."

"That is absurd," Gamus said. "What did Arrius say when he heard those words?"

"Arrius?" Marcus said. "Why would he care?"

"He is a fellow believer," Gamus said. "He is my sister's child."

"Ah," Marcus said. "That explains it."

"Explains what?" Gamus said.

"The easy kinship between the two of you, and why he protects me," Marcus said.

"That he does, my friend, that he does," Gamus agreed. "But what of the boy?"

"Hello?" Nona called, making them both jump at once, her booming voice nearly shaking the amphorae in their stands.

"Ah, my sweet, quiet wife," Gamus said, laughing, "you startled Marcus."

"You jumped, too," she said, laughing. "But what *of* the boy, Marcus? Where did he come from, and what is he doing with your company?"

"I'm going to need your help," Marcus said. "Can you keep the boy here for a few days?"

Nona and Gamus looked puzzled.

"I am being followed. I know where his mother is, and I want them reunited, but it will take a few days before I can safely take him. I don't trust his father."

"I'm happy to do that," Nona said. "But the poor mother."

"And, Gamus, I need these men so sleepy that they don't wake until late morning. I want them heading back to the barracks worried that I came for them, and they were too busy sleeping to come with me."

Gamus laughed. "I can do that," he said. "There is nothing like Nona's hot bread and rich cheese and warm honeyed milk. It works every time."

"Good," Marcus said. "I don't want them asking any questions about what I did with the boy. I want them to assume that I turned him over to the proper authorities in the first light of morning."

"Done," said Gamus.

"Thank you, my friend," Marcus said.

Gamus piled a platter full of piping hot bread and soft white cheese and carried them out to the hungry men.

Nona smiled behind him. "He will take care of them, don't you worry." At that moment, the small boy, Flavius, awoke from his corner mat and began wailing.

When they reached him, he was drenched with sweat.

"Have no fear," Marcus said to the squirming, flailing child. "You are safe with us."

The boy looked right through him and wailed.

Marcus looked back at Nona.

"He acts as if he doesn't see me," Marcus said. Was the boy out of his mind? Had he been driven to the brink by the chaos in his life over the past few weeks, the crowning blow being taken from his home in the dark of the night?

"Night terrors," Nona said. "He doesn't know who we are. My oldest had them. Sometimes he would wander around the house mumbling some sort of garbled nonesense. Leave him be and he will go back to sleep."

At that moment, just as she predicted, the boy stopped wailing, looked out as if he were seeing a pleasant vision, smiled, lay back down and slept.

"The sweet thing. I would prefer to keep him here for good," she said. "I miss my boys."

"I think his mother might find that a bit painful," Marcus said.

"The mother?" Nona asked, her eyebrows raised high. "How do you know the mother?"

"As I said, it's a long story," Marcus said.

"And you need to think it through before you feel like

talking about it? Well," Nona said, "I have all night," and she smiled at him.

Marcus relaxed. He needed to talk with someone. He needed to think clearly about this, and sometimes thinking clearly meant talking it out.

She sat across from him and prepared to listen.

"She is beautiful" were the first words out of his mouth. He stopped himself, and looked at her.

"Ah," she said, "you like her. I thought there was someone, so this is the someone."

Marcus wished he could pull the words back into his mouth. He hadn't wanted to lead with that statement. He had wanted to get there a bit more rationally, easing his way in, but his heart had spoken before his brain could catch up.

"I do think of her. But she is the mother of three children," he said, his face tight with worry.

"And that makes her unlovable?" Nona asked.

"Just not the woman I…" Marcus's words trailed off into silence.

"Ah, a sullied woman," Nona said. "You've been listening to our friend Callus, I fear."

"Maybe," Marcus said, "but it has always been my dream. Starting a home with a woman, having our first baby together."

"You sound like a woman," Nona said.

Marcus grew red hot at this. "A woman?" he asked, horrified at the thought.

"Yes," Nona said. "You are dreaming the dream of a woman, which means you are ripe for marriage."

"It's odd?" Marcus said.

"No, it's not odd, it's perfectly normal. It's what all young men do—some older than others—when they are ripe for marriage. How old are you?" she asked.

"Thirty and seven," he responded.

"Good," she said. "You are at the perfect age for marriage. Past the age of stupidity, but not yet set in your ways. Any woman who marries you will be blessed indeed."

Marcus glowed under this praise. It felt good to be able to talk freely of his thoughts. His brain had felt like foreign territory since he had first met Annia.

Pleasant foreign territory, but foreign territory nonetheless.

"I met her when I was sent to take her baby to be exposed."

"Ordered by her sour former husband?" Nona asked. "I am guessing he had accused her of adultery and had her banned from the house, then divorced her and married a younger, wealthier woman?"

"Yes," Marcus said, amazed. "How did you know?"

"It is an old and very, very tired story," Nona said. "It has happened more times than I want to say. But the added twist is the pregnancy and exposed baby. This man sounds like an abomination even beyond the abomination that is Rome itself."

"He is," Marcus agreed.

"And what does all of this have to do with the boy?" she asked.

"His older brother watched me from the window when I reported on having safely taken the baby to be exposed. He chased me down. I think the little fellow had it in his mind to kill me," he said.

"Spunky little thing," Nona said.

"And he almost did kill me, but I was able to save myself and reunite him with his mother."

"Happy to know you had skill enough to escape from

a child warrior. That's what our taxes go to support, I suppose." Nona was laughing.

"Yes," Marcus said, smiling. "It's true. I barely escaped with my eyes intact, I will tell you that."

"Vicious as well as spunky, then. That bodes well for him and his future as a Roman Legionary," Nona said. "But go on. Put the puzzle pieces together for me."

"Galerius doubted me, doubted that I had actually exposed the baby. Your Arrius told me of his doubt. When Galerius called me back to take the youngest son, accusing him of being a flesh eater, Arrius warned me that it might be a trick. Which is why we are here."

Marcus stopped as if he were finished.

"And," Nona said, "what does all of this have to do with the mother of the little boys?"

"I promised her I would bring her boys back to her," he said.

"Well, it looks as though you will be able to fulfill your promise," she said.

"Yes," he said. "That is true. But Father believes I should send them all away from the house. He fears their presence will endanger the lives of the other women and their babies."

"And," Nona said, "he is right. But, the child must be reunited with his mother. I will take him there myself. You will stay out of it."

"Thank you, Nona. And I will think of a plan to get them somewhere safely away from Rome."

Marcus left the safety of Nona's house and set out to complete his night patrol and his duty to keep the streets of Rome safe. He was alone. His men had, as hoped, fallen asleep over the table, content in their knowledge that their commander was happy with them. The streets were quiet by now. There was little need to wake them.

And for the first time in a very long while, Marcus prayed as he walked. He prayed to be forgiven for doubting his mother's mission. He prayed for forgiveness for valuing his own selfish desires above the safety of those in his care. He prayed for protection for himself, his family, his men. And he prayed for Annia and her babies that he might be able to keep them all safe.

Chapter Nine

Marcus arrived at home early in the morning after his night duty. He was certain he had not been followed. At least not this time. The streets were still quiet, the sun not yet up. Marcus wanted to be there when Nona brought Flavius to Annia. He told himself it was to be certain the mission was complete and Flavius delivered safely to Annia. The reality was that he couldn't resist being there to experience the joy of the happy reunion.

The sleepy old guard lifted the heavy latch and swung open the wooden door. The dogs gave a half-hearted bellow, but burrowed more deeply into their blanket when they realized it was only Marcus.

He heard the swish-swish sound of someone cleaning the mosaic tiles. The sound blended with the soothing sound of the tinkling fountain, and Marcus wondered who was working so early.

Changes in the household routine were unusual.

He recognized the brown curls peeping from beneath a headscarf. His heart did a little leap.

"Annia?" he said.

She swiped her forehead with the back of her hand and looked up at him.

Her smile filled the room.

"Marcus!" she said. "Just in time to help me with the morning scrub."

He loved her sense of humor. She was a lady born, her father a patrician, and here she was, scrubbing floors.

And she seemed charmingly adept at doing so.

"Why are you scrubbing at this hour of the night?" he said, though dawn spread a pink light on the garden pool.

Annia laughed. "Your mother is concerned that too many women and children around your father's clients will bring unnecessary attention to her mission. So she wants us to finish our work in the front of the villa before the clients begin coming."

Marcus felt a jolt of shame. This was his own doing. Had he not made the deal with Galerius, his mother would not have felt the need for this safeguard.

"Look," she said, pointing proudly at a corner of the colonnaded porch.

At first all he saw was the water she had spread liberally around the tile flooring. "Was there a flood last night?" he teased.

She smiled, and he sloshed through the puddles she had created to examine the corner more closely.

Even in the dim light he could see the freshly cleaned tiles glistening and sparkling. The blue tiles glinted, and the white tiles gleamed. He was fascinated. He looked down at her, his eyes brimming with admiration.

"Your gifts amaze me. I did not know cleaning was among them."

"Come here and I'll show you how I did it," she said, still smiling.

He followed her, a willing servant.

If she could clean like a slave and maintain her dignity,

and her sense of humor, so could he. He shed his shoes and began working alongside her.

She sat across from him, the bucket between them. She handed him a part of her rag. "Here," she said. He gazed at her, charmed by her servant's attire. She splashed a little water in his face and giggled.

"I'm sorry," he said. "I am trying to get accustomed to the lady patrician I met a few nights ago scrubbing floors like a slave."

But it was more than that, and he knew it. She was lovely, more so because she was as good as she was beautiful. She scrubbed floors as cheerfully as if she were hosting a grand banquet, and he guessed her to be equally comfortable in either position.

"You are surprised that I know how to scrub floors?" she asked, her eyes dancing.

"Yes," he said. "I must say, yes."

"In Britain, things were not always as clear as they are here," she said. "Reliable servants were hard to come by. The slaves were so sullen that my father wouldn't keep them. He hired his helpers, but if there was a festival or holy day they didn't show. We took over their chores."

His eyes widened. "What chores did you do?"

She laughed. "Everything you can imagine and more. Harvesting crops, grinding wheat, baking bread."

"Shearing sheep, combing wool," he added, smiling.

"Yes," she said, "and everything in between."

A woman who could literally do anything. He had never been so comfortable in a woman's presence. It was an unusual feeling.

They worked together companionably. She showed him how to sprinkle a little sand on the tile first, then scrub it with water, dry it with rags, sweep up the sand and polish it with a rag dampened with vinegar water.

"You are doing good work," she said, beaming with satisfaction at his glistening corner of tile.

Before long, they had cleaned the entire perimeter of the peristyle garden and pool. All that was left was the area directly in front of his father's office.

"So tell me," she said, sitting up from her scrubbing and staring directly into his eyes, "what is your ambition?"

He was so surprised by the question he knocked over the sand bucket.

She laughed. "I didn't mean to frighten you," she said. "But, I've been around enough Romans to know that ambition is born and bred in them. What is your dream?" she asked.

He felt his face flush.

"That much of a secret, is it?" she asked teasing him.

He laughed nervously. "My dream is to become prefect of the Praetorian Guard, to keep the emperor safe."

She was silent as if measuring his words.

Sharing his ambition made him uncomfortable. He turned his attention to sweeping up the spilled sand. Had he betrayed her? Together they scrubbed the remaining section.

"It seems a courageous dream," she said.

But what was he willing to sacrifice in order to achieve his dream? Annia and her children?

He shook off the uncomfortable thought and justified it with this: at least here in his father's villa he could protect her.

Marcus felt eyes upon him and looked up to see his father's Greek steward watching them.

"Good morning, Philip," Marcus said.

"Good morning, sir," the steward said, his eyes betraying nothing. "Your father will need to speak with you."

"Is he up and ready?" Marcus asked, knowing the answer to this question. His father preferred an early morning walk around the perimeter of his land. He said it refreshed him and made him ready for his day.

"Yes, and he will be here soon," Philip said. "May I find someone to finish this business?" He pointed a finicky finger to the tile Marcus and Annia were joyfully scrubbing.

"No, Philip, but thank you. I will be ready when Father arrives." Was the steward shielding him from relations with Annia?

"He is expecting visitors," Philip said. "Candidus Marius and his daughter."

Marcus flinched.

"Thank you, Philip." The steward did not want Marcus seen cleaning like a common slave by his father's visitors.

"What time shall we expect the visitors?" Marcus asked.

"Not until afternoon," he said.

He hoped the visitors would arrive after Nona and her surprise, and not before. He did not want to miss the reunion.

Worry replaced his simple joy in cleaning with Annia, and now it was a matter of helping her finish the floor as quickly as possible.

They worked in silence, and when they had finished, Annia smiled at him.

"Thank you," she said. "I would not have finished this without your help. I underestimated the enormity of the task."

He smiled and wiped his own forehead. The morning had turned hot.

He wished to follow her, to help her with all of her tasks for the remainder of the day.

"Marcus?" It was his father. "I need to discuss a few things with you before the benches are filled with clients."

His father smiled at Annia, and Marcus had no choice but to follow him into his office.

"I will find you later today," Marcus said. And that was a promise.

She smiled back at him. His heart responded with a leap, and he had to quiet himself. It was his duty to protect her and her family. Her reunion with her sons here, under this roof, would have to be short. It was too dangerous for them to stay. He hoped his father could help him figure out a solid plan. This was not a good day for visitors. He wished father's friends were coming another day. Or not at all. He knew his father's friend wished to make an alliance between Marcus and his daughter, Cassia. Marcus was not interested.

"Can we swim in the bath, Mother?" Cato asked when Annia found him beside the bathing pool.

"Yes."

"May I teach my new friend to swim?"

"Let's ask his mother first, and if she says yes, then let it be so," Annia answered, smiling at her child.

When the mother agreed, Cato and the boy flew to the pool.

Annia could hear their splashing and laughter out near the sheep pen where she had set up stations for felting the wool.

She was thankful for the diversion for Cato. It kept him from planning ways by which he might save his brother.

Still, even last night before he slept, he talked of how he would one day sneak out and kidnap him from their father's house. Annia was tense until she heard his peaceful, even breathing—the rhythm of sleep.

It was then, when he slept, that she felt some peace. It was then that she prayed for all of them.

Including Galerius Janius and his new wife.

She prayed that they would draw close enough to the one God that they would receive His peace.

Perhaps, in this way, her son could be safe in their home.

It had taken her a long time to be able to pray this prayer.

The anger and the pain she felt when Janius told her he didn't love her, he never had loved her, had been bad enough. She had lived with that pain for years.

But when he divorced her, accused her of adultery he knew had not happened and kept her sons away from her, her fury was boundless.

And when the last straw fell and he had ordered Maelia exposed, forgiving him and praying for him had been a groaning struggle.

But the Master had said it was easy to love those who loved you.

Drinking the living water, drawing close to Him, would enable you to pray for those who persecuted you.

And He was right.

Praying for Janius lifted the hatred from her heart and replaced it with a peace beyond understanding.

Annia walked past the boys, happy in their swimming, the early morning sun shining kindly upon their faces. She made her way to the sheep pen and makeshift felting stations.

Annia's deep fear was that if she didn't make herself useful Scribonia would insist she go away.

Annia wasn't yet certain of the rules for living in this lovely estate.

She'd never actually seen Scribonia send someone

away, but it was hard to be truly comfortable when she feared at any minute she would be asked to leave.

So when Annia found that the other women in the villa were pleased with her work, she felt a slight relief.

"Spinning our own wool on hand spindles and making our own ink would make us less dependent on outside help," Lucia had explained to Annia. "And Scribonia believes the more self-sufficient we can be, the better it is for all of us."

It seemed that Scribonia's mission was to give the women a safe place to raise their children and offer them the tools to be successful if they ever needed to live on their own.

Annia spent the rest of the morning fulfilling Scribonia's mission of self-sufficiency by shearing more sheep. The work occupied her mind, but it also made her look forward with relish to the noon meal.

"The more things we are able to grow, produce and craft here within the walls of this villa, the less dependent we are on goods and services from the outside," Scribonia explained to Annia as they ate their midday meal.

"I don't like life in the city of Rome. In the heart of the city, I fear people are becoming too dependent upon others to do the simplest things, things that could give them the pleasure they sorely need," Scribonia said.

Basso agreed. "When I was a girl, we grew our own food in a little back garden. Now everyone buys their food. All of it."

"I believe this is why they become lazy and depressed. Because they are too busy to work the land and get the self-satisfaction of supplying their basic needs," Scribonia added.

Basso agreed.

Annia listened to the women. She herself had never even considered the life of the workers on the street.

In Britain, they had grown their own food. And it was true. Even the poor were happier in Britain. She had never wondered why, never considered being dependent upon others, for the simplest things might be a cause for unhappiness.

"Did you know," Scribonia continued, "that a majority of the workers in the city never even cook their own food? They eat food served up at the shops on the streets cooked right in front of them. Why, it costs a cobbler two pairs of shoes—his entire morning's work—to buy his lunch. But he is helpless to change it. To cook the only beans he can afford to buy, dried garbanzos, he must keep his fire going for two hours. He isn't home that long, and his wife is working as hard as he is. It's a terrible situation."

Annia knew Scribonia was right. The shopkeepers were so busy trying to pay the rent on their *insulae* and shop fronts that they had neither the time nor the energy to save money.

"If people lived closer to the land," Scribonia said, "they would not be so worried about having the latest hairstyles, the latest fashions, the latest floor coverings."

The women went on to criticize the ostentatious show of wealth represented by the rich when they insisted on eating lying down rather than sitting up like normal people.

"What sense does it make? To lie down and eat, you have to have someone feeding you," Scribonia said.

"That is the point, *domina*," Basso added, "to show off how many servants you can afford. If you are so rich that you have someone to feed you, then you are very rich indeed."

"Save me from a time when I am so soddish that I can't even feed myself," Scribonia said.

Annia would never admit that in her home—before she was divorced by Janius—that is exactly how they took their evening meals. They lounged on eating sofas and were fed by house slaves.

Annia preferred the tables with folding bench seats at Scribonia's villa to the ones at her former abode.

It was ever so much easier to sit and talk to people when you were sitting up rather than lying on your side.

She wondered what Marcus thought. Did he see lying down as habit of the decadent rich? She suspected so.

Annia liked Scribonia. She liked her common sense, and her fierce independence. She liked that Scribonia had seen the emotional pain caused when a woman carried a baby for nine months and then was forced, against her will, to watch that baby be taken to be exposed for death or slavery.

"I have rarely seen my Marcus as happy as he was shearing sheep with you yesterday," Scribonia said.

Annia's breath caught. She had not realized they were being watched.

"It was one of the funniest things I've ever seen," Scribonia continued, "better than any play. Why, when he went to chase those sheep and they headed in three different directions, I had to stuff my *palla* in my mouth so he wouldn't hear me laughing."

"Oh, dear," Annia said. "I didn't mean to make a fool out of him. I just needed those sheep in the water before I sheared them."

"Yes, my dear, and it was your very sincerity and your need to get the job down without any foolishness that made it all the funnier. My son would have done anything for you. That was clear."

Annia blushed.

Just then there was a booming voice in the front of the villa. It filled the atrium and bounced into the eating area. Annia, Scribonia and the rest of the women and their babies and children stopped and listened.

Annia checked to make certain Cato was there. He was sitting with little Julius. She thanked God he had found a friend, and had not thought seriously about rescuing his little brother, except at night, when he really missed him.

A titter went through the women. Annia looked up to see why.

A woman approached the door. Her body was shielded by the rows of heads between Annia and the entranceway. A tall man stood behind her, though in the shadows, Annia could not see who it was.

Annia's attention turned quickly to Cato, who suddenly jumped up and ran across the dining room.

Her heart dropped. Had he chosen this moment to leave? Was he running away? Then she saw the look on his face.

Surprise.

Delight.

The woman had stopped, and Cato was running toward a tiny figure emerging from behind the woman.

The tall man was Marcus, and he was beaming.

Annia jumped up, her feet moving without her brain having to say anything. She ran as if the wind was her ally.

"Flavius!" she called. "Flavius!"

When he heard his mother's voice, he ran toward her, Cato close behind.

Flavius jumped into Annia's arms at the same time the commotion peaked, and Cato wrapped his arms around them both.

"My babies," Annia said, tears rolling down her cheeks. "My babies."

She looked up at the woman moving toward them and said, "I don't know who you are, and I don't know who sent you, but I can't thank you enough."

The woman pointed behind her. "Marcus sent me with the boy," she said. "He said he made a promise to you, and he isn't one to break promises. My name is Nona, and you are exactly as he described you—a tiny beauty."

Annia looked up at the woman and smiled, tears blurring her vision. "Thank you!"

Marcus grinned at her, bowed his head and disappeared.

"Now, then," the woman said, "I'll leave you time alone."

Scribonia had walked up and hugged the woman warmly. "Nona, my friend," she said, "I'm sure there is a story here. You must come sit and tell me all about it."

After finishing their meal, the boys played happily in the pool. They talked animatedly, catching up on the days they had been apart. Though Annia wanted to stay with them, not leave them for even a moment, she wanted to thank the woman who had brought Flavius home safely.

She knew she would find her in Scribonia's small office next to her husband's.

The atrium was pleasant in the middle of the day. The world outside sweltered in the afternoon heat, but here the marble was cool and shady, the water of the *impluvium* making a pleasant gurgling sound. It sounded just like Annia's heart felt. Happy and content.

Annia paused to hear the birds sing. It was as if they were singing to her.

Annia heard the women, Nona and Scribonia, talking.

She didn't want to be rude and interrupt them, so she took a polite seat on one of the marble benches and waited for a break in their conversation.

"He said the right thing to do was marry an unmarried woman," Nona was saying. "My husband and I made it very clear to Marcus that there are other ways to find joy. My husband's friend can be a bit stiff, sitting at our table the way he does, twisting and untwisting those long skinny fingers…."

Annia's hand went to her chest, and she grasped the bronze pin holding her *palla*.

Of course Marcus wanted an unmarried woman. Of course he thought it only right to marry one. Why would a man like Marcus Sergius be interested in a divorced woman with three children?

She wanted to walk away. Her pain upon hearing the news that Marcus wished to marry a woman who had never been married before was so palpable that she didn't think she could utter the words necessary to thank Nona for her kindness.

Just then there was bustling at the villa's front entrance, and Annia saw a great crowd of people enter. Filing in as if in a grand procession were four footmen, followed by a man whose purple stripe down the center of his tunic made it obvious he was a senator. Completing the train were four more footmen, and a woman so beautifully dressed in billowy sky-blue silk that Annia put her hand over her mouth to keep a gasp from escaping. The woman was followed by three lady's maids. Two brawny slaves guarded them all.

Philip bustled in behind them and made his way around the train of people, excusing himself. He stood guard at the entranceway to the office of Petronius Sergius.

The steward gave Annia a withering sideways glance when he saw her seated on the bench.

Why did he dislike her?

The footmen, lady's maids and slaves lined up on either side of the office, making way for the senator and lady to walk in.

Annia was stuck. She could not easily get up and move, for she was hemmed in on all sides by people. She could see the lady in a crack of light between the footmen. Up close, she realized the lady was only a girl of eighteen, not really a lady, but wealthy nonetheless. Perhaps she was the senator's daughter?

"Ah, Senator Valentius," Petronius Sergius said, welcoming them both. "And your lovely daughter, Cassia. So lovely to see you both."

Annia heard the sound of servants opening folding chairs and sliding them up to Petronius Sergius's desk.

"I can't thank you enough for all you've done for Marcus," he said.

Yes," Marcus said. "You have been a true patron, and I hope I will be able one day to repay your kindness."

Annia's heart beat loudly. She'd not seen Marcus. He must be standing right beside his father. She wished she were anywhere but here.

"Think nothing of it," the senator said. "It was the least we could do. Marcus is on his way to a position of great power. It would be an honor to enjoy a family alliance."

"Philip, please take our friend Cassia to my wife. I'm quite certain she will be bored with our conversation."

"Yes, yes, of course," the senator said, agreeing heartily.

The girl's cheeks were bright pink when she was led past Annia and into Scribonia's office.

So this was how it was. Annia tried to calm herself.

She tried to be happy for Marcus. This would be the woman he would marry. She was lovely. Annia felt a painful catch in her throat. Why did she care? Of course Marcus had a wife picked out for him. He was long past the age of first marriage.

"Annia!" A familiar voice broke through the silence that now reigned over the courtyard.

Marcus sat down beside her. "You are the very person I'm looking for," he said, his cheeks pink, the excitement in his voice clear. "How is Flavius?" he asked.

"Oh!" Annia said, forgetting all about Cassia in her delight at remembering her precious child. "It is the most wonderful thing that has ever happened! How did you do it? I can never thank you enough!"

"Yes, but there is something else," he said, his voice dropping.

Annia blinked quickly. "I've heard," she said, her voice formal, her smile forced. "I'm very happy for you."

Marcus looked at her quizzically.

Annia looked away, fighting sudden tears she didn't understand. Was she crying out of joy for having her boys with her? That's not what it felt like. Something was troubling her. Fear? Or did it have something to do with Marcus? She had never given coherent thought to the things she felt for him.

"Annia, something is troubling you. What is it?"

"Why, Marcus," a female voice broke in, startling them.

"I thought I heard your voice." It was Cassia. She had not yet gone into Scribonia's office. Instead, she took both of his hands, and pulled him up off the bench.

She didn't even seem to notice Annia sitting beside him. Annia was in servant's clothes and, therefore, invisible to a senator's daughter. Annia knew she herself had been guilty of similar oversights.

Cassia took Marcus out to the peristyle garden, chattering gaily as she pulled him along. She chose a bench on the farthest end of the garden.

Annia stood and backed away, then headed in the opposite direction, but stopped, realizing in her haste she had forgotten there was but one way to the back pool and fields beyond. The only way she could get back to her quarters was to walk in front of the couple cozily ensconced on the garden bench.

She yearned to get back to her children. She could simply walk by them, like the servant she was. But Philip stopped her.

"While you are here," he said, and handed her a polishing cloth.

She looked at him, trying to read his meaning. The look on his face was kindly understanding.

"The children have all gone to pick olives in the back grove," he said.

Was he trying to put her mind at rest?

She nodded. "Thank you," she said.

And then, he left.

"The girl is lovely," she overheard Scribonia say, completely unaware of the drama unfolding outside of her door. "Her husband was an oaf and a fool. He knew her to be faithful to him—his spies were all over the house, reporting back to him everything she did."

"So I've heard," Nona said.

"The day the baby was born, I walked into his chamber and laid the baby before him. It was the third baby I had laid before Galerius Janius. It was a formality, really. But even then, he was entertaining his new wife-to-be and was furious that I had brought the baby in."

With a jolt, Annia realized they were speaking of her, of her baby. And now she couldn't leave. She busied herself polishing the large urn that stood outside the door. Was this what Philip intended? The urn was as big as Annia, and hid her well.

"'Child of an adulterous woman,' he said when I laid the baby down.

"One of his slaves said, 'Oh, no, master, this is your child, of this we are quite certain.'

"It was one of his house spies. When the poor man spoke, Janius was infuriated. 'Lying thief,' he roared, and had the slave taken directly to the slave market to be sold," Scribonia finished.

"No," Nona said. "Why, that is horrible."

"Yes," Scribonia said, "it was. But my husband heard the story and bought him. No one else was going to. He was not a young man and had served his master and his father before him since he was a boy."

"The poor man. I am so glad you bought him," Nona said.

"He didn't fetch much of a price at the market," Scribonia said. "Poor man. We set him free at once. His fondest desire is to go to Britain and live among his relatives."

"And why is it that Marcus despises Britain?"

Marcus despised Britain? Her home? The news brought new pain. It also stiffened Annia's resolve.

It was very clear to her. To get Marcus out of her heart and mind, she would have to be far, far away. She loved her homeland. There she would be able to forget Marcus. Annia would go home to her mother and father. Britain was the perfect place to go. Besides being far away from Marcus, it was the only place where her children could be safe.

But what she heard next made her more frightened than she had ever been in all of her life.

"I've heard it was not enough for her to be rid of the boys. Even now, I fear she has spies searching for them," Nona said.

"But why?" Scribonia asked.

"The marriage between Janius and his new wife was *sine manu*—she still legally belongs to her father—as does her fortune," Nona responded. "But she has promised to change the status to *cum manu*—under the legal guardianship of her husband—if Janius will get rid of his other three children. She says they must be dead, not simply taken by slave traders, or her father will not agree to it. Only if the inheritance goes to their new son, and him alone, can she rest safely without the *sine manu*."

Annia's heart was beating wildly now. She had to go immediately and find the safest place to take her sons. Britain, place of freedom.

She had no time to even thank Nona.

She had to gather her sweet children. She had to find them a safe place. Far away from Rome. Now.

Action would keep her from having to think. Action would give her heart a chance to heal.

Chapter Ten

Cassia was a sweet girl, Marcus thought as he struggled for sleep in the hot barracks, but compared to Annia, she seemed a mere child. The fact remained. His father wanted him to marry Cassia and so did the senator.

Was that the price of a position as prefect? The senator arranged for Marcus to have an audience with Claudius himself. Marcus was closer to gaining the position than he had ever imagined.

Marcus thought of Annia. He remembered the joy he had felt working side by side with her, cleaning the sheep, scrubbing the floor. They'd shared none of the traditional courting rituals—the dinners, the walks, the family gatherings—and yet he felt a comfort with her. She made him feel for the first time that a family, a wife and children could be something he would enjoy, something he even eagerly anticipated.

When a young messenger called out to him, Marcus woke from his dreams of Annia, and back to the present hot summer day in the barracks of the *Vigiles*.

"Yes," Marcus responded. The boy was about ten, the same age as Annia's oldest.

"My uncle sent me," he said, breathless. "They've taken Arrius Pollio, my brother."

"Who has taken him?" Marcus asked.

"I believe it to be in this note," the boy said, and handed Marcus a paper that had been neither folded nor sealed, so hastily had it been written.

Marcus read it. The note confirmed the boy's message. It did not look like the handwriting of Gamus.

"If this is true, where does your uncle want me to meet him?" Marcus asked, studying the boy carefully.

"At the baths," the boy said. "Outside the bathhouse."

The boy looked very much like Arrius Pollio. Marcus guessed Gamus had sent him. But why would Gamus send an unsealed document written by someone else?

"I will be there," Marcus said.

"Thank you." The boy turned and sprinted in the direction of the baths.

Who would kidnap Arrius Pollio, and for what reason?

He gathered his things—he would be going straight to night duty after the bath—and strode quickly to the bathhouse.

This was the time of day he might normally find a bath relaxing. If someone wanted to share information unobserved, the bathhouse was, ironically, the place to do it. One hardly noticed who talked to whom. Was Gamus waiting for him there?

The bathhouse was large and beautiful. It rose from the street like a palace and was open to all, rich and poor, young and old.

It was, his mother said, the way the empire kept the masses from rioting. Providing beautiful public bathhouses, theaters and plenty of water.

Whatever the reason for the baths, Marcus was grateful for them. On a normal day, he loved the easy camaraderie of the people within. Everyone talked to everyone, and many business transactions occurred while patrons were being oiled and scraped or simply relaxing in the warm or cold baths.

Today would not be a normal day.

Marcus stood at the door and looked for Gamus. In the morning, the bathhouses were reserved for women only, in the afternoon, men. Marcus could not recall ever arriving at this hour. The women had not yet finished their time.

He was relieved to see he was not the only man there. A line of men stood waiting at the door for their turn. He scanned the line, but Gamus was not there.

Soon, the line began moving into the outer room of the bathhouse, where the men would shed their clothes and hang them while they relaxed first in the hot room, followed by the warm room, the steam room and finally the cold room.

Marcus liked the cold room best. Nothing was more invigorating than jumping into cold water after the heat of the steam room. Today he was wary. Where was Gamus? Marcus worked hard to keep to his normal bathing routine. He did not wish to draw attention to himself.

He finished his bath ritual and dressed. Still, no Gamus.

He walked around to the front of the bathhouse.

Marcus looked around him, every muscle in his body taut. Gamus was not one to keep him waiting.

Marcus feared for Gamus's safety. In normal circumstances, Gamus would send a messenger to let him know that he would be running late.

Marcus got a prickly feeling in the pit of his stomach and turned to search for his friend.

"Going so soon?"

Marcus looked around for the speaker.

Galerius Janius looked out at him from a heavily brocaded litter.

Janius motioned Marcus over.

"Come here," he said. "I have business I need to discuss with you. I see you got my note."

"What business have you with me?" Marcus asked.

"You are wondering why I'm here?" Janius said, his tone so jovial it made Marcus's skin crawl. "A very good question. Of course, it's not for the baths. I have my own private bath."

Marcus was silent. Did this odious creature have Gamus?

"Well, my business is this. Aren't you the man who stole my son from my house three days ago?"

Marcus jerked as if scalded. "You ordered he be taken and arrested."

"Have you any proof?" Janius asked, smiling, oblivious of the slaves holding the litter as rivulets of sweat poured down their temples.

"I hear someone has done you a favor and you will be talking to the emperor himself. I would hate for that little plan to be spoiled."

Marcus chastised himself for not saving the note the slave boy had delivered to him.

"So," Janius said, "you are going to lead me to my son, or you are going to bring them to me."

"Bring who to you?" Marcus asked.

"My precious sons, Cato and Flavius. I need neither their mother nor her brat."

Marcus tensed, and Janius noticed. "So the seductress has enticed you, as well? I'm so sorry. She will cheat you as she cheated me."

Did the man truly believe Annia had committed adultery?

Had she?

"Now, run along," Janius said, as if speaking to a child. "You bring me my sons, or I will make certain that your father's villa is burned to the ground."

In that moment, Marcus knew that Janius was bluffing. His father's estate was built of marble and concrete. It would take more than a fire to bring it down.

They must have lost the trail at Gamus's place.

Nona and Gamus. Where were they?

"Not to worry about your friends Nona and Gamus. They are quite safe, probably walking home now, along with Arrius Pollio. His brother was willing to do anything to save him. Even lying to you about meeting me here. Of course, I assured him you wouldn't be hurt."

"Do you ever tire of playing the villain?" Marcus asked.

"Oh, no, not at all. It rather suits me, don't you think? Anyway, your friend Gamus tried to be the brave one. But he is an old man and easily deterred. We only had to threaten to hurt his wife, and he talked readily, telling us how kindly he treated the boy."

Janius motioned to his slaves. They moved forward, their heavy burden straining their muscular bodies.

The hot taste of anger rose in Marcus's throat. "I don't know what you are working to achieve," he called after Janius, "but I know this. In this game, you stand to lose far more than I."

The sound of Janius's laughter spilled from the litter and onto the street like shattering glass. His slaves grunted as they carried their burden.

Marcus sprinted toward Gamus's shop.

He found the merchant and his bedraggled wife limping down the street toward their home.

Seeing Marcus, Gamus called out, "Tried to get us killed, did you? But we are much tougher old birds than you thought." Gamus laughed, and the laughter softened his face and made Nona laugh, as well.

"Ouch," she said and stumbled. "It hurts to laugh."

Marcus rushed forward to catch her. "Are you injured?" he asked, but she brushed him away.

"No," she said, "only my pride. That, and I'm very, very tired. We must have walked ten miles."

"Don't exaggerate, Nona," Gamus said. "It was barely a mile."

"Well, it felt like five," she said, huffing. "And it's hot out here. Very, very hot."

Gamus laughed. "That it is."

Marcus admired the wisdom in their humor. They were being cautious, so as not to draw the attention of anyone on the street that might be listening.

They moved into the shop's sheltering cool. Gamus closed and locked the door behind them.

Inside, they went straight to the cellar. The couple sat heavily on the folding stools stored against the walls, and Marcus stood to listen. He was too nervous to sit.

"Sit down, lad," Nona said. "We've had enough interrogation to last a lifetime."

"Nona is like a star in the sky," Gamus said. "She is a clever woman, more clever than I imagined. When they came looking for the boy, she dressed him like a girl, more quickly than you can snap your fingers, before the soldiers could even find her."

Nona laughed. "That I did. I always wished to have a girl and, instead, I got two battle-hungry boys. I even had some clothes and a doll stored away for a little girl. I pulled the doll down when I looked through my things for old toys the boys played with. Then all I had to do when they came in for him was dress him in a *stola* and thrust the doll in his hands. He took it willingly, and the men, stupid sods, didn't even look twice at him."

Gamus smiled broadly.

"I'm thankful neither of you is seriously hurt," Marcus said. "Who took you and why?"

"Oh, just some street roughs hired, I'm sure, by Galerius Janius. They wanted to be certain that the boy was far, far away. When I told them I'd made a little profit off the boy selling him into slavery, they got all greedy eyed. I told them I had the money in my pocket from the sale and if they would like me to share it with them, no one would be the wiser."

"He's a smart one, my Gamus," Nona said. "They tripped all over themselves reaching for the money Gamus held out to them. We walked away while they were arguing among themselves over who got what."

"So they came into your house that night and took you away?"

"No, no, no," Nona said. "The ruffians came today, just a few hours ago."

"The soldiers came the night you left the boy," Gamus clarified. "They left before the sun rose."

"Then," Nona continued, "I took the boy and we stayed at my sister's house until I felt it was safe to take the boy to his mother."

Marcus remembered the reunion. He could still see Annia's eyes sparkling, surrounded by her boys, cradling Maelia in her arms.

Nothing was so beautiful to him as Annia holding her baby, her sons beside her, her face glowing.

Pure joy. Would he ever know a joy that pure?

His joys had all been on the battlefield. The joy of conquering a city, of expanding an empire.

But now he wished to learn new joys. He believed this woman, Annia, could help him.

She wasn't the woman he had planned on, that was certain, so why couldn't he get her out of his mind? He could see her now, nearly dancing with joy.

"You saw her. She was so happy she danced, Marcus," Nona said. The woman had the most uncanny way of knowing his mind. "I told her you followed through on your promises. I think she understood."

Marcus smiled his response. But then his face clouded with worry.

"He said something," Marcus said, his voice cracking like an adolescent's.

Nona looked at him. "What, son? What did he say?"

"He said that she had slept with someone else, had been completely unfaithful."

"Of course he said that," Nona said. "It's the only way he could get rid of her. But you know, Rome is big, but Rome is small."

"What do you mean by that?" Marcus asked.

"What I mean by that is that I know she has never been unfaithful, if that is what you are thinking."

"How would you know that?"

"My sister is friends with her cook. She says Annia was the sweetest thing the house ever knew. She claims Galerius Janius is a greedy, self-interested pig. She says that he became that way because his father told him he would never amount to anything."

"Are we supposed to feel sorry for him?" Marcus asked.

"No, not at all. It's just nice to know why people are the way they are. He has to prove to himself and everyone else that he will amount to something. He believes power is success and power is for sale."

Marcus had the strangest feeling that those last words were meant for him.

Didn't he believe that power was for sale, and wasn't that the very reason he had gotten involved in this mess in the first place?

What if Annia discovered the real reason he had come for the baby? Because he wanted to advance his career.

"Now, it seems, there is a new worry. But I'm confused, and maybe you can clear it for me. Does Galerius Janius want the boys back or not?" Marcus said.

"Why would he want them home?" Gamus asked. "It's clear that he uses them as pawns in his political game."

"That much is evident," Marcus said. "I can't imagine why he would want them other than keeping them away from Annia."

"He is certainly doing that," Nona said. "But I believe his primary concern to be convincing his new wife that his boys will never get their hands on any of her money. In order to convince her, he has to kill them."

"The only way to protect them is to get them as far away from Rome as possible," Gamus said. "It's clear to me what needs to happen, son."

Marcus listened.

"I've told you before the threat is becoming more menacing every day. Christians are going to be forced to leave Rome. There is controversy among the Jews and believers, you already know that. But Claudius is being advised that we all need to go."

Marcus felt a sickening lurch. Would he lose his position before he had ever even gained it? This could change things completely.

"What is your point, exactly, Gamus?" Nona asked. "I

know you are saying something. I'm just not sure what it is."

"My point is that you have to get Annia out of here as quickly as possible. She and her boys must go," Gamus said.

"My father agrees. Where do you advise me to take them?" Marcus asked.

"You mustn't take them anywhere. But you must send them to Britain. For Annia, I believe this will be easy."

"My sister says Annia's mother and father are both still in Britain. She will be happy to go home," Nona said.

"If she goes, I go, too. She needs my protection," Marcus said, stubborn in his disappointment that Gamus believed he should stay here. His memories of Britain were unpleasant. But sending Annia there alone and unprotected was even more so.

"No, you can't go yet. You will have to convince your mother that she, too, must go. Your father is not in so much danger. He is not a prominent believer. Your mother is."

"How will we find homes for all the mothers and babies?"

"That is something we will have to work on," Gamus said. "I will help you. But for now, you must go and get Annia and her children safe passage on the next ship headed out of the harbor for Britain."

"Go, my child. My prayers are with you," Nona said. "We all do foolish things. God has a funny way of taking the bad and making good out of it if we will let Him."

"I want to believe that," Marcus said. He had done something reprehensible. He had taken gold coins from a man who meant him to harm many people. He needed forgiveness.

"That is what faith is all about." Nona smiled and kissed his forehead.

He felt forgiven.

Chapter Eleven

There were two people that Annia needed. Virginia and the slave that Scribonia and her husband had purchased from Janius.

Annia picked up the bronze needle, gold embroidery thread and purple wool band. She threaded the needle and began working on the series of leaves intertwined with birds and flowers. She tried to remember exactly the picture her own mother had embroidered on the purple band of her first toga and copy it. She would never be the artist her mother was, but embroidering gave her peace.

First, Annia needed to know who exactly the man was who had been so loyal to her that he had been sold. Whoever he was, she was happy to know he would be her ally.

She felt Basso could help her.

Basso was in her garden, weeding.

"What is it, *domina?*" Basso asked. "What can I do for you?"

"There is a man here, a new one. I believe he was purchased at the slave market either last week or the week before by Scribonia."

"Ah," Basso said, "you must be speaking of Titus."

"Titus?" Annia said. Was it true? Her Titus? Annia

had brought Titus with her from Britain when she came to be married.

And he certainly wasn't an old man, not yet. He was only a few years older than Scribonia and Petronius Sergius. If it was the Titus she was thinking of, he was just the man who could help her and her children get to Britain.

"Where is he," Annia asked, trying to keep the excitement out of her voice, "this Titus?"

"He is right here, *domina.*" Basso pointed to the garden, where her very own Titus stood watching the boys swim.

Annia was so relieved to see someone familiar, someone from home, and someone who genuinely loved her that her knees nearly buckled.

"Mother," Cato called, seeing her talking with Basso. "Mother. I was hoping you were going to go back to your sheep this afternoon and walk through the garden and beside our pool. Look who we've found. It's our old friend, Titus."

The boys both jumped from the pool wriggling with excitement like little fish, their tanned bodies glistening with water. They jumped up and down beside Titus, though not so close as to wet him. She was happy to see they were minding their manners in spite of their excitement.

"Titus," Annia said.

"Oh, my lady," Titus answered and hugged her as if she were his own child.

"We are a long way from Britain," Annia said, holding back her tears.

"Yes, my lady, a long way. But I plan to return as soon as I can."

"Do you?"

"Yes. I had saved enough money to buy my freedom when Galerius Janius sold me. When I told Petronius Sergius, he saw to it that my money was returned."

"Galerius Janius is a charlatan," Basso put in. "But Galerius Janius can't cheat our Petronius Sergius, that's for sure."

Annia smiled at the thought of Galerius Janius being forced to part with gold coins.

"But I couldn't leave without saying goodbye," Titus continued.

"I'm so glad you waited," Annia said, and pulled him aside. She waved to the boys. "It's fine, boys," she said, "go on back to the pool and play. It's a perfect day for swimming."

They both looked at her suspiciously. "Why, Mother?" Cato asked. They did not want to miss out on anything.

"Because we are going on an outing soon. Get your swimming done while you still can" was the only excuse Annia could think of to keep his attention off her conversation with Titus.

Titus and Annia walked together to a bench at the edge of the garden, far enough away from prying eyes and ears to be able to talk privately.

"I've overheard something that has brought me great fear," Annia said.

"What is it, my lady?" Titus asked.

"I fear Janius is hunting the boys, hunting them down like prey. Has he no love for them? Why would he want to hurt his own flesh and blood? Why?"

"Oh, my lady, the world is beyond my explaining. Galerius Janius, he said…" His words broke off, and he looked around as if he had heard something. He stood.

Marcus Sergius, the last person Annia wanted to see, took Titus's place beside Annia.

Annia stiffened and pulled away.

"Why do you pull away?" Marcus asked.

"I was talking to Titus," she said. "I need…"

"She needs help getting her boys to safety," Titus finished for her. "I am willing to do everything I can to guarantee safety, but I fear the little that I, a former slave, can do to help you will not be enough."

"What, then?" Annia cried. "If I could just get to Britain, to my father's villa, he could keep us safe."

"It is a long way between here and there," Titus said. "I wish I could do more."

Annia closed her eyes. "I wish I were a man," she said. "If I were a man, I could do what needs to be done!" She shook with rage and frustration. "I would find a way to keep my children safe. I would fight to the death to protect them."

"Yes," Marcus said, "I know that. And you have done much to protect them already. But now, you must let me help you."

"How can you help me?" she asked. "You hate Britain. You never want to see it again." She threw a hand over her own mouth. The words had slipped out before she could stop them. Anger, frustration and very real fear clawed at her insides. She had never felt so desperate.

Marcus put a gentle hand on her shoulder and looked deeply into her eyes. "I don't know what you have heard about me, but this is what you can trust. I am not going to let anything happen to you or your boys. Do you understand me?"

At this, Annia dissolved into tears. Marcus wrapped his strong arms around her, and she relaxed in his arms. She sobbed until her sobs turned to sniffles and then stopped altogether.

She sat up, dried her face on her *palla* and said, "You can keep us safe? You can protect my children?"

He lifted her chin with a gentle finger and said, "Yes."

"Yes," she said, as if repeating his word gave her courage. She smiled a tentative smile. "How?"

"I don't know," Marcus replied, "but I will."

She felt herself relaxing in his promise. But she knew that she must protect herself, as well. It was important that Annia not allow herself that helpless feeling again—that feeling of trusting Marcus completely to hold her, to be strong for her, to take care of her and her children. She must remember that it was only for a short while, until he got them to safety. For a few seconds, it had felt so good to pretend that this man could take care of her and her family forever, but she knew it couldn't last. He was promised to someone else.

"I must go and speak with my father," Marcus said. He looked down at Annia. "I will see you soon."

Annia hated the thrill that went through her stomach. It was very sweet of him to comfort her. But she was certain that was as far as it went.

Titus and Annia watched Marcus take his leave, ruffling the wet, curly heads of the boys as he walked by the pool.

Annia let the boys play in the pool for a while longer than she had planned. It felt good to sit and think while Titus napped in the warm afternoon shade.

Titus awakened with a jerk and turned to Annia. "Petronius Sergius doesn't want his son doing anything foolish trying to save you."

"I know," Annia said. "I heard it myself just a few days ago. His father has already picked out a young woman for him."

"That may be," Titus said. "But from what I have just

observed in the young man himself, he would gladly risk his life for you."

"I've just heard Scribonia talking with Nona, and Nona said that he wanted…" The words were almost too difficult for Annia to spit out. "…an unmarried woman. Besides that, he is already promised to Cassia."

"Well, my lady, all I know is what I have seen." Titus grinned and nodded toward the garden gate directly behind them.

Annia looked over, and there Marcus was, again. He now looked relaxed and happy. Whatever his father had told him had calmed him.

She felt an uncontrollable anger. In the next instant, she shivered with excitement. She was infuriated by the complexity of her emotions. She didn't know what she wanted to feel, nor what she should feel.

She glanced at the boys playing happily in the pool.

Marcus Sergius, his short blond hair shining like a halo above his head, his eyes dancing, approached them.

"You were listening," she said, her words clipped.

"No, I wasn't," he said.

Annia tried to think of what she had said, and what he might have overheard.

"I owe you thanks," she said. Simple was all she could summon.

"You owe me nothing," he said, his face a play of obviously painful emotions.

What was he fighting? He was promised. That was it.

"I need you to go with Titus to Britain," he said. "Father agreed with Titus about Galerius Janius."

Her eyes narrowed. "But you can't go?" Was he so eager to send her away alone?

"There are many things I need to tell you. Father just received word that I've been made prefect of the *Vigiles*."

Annia's breath caught. "Oh, Marcus. It is what you have always wanted. The position will take you to where you want to be—prefect of the Guard. That is the best news I've heard."

Her eyes shone. "It's not yet prefect of the Praetorian Guard," he said. "But it is a step in that direction. You are right. I believe that if I do a good job as prefect of the *Vigiles,* I will be eventually earn the position of prefect of the Guard."

"I know you can do it," she said. "The emperor merely needs to see you in action, and he will be quick to appoint you to be prefect of the Guard!"

Marcus smiled back at her, but there was something else, something he wasn't telling her. She could feel it.

"What is it?" she asked.

"I think it would be best if we prepare you and your boys to leave Rome immediately. I think Galerius Janius will not rest until you are all gone."

Of course. Once she was gone, it would be so much easier for him to follow his dream. He could stay here in Rome, marry Cassia and settle into a life of ease.

"How soon can we leave?" she asked, hiding her pain, resigned to make the best of this new situation.

"And, my father has just told me that things have become more difficult than we even knew," he said.

"How can things be more difficult than what you have just told me?"

"It is being rumored that Emperor Claudius will make a formal decree in the next week banning all Jews and believers from the city of Rome."

"No. That can't be," Annia said. "Why, Claudius is the most tolerant of us all. He has close ties to Herod Agrippa, or so I have been told."

"Yes, but there has been talk of riots and anarchy in the

Jewish quarter. Jew against believer and believer against Jew."

"But why should that affect us?"

"For decades, Jews have been allowed to worship the one God and not bow down to the emperor—they were given permission to worship in the traditions of their ancestors. But believers have only recently chosen to worship Christ over the emperor. And Claudius can't discern Jews from Christians. So he is getting rid of us all."

Marcus would be prefect of the *Vigiles,* and that meant he would have to stay in Rome.

"Can't we wait until the order is real?" Annia asked, though she knew she was grasping at feathers in the wind.

"No. If we do that, we will have a very difficult time getting Mother and all the babies out. Already, the task will be difficult enough simply convincing her she needs to go. I have to send those who wish to go first. You are lucky. You have a home in Britain. Claudius really doesn't care what you worship when you are there. You are too far away to cause him any trouble."

"I understand," Annia said, trying to think more rationally. Leaving Marcus would be difficult. But, perhaps, only temporary? "And what of the others, what of the women here? Do you need for me to take anyone with me? We have plenty of room at our villa for at least a few of them and their babies."

Marcus looked very relieved. "I was so hoping you would offer that," he said. "We have a villa there, as well, but I fear that it is not quite large enough to hold all the women we have here."

He looked off into the distance. "What I fear most, however," he said, "is that I will not be able to talk my mother into leaving. I fear that she will insist on staying. Her work is here, she will say."

"Can't your father convince her?" Annia asked.

"No," he said. "My father believes in her mission almost as much as she. I suspect what will happen is that as soon as we take as many women and babies as will go to Britain, she will fill the villa up again with new babies."

Annia smiled. "She is a great woman, your mother."

Marcus looked at Annia. "That she is. I just hope she is able to protect herself. She can't afford to be foolish. There are too many lives at stake."

"Do you believe she will see that after a while?" Annia asked.

"I hope."

"And what of you?" she asked. Hoping, praying that he could come with them, that all of them could escape this place. But she knew better.

"My duty is here," he said, avoiding her eyes.

Chapter Twelve

"We can't get a boat out for three more days," Marcus said. "In the meantime, there is something I want you to see."

Three days? That was all? And then she would never see him again. He would marry Cassia and stay in Rome and enjoy his new position.

"I have a lot to do," she said. "I have to finish combing this last bit of wool. We are finally finished with all three fleeces. Washed, pulled and combed. I'll take some on the boat and spin it. It will keep all of us busy on the long journey. And I haven't even started gathering food and clothes for the children."

"The children will be fine, and you will have plenty of time to prepare everything. Come with me this evening after the children are fed and put to bed, and I will show you."

She couldn't resist him. And it infuriated her.

Annia finished the last of her combing, gathered the neat piles of combed wool and laid them carefully in the cloth bags Marcus had brought for her. She slung one across her shoulder, picked up Maelia and handed Marcus the other two to sling across his shoulders.

"It's too hot to be carrying around this much wool," he said, laughing as he shouldered the bags.

She didn't feel as at ease with him as she had felt before. She didn't want to fall for a man she had no hope of being with. His duty was to Rome and the emperor, and Cassia, not to her.

Before they reached the garden door, they heard giggling and splashing.

"Those boys," Annia said, relieved by their joy. "They think they are fish. It is hard to keep them out of that pool."

"It's not just your boys now. You'll see," Marcus said, holding the heavy wooden villa door open for her.

And Marcus was right. It wasn't just her boys in the pool. Lucia and Julius had joined them, and it looked as though Cato was busy giving them swimming lessons.

"See," Marcus said, "I told you they were having fun. And, like their mother, working at the same time."

"Do this," Cato said, instructing Lucia, and put his face down in the water.

Lucia obediently followed suit. Her bright red hair swirled just beneath the water's surface.

Julius looked at Cato and followed his lead, placing his little face down in the water, then lifting it, coughing and spitting. It was clear Julius was willing to do anything his new hero was doing.

"You can't breathe under the water, Julius," Cato said, and shook his head.

"I wasn't," Julius returned, his eyes blazing.

"It looks as though Cato has found a friend," Marcus said, smiling.

"I pray Cato is always conducting himself honorably when his little friend is following," Annia said.

Lucia popped up from underwater, laughing, water

bouncing off her springy red curls. "I held my breath underwater!"

She noticed Annia and Marcus, and said, as if explaining herself, "I decided that if Julius and I didn't learn to swim as soon as possible, the two of us would eventually drown. He shows no intention of staying out of the water. Flavius and Cato have each fished him out at least once."

"Learning to swim is a very good idea," Annia agreed.

"I'm teaching Julius, Mother," Flavius called. "See? Come here, Julius." And Julius moved closer to Flavius.

He allowed Flavius to lay him on his back in the water, holding him up with one hand. Julius stared solemnly at the clear blue July sky.

"See, Mother?" Flavius said. "He's floating. Watch this."

Flavius whispered something to Julius, and Julius smiled. It was clear Julius had two heroes.

"Ready?" Flavius said, and then let go of Julius. The child bobbled for a moment, then floated atop the water like a little cork.

"Good," Annia called to the boys. "That is wonderful, Julius. Good job teaching them, Flavius and Cato. You may very well be saving their lives."

"Watch this, Annia. I can do a lot more than hold my breath underwater."

Lucia propelled herself toward the middle of the pool, paddling like a dog. Julius followed closely behind, splashing as hard as his hands would allow.

"Why did no one ever tell me how happy swimming could make you feel?" Lucia asked when she had reached the other end, Julius close behind.

They all laughed.

"By tomorrow afternoon," Cato said, "they will be

swimming the way you're supposed to swim. They learn fast."

Lucia and Julius beamed as if they had been given an ivy crown.

"Be sure to teach Lucia how to save people in the water," Annia said.

"Don't worry," Lucia said. "I've already made that request."

"Someone here besides Basso must be able to save babies from the stream," Annia said.

"Yes," Lucia said, "and I plan to teach anyone willing to learn as quickly as I can."

Annia threw Lucia a puzzled look. "That's lovely. The more able to swim and save lives in this villa, the better," she said.

"That's not what I mean," Lucia said. "I'll have to teach someone else. I'm coming to Britain with you."

"Really?" Annia asked. A friend on the journey home would double her joy.

"Oh, Lucia. I am so happy," she said. Annia held her arms out to hug her wet friend.

"I decided yesterday," Lucia said, "when Scribonia asked if anyone wished to go. So far, I am the only one. Everyone else has heard such stories about the wilds of Britain—the men painted blue, beating their shields, tall as giants—that no one else would go. But I knew that if you were from there, it couldn't be so bad."

"You will love it," Annia said. "It's not like Rome, where the sun blinds you. There, the sky is a softer blue. Most of Britain is densely wooded, and in spring, full of bluebells and primroses. But," she added, her voice taking on a warning tone, "it is not warm very often. It is cool most of the time. Not painfully so, but cool."

"So all that wool will be put to good use?" Lucia asked, teasing her.

"Ah, yes," Annia said. "You will become the wool-working queen after we've been there for a few winters."

"I look forward to it," Lucia said, rolling her eyes, but smiling.

"I wish you could meet my friend, Virginia," Annia said. "I wish she were coming, too. What fun the three of us could have together. You would love her, and she would love you."

How could she find Virginia so that she could go with her, as well? Annia wondered if Virginia might possibly still be back at her modest villa on the outskirts of Rome. It couldn't be too far from here.

"Do you think it would be too dangerous to go back to my villa and get Virginia?" Annia asked Marcus.

"I'm working on that," Marcus said. "I've got people watching your villa to see if it's safe."

"Is Virginia still there?" Annia asked, her joy bubbling over her words. "Although I'm not sure where else she could have gone."

"Yes, she is," Marcus said. "And, according to a very reliable spy, she works very hard keeping it clean and beautiful."

"I hope she is not alone," Annia said. "Did any of the servants stay to help her?" She worried for her friend and knew that she would do everything and more to keep the house safe, clean and ready for Annia's return.

Virginia had always done more than asked, putting Annia's comfort before her own desires. Yes, she was a slave, but being a slave did not necessitate loving your mistress.

The bond between the two women had grown stronger over the years. Only Virginia understood the pain Annia had suffered over the many years knowing Janius loved only her money.

Virginia had carried her through the heart-killing pain of being thrown out of her house and wrenched from her boys.

Virginia had reminded her that her hope had to be in the Lord and not in men.

"Titus has gone to help her," Marcus said. "I believe he intends to marry her as soon as she gains her freedom."

"That is perfect," Annia said. "I am so happy."

And she was. It made her feel safe to know that not only did she still have a safe home of her own, even if she couldn't go back and live in it, but it was filled with people she loved and who loved her.

"Come on, then," Marcus said, turning her attention from Virginia. "We will take time for baths and then be ready for the evening."

"Baths?" Annia said. "Indeed."

In one swift movement, she pushed Marcus into the bathing pool.

Quick as a flash, she shed her outer layers of clothing, right down to her undertoga, laid Maelia on the little garden bench, making certain she couldn't wriggle off, and jumped into the pool landing beside him.

"You didn't expect that, did you?" she said, turning to laugh at Marcus's surprise. "You can swim, right?" she asked, a small shadow of worry crossing her face.

"Across the Mere Internum from Italia to Corsica if I have to."

"That, my good fellow, is quite a boast," Annia said, splashing him in the face for his overwhelming pride.

"Mother," Flavius said, "race him."

"Sounds like a challenge to me," Marcus said.

He climbed from the pool, shed his outer garments,

made his way to the far end of the pool and stood waiting for her.

His chest was that of a seasoned Roman soldier, massively strong but scarred.

"Ready?" he asked, taunting her with a mischievous glint in his sparkling green eyes.

"I've never been more ready in my life," she teased.

"Come on, then," he said, nodding as if he were already the victor.

Annia pursed her lips. "You think you can win?" she said. "You've never seen me swim."

"The challenge is accepted," Marcus said.

Cato, Lucia, Flavius and little Julius moved aside, laughing at their playful taunting, eager to see who would win. They took seats on the edge of the pool, their feet dangling in the water.

"I'll be the judge," Cato said.

Annia pulled herself out of the pool and stood at the edge next to Marcus, ready to dive in.

"No," Cato said, "the pool is too shallow and short for diving. You'll have to begin in the water, touching the side of the pool."

"A wise judge," Marcus said, "saving lives." It was clear that he admired the child for his foresight.

"Good boy," Annia said. "You kept your mother from being a fool."

"Now," Cato said after they had climbed back down into the cooling waters and stood tense and ready to go at its edge. "Champions, begin!"

Annia and Marcus kicked off the side of the pool, and Annia took the lead.

"Swim, Mother, swim," Flavius said, and Julius took up the chant.

"Someone has to yell for Marcus," Lucia said.

"I can't yell for anyone," Cato said. "I'm the official. You will have to."

"Swim, Marcus, swim," Lucia said.

By the middle of the pool, the race was close. The water was Annia's safe place, and she had been swimming since she was a child, so she was lithe and quick.

"You can win, Mother, you can," Flavius yelled.

They raced past Flavius, who stood on the center side of the pool, and Marcus began catching up.

"You can win, Marcus," Lucia yelled. "You are gaining on her!"

They were almost to the end, and it still was not clear who was going to slap the pool edge first.

Cato stood at the end of the pool leaning down, close to the edge so that he wouldn't miss the first hand.

"I think she's going to win," Flavius said, echoed by Julius.

Annia pulled forward.

"Win, win, win," the boys chanted.

But it was not to be. Marcus was bigger and stronger and, it turned out, faster.

His hand slapped the edge a short moment before Annia's.

"And it's Marcus, the winner and champion," Cato said, holding Marcus's hand up in victory.

Marcus turned to Annia, eyes wide. "You meant it when you said you were fast," he said, laughing, the water pouring in streams down his face. "I've never raced a woman, and I've never seen one who could swim so fast."

Annia hated losing, but she was pleased that she had come so close to winning.

"We forgot a crown," Flavius said. "Marcus needs a crown." He ran to the ivy growing up the garden wall, broke off a vine and twirling it quickly into a crown, turned and placed it on Marcus's head.

Annia shook his hand. "Congratulations, champion," she said, her face a wreath of smiles. "But next time, the honor will be mine."

They played in the water for a while until Maelia began making tiny sucking noises that soon turned into grunts, then full-bodied cries.

"I think you are being summoned," Lucia said.

"I think you are right," Annia said. "It appears my swimming for the day is complete."

"See you in the atrium as soon as you feed her and get dressed," Marcus said, smiling. "Wear your best *palla*." He winked.

Annia felt giddy as a girl. She picked up Maelia and walked as quickly as her legs would take her to her room, where she fed Maelia and dreamed of a family where the father loved the mother.

Chapter Thirteen

The sun had not yet set when Marcus offered Annia his arm. They walked out of the villa and into the golden hour of late afternoon.

A shadow behind her made her catch her breath and turn.

"Don't be alarmed," he said. "I have a few people watching."

"For the boys?" she asked.

"Yes," he said. "They will be safe, and we will not be followed."

"Thank you," she said, and meant it.

The evening promised to be perfect. A breeze cooled the summer-hot street, and the people they passed, their day chores done, were cheerful, hurrying home to their families or to meet friends for dinner.

Marcus led her through the gilded afternoon to a corner of Rome where she had never been, where there was no chance of her being seen or recognized.

The street felt familiar, though it wasn't. The sights, sounds and smells took her back to a place from her girlhood.

She felt she was in the heart of the little village near her home.

The people in this corner of the city that was Rome were dressed in the clothes of Britain. The women wore capes rather than *pallas* and the men lace-up buckskin boots like the shepherds of her homeland.

There were cheese shops and wool workers' shops, and the accent she heard on the sidewalks reminded her of her mother.

"What is this place?" she asked Marcus, looking around her in wonder.

"I thought you might like it," he said. "This is called Little Britain, where freedmen have settled with others from their homeland."

"It's wonderful," Annia said. "How did I never know?"

He led her to a storefront. Just beyond the vendor's wares was a secret gate, leading to a garden beyond.

The sweet scent of lavender wafted through the iron gate, adorned with complicated circles and knots and sprinkled with bronze-work leaves.

The gate, so similar to the one guarding her girlhood garden, stopped her. She touched the filigreed knots and leaves, running her fingers over them, relishing their familiarity.

"Close your eyes," he said, taking her hands in his and opening the gate.

"Where are you taking me?" she asked, but her excitement at being among people and things that were so familiar made her trust him to take her to a place that would bring her joy. She was not afraid.

He led her down the garden path, the scent of lavender growing stronger and placed her hand in the hand of another. A woman, Annia was certain, her hands soft and small.

"Open your eyes now," the woman whispered.

Annia was in a cool white room surrounded by floating curtains where the woman's dreamlike hands helped her slip out of her street clothes and into a garment that was made of a light, silken material. The dress reached her toes and floated and swished around her legs when she turned.

Other women surrounded her and silently caught her hair up in an elaborate braid and sprinkled it with a light golden powder so that it sparkled in the candlelight. They placed soft kidskin dancing shoes on her feet and rubbed her arms and shoulders with scented oil.

They led her out onto a green lined with glowing lanterns and adorned with a silken canopy.

When they led her beneath the canopy, she heard a familiar drumming. The drumming was joined by a pipe, and soon strings echoed.

The familiar music took her back to summer nights round dances on the village green, nights of mystery, joy and laughter.

She remembered watching her parents dance and being at once delighted and a little frightened by the seriousness of her mother's face as her father led her, gracefully navigating the complicated rhythms and patterns of the dance.

Marcus held his hand out to her. She trembled when she took it. Did he invite her to this ritual with full knowledge of its meaning?

This was the harvest dance, a courtship dance, the round dance of God and life and love.

He couldn't know its true meaning. If he did, he would not be dancing it with her.

Her foot tapped to the rhythm of the drum, and before she could think any further, she took his hand and together they claimed their space in the middle of the circle of dancers.

As they faced each other, waiting for the dance to begin, Marcus's face was at once serious and kind.

Annia looked deeply into his eyes, captivated by this man who had woven for her an evening so beautiful that she would remember it always.

The dance began.

Marcus stepped forward, bowed and touched both his hands to hers, palm meeting palm, just a touch, then withdrew and stepped back.

Annia stepped forward and curtsied. She made a half turn, then another, her silken gown flowing like gossamer around her feet.

She held her hand out, palm up, and waited for Marcus to meet her hand and pull her to him, then back again, forward and back.

The pipes and strings joined the drums, and now Marcus and Annia turned to the side, circled each other, bowed and lifted one arm then the next, keeping their eyes on each other until they turned away, then back again.

The dance was somber at first, prayer-like, and then the music's tempo increased and the circles became faster and faster, the dancers swirling until they were dizzy, their feet keeping quick jostling time to the music.

When the dance was finished, they laughed and then stood still and waited for the next dance.

This one was much slower, and the dancers swayed and melded together until it was difficult to tell them apart.

The dips and turns of this dance were done while Marcus held Annia securely about her waist. Annia leaned back, Marcus's arm holding her tight. Marcus leaned over her; then they stood tall and pressed together, side against side.

This dance was far more complicated and required Annia to have perfect trust of Marcus holding her safe. The dips and lifts were dramatic, and if their timing was off, Annia would surely fall.

But there was no such confusion. Annia and Marcus danced as if they were made to be with each other. Annia pressed her tiny hands firmly against Marcus's big, strong hands, giving him a solid partner to work with.

She looked up into his eyes, and his smile melted her.

Any resistance she might previously have felt to his charm disappeared by the end of this dance.

"Is there someone else?" he asked.

She looked up at him, understanding exactly what he was asking, but she didn't answer. She couldn't. Even if he weren't promised to someone else, was there room for her in his quest to be prefect?

In the final dance, the circle of dancers entwined upon itself. Original partners lost each other to other partners one, two, three, four times before being reunited in a twirling, swirling circle.

Just as the music pushed them together, it pulled them quickly apart, and they were on the arms of others, passed from one to the next at opposite ends of the circle from each other. Again, a slow weaving, at the end of which they found each other, embraced, twirled and in a final triumph, Marcus lifted Annia high in the air, turning three times.

Slowly he let her down, and she stood securely on her own two feet.

Each was breathless. Each silent.

They looked at each other, and Annia knew she would never feel this way about anyone else. But did he feel the same?

The music quieted, and the dancers congratulated one

another, and then went back into the dressing rooms to change back into their own clothing.

When they walked back home, Annia said, "What was that place? It was wonderful."

Marcus responded with only three words, "Yes, it was."

"And how did you learn the dances?" she asked. She had not danced them since she was a girl.

"I haven't danced them since I was a boy," Marcus said. "We moved from Britain when I was ten and Father was offered a job with the imperial government."

"How did you find this place?" Annia asked.

"I was trying to avoid being followed by Janius's spies, going home a completely different way, and I happened upon this neighborhood. The people here, for the most part, were born and raised in Britain. They live in this neighborhood and keep the old ways as best they can."

"Well, it appears that what Janius meant for evil, God used for good. I haven't had that much fun since I was a girl."

Marcus's smile told her this response was what he had hoped for.

Chapter Fourteen

The following morning, Marcus was able to take Annia to her modest villa on the outskirts of Rome.

Annia decided that for the remainder of the days she had left in Rome, she would enjoy his company. When she returned to Britain, she would never see him again.

"If I had realized how close my own little villa was, I would have gone myself," Annia said.

"Yes," Marcus said, "I know that, and it was important that you didn't know. I knew if you did go back, there was a very good chance you would be found then followed back to the villa and your children taken. Your villa was watched for several days after I came for Maelia. But Janius seems to have lost interest in the hunt."

Annia's cheeks were sore from the smile she had worn since she woke up. She was so eager to see her friend Virginia she could barely contain herself and hardly heard what Marcus said.

"I hope you are this happy to see *me* someday," Marcus said, teasing her.

"I've never had a friend like Virginia," Annia said, hiding the thrill she felt at Marcus's words. "She is closer to me than a sister."

"I see that," Marcus said.

"But wait," Annia said. "I've forgotten something."

"If it's your children, you didn't forget them. They are being kept under the watchful eye of Lucia," Marcus said. "And I suspect my mother is fighting with her over the watch. I think she planned to relieve Lucia of her baby-tending duties so that she herself could take over."

"That is kind of your mother," Annia said, and meant it. But she was distracted.

She stopped on the side of the road only a few yards from their destination.

"We must go back," she said.

"Whatever for?" Marcus asked. They were so close to the villa now, he could have thrown a stone through the round bronze doorknockers.

"Her manumission papers," Annia said. "I want to present them to her as soon as I see her."

The papers granting Virginia her freedom had been drawn up by his father's clerk and signed and sealed with the official state seal.

Virginia was a free woman.

"Oh, I must go back and get them," Annia said. "I want to hand them to her."

Marcus shook his head. "Can't you just tell her you have them?"

"No, it's not the same," Annia said. "I have to hand them to her, physical proof that she is a free woman."

"If it's that important to you, then by all means," he said, "let's go back and get them." He shook his head again in mock exasperation. "Women," he said. "Such strange and wonderful creatures."

Annia laughed, took his hand and ran. He was forced to run with her or let go of her hand, which he didn't seem willing to do.

Within a few minutes they were back at the front of the villa, manumission papers in hand.

Annia knocked at her own front door, which she was quite certain was bolted from the inside, then stood waiting.

The door opened, and Virginia's sweet face peered from behind.

"Do I know you?" Virginia asked, a gleam in her eye, her smile reaching practically from ear to ear.

Annia lifted her off the ground and swirled her around in an enthusiastic hug.

"I've missed your enthusiasm," Virginia said, picking herself up from the floor where the two of them had fallen in a heap. "I'd forgotten what it was like to be knocked over by a giant six-month-old sheepdog. Thank you for reminding me."

Marcus laughed as hard as Annia. Virginia's lively spirit made clear that in her presence there was no need for pretense.

She hugged Annia hard, and they stood, clinging to each other.

Virginia looked up at Marcus, squinted, wrinkled her brow and said, mocking his deep, gravelly voice, "Marcus Sergius Peregrinus? Aren't you the one who took her away?"

Annia laughed outright at her. "Yes, he is," she said. "But now he's brought me back. I'd like to introduce you to my friend Marcus Sergius." She stepped away, giving Marcus a little push forward. She wanted to see if Virginia saw what she saw in this man. She trusted Virginia's instincts.

Marcus obliged, stepping forward and greeting Virginia.

He took her hand gently and looked into her eyes. "Annia has told me of your kindness."

"Oh," she said, looking back to Annia in approval, "nice, very nice manners." She winked at Annia when he kissed her hand, the *basium* no small surprise.

"Good hands," she said, pulling his hand to her and holding it up in the sunlight to examine. "Yes," she said, growing more serious by the moment, "a soldier's hands. See the calluses, here and here." She pointed as if examining a scroll. She looked up at Marcus.

A prickle of anxiety moved Annia closer to Virginia's side. She had known Virginia since they were girls. She could tell that Virginia did not trust Marcus.

"It's where he held his *gladius,*" she said, showing Annia.

Annia nodded. "Yes, of course," she said, curious as to why Virginia felt this minute inspection necessary.

Virginia looked up at Marcus. "Let me see your other hand."

The atrium grew very quiet.

He held his hand up to her obediently. Marcus was wary but friendly.

"Ah, yes," Virginia said, "and here, a callus from your shield. You used it as a weapon, in many battles, did you not?" she said, backing away as if examining the rest of him.

Marcus raised his eyebrows and nodded. "How do you know so much about the hands of soldiers," he asked, his curiosity overriding his good manners, "and why this close inspection? You seem to be looking for a birthmark. I have none."

"What I am searching for in you is not for you to know," Virginia said, and for just a moment, anger blazed in her eyes. "If I find it necessary to shield my mistress from those I do not trust, I will do so, and I certainly don't need your permission."

"He's safe, Virginia," Annia said. "He's not going to harm me or you. He saved my life and that of Maelia," she said, looking back to Marcus for confirmation.

"And look, Virginia. Look at what Marcus was able to help me get," Annia said, pointing to the papers in Marcus's hands.

Annia took the manumission papers and held them out to Virginia, hoping to change Virginia's focus from Marcus to freedom.

"You are my dearest friend, and I couldn't think of anything better to give you. Please accept this as a token of my deep love for you."

She handed Virginia the papers.

It worked. Virginia took the papers, her eyes wide with surprise.

She moved into the sunniest patch of the atrium and sat on a bench and read every word.

When Virginia had finished reading, tears trickled down her face. She batted them away. Not one to show emotion, she waited until she had regained control, then turned to Annia.

"Thank you," she said. She folded the papers neatly and secured them in the flat leather pocket she had sewn herself and attached to her belt.

Annia smiled and nodded. She kissed Virginia's cheek.

"Now, then," Annia said, "are there any forthcoming changes in your life that you would like to share with me?"

Virginia blushed this time. "I suppose you have already heard, or you wouldn't be asking."

"Tell me everything," Annia demanded.

"Like what?" Virginia asked, but her glow told Annia

she was bursting to share. "Titus and I are going to marry."

"When?" Annia asked.

"As soon as we get home," Virginia said. "Our real home. Caledonia."

Annia's face fell. "Oh," she said. "I'm so happy for you. But Caledonia? It is so far away, so far north from our villa in Britain."

"It's his home, Annia. Just as you long for Britain, he longs for Caledonia."

"But what of your home?" Marcus asked.

"I was taken as a young girl when my village was burned and my parents killed. I was blessed enough to be rescued from the menacing hands of soldiers by Annia's father."

Annia reached for Virginia's hand and squeezed it.

"He took me to your home and treated me like a daughter, and for that, I will be forever grateful. But I want a family of my own. I want to have a mother and father, sisters and brothers, even if it is only through the bond of marriage." Tears glistened in Virginia's eyes but did not spill.

Annia nodded. "I understand," she said. "Very much. Well, then, I shall enjoy the weeks we have left together until then."

"As shall I," Virginia said. "I've missed you."

"We have much work to do," Annia said. "Two days to pack all of our things and begin our journey."

"Will you be coming with us?" Virginia said, addressing Marcus directly.

"I had thought not at first," Marcus said, "but now, it seems, my father wishes that I go and prepare the villa for my mother and the rest of the babies and their mothers."

This was news to Annia. "Oh, Marcus," she said,

"when did he tell you?" She was giddy with joy. She would have at least a few more days with him in Britain before the inevitable happened and he returned to Rome.

"This morning, before you were awake," he said. "Father has heard more news and believes the expulsion to be imminent."

"What expulsion?" Virginia asked.

"The expulsion of the Jews and Christians from Rome," Marcus answered.

"Well," Virginia said, "better now than last month. We have already booked passage for a journey of our own. Titus planned to use all the money he has saved to buy me from you."

"He must love you deeply," Annia replied.

"Yes," Virginia said, her cheeks glowing. "And now we can use his savings to buy land and build our own house and farm."

Annia looked at her, her face a wide-eyed question. "But how do you know we are traveling together?"

"Because," Virginia said, "Titus has booked passage for all of us at the request of Marcus's father."

"So," Marcus said, "you pretended I was a stranger, knowing all the time who I was?"

"Do you think I would have opened the door for you otherwise?" she asked.

"Certainly not," Marcus said, laughing. But there was a tightness in his voice that Annia had not heard before. "I see why she is your dear friend, Annia."

Annia nodded. "She notices everything."

Marcus said, "I will leave the two of you to your packing. I will be back at the noon hour to collect you, Annia, and take you back to your children."

Annia nodded.

Marcus looked once again at Virginia. Did he seek approval? "Good day," he said. "It was very nice to have met you under much more pleasant circumstances."

"And you," Virginia said graciously with a slight nod.

Marcus left, and Annia turned to Virginia. "You have many secrets," she said.

"You still need my protection," Virginia replied. She turned on her heel and looked back over her shoulder at Annia, who was shaking her head. "Come along, then, mistress. We have work to do."

"Mistress no longer," Annia said, linking arms with Virginia. "Just friend."

For Marcus, the joy was mixed. He had postponed his meeting with the emperor because of this most recent news. Marcus was, after all, a believer. He had decided it best to travel to Britain before that particular bit of information was revealed to the emperor.

Officially, he was traveling as an emissary to check on the progress made on organizing fire brigades in the colony of Britain.

If his work was good, he would have something in hand to present the emperor as a token of excellent service proving his worth for his new job as prefect.

But Marcus knew Annia would be staying in Britain.

Marcus yearned to be prefect. He still wanted that glory. He couldn't deny it. Nor could he help it. It might be that he would marry Cassia in order to be prefect. Possibly, as prefect, he could help Annia and the rest of his family secure a safe place in the empire.

Or so he chose to believe.

Chapter Fifteen

On a clear day in midsummer, after two months' travel over land and sea, the ship's captain announced that they would make landfall on the southern coast of Britain within a day if the weather cooperated.

The children were ecstatic, as were the adults. Annia would be quite happy to never look at the sea again for the remainder of her days.

She picked up the bronze needle, gold embroidery thread and purple wool band. She threaded the needle and began working on the series of leaves intertwined with birds and flowers. She was almost finished.

The journey by sea had been far more pleasant than Annia had expected. She had plenty of time to work on the band of Maelia's *toga praetexta*. She couldn't wait for her mother to see it. She would never be the artist her mother was, but embroidering helped pass the time.

One sailor pointed out southern Lugdunum, the coast jabbing out into the sea, almost meeting the southern coast of Britain and their port.

Another sailor cautioned Annia, "This part of the sea is known for its unpredictability."

"How so?" Annia asked.

"On a clear day, a gale can blow up so quickly that you don't know it's coming until it's gone," he said, climbing back up the mast to check the sails.

Annia noticed the rest of the sailors getting more anxious the closer the ship came to Britain.

"Many a time we've gotten this close to land, and a storm has blown in and set us back out to sea for three days or more," the sailor said.

"Keep your babes close," he advised. "Be sure they have something that floats."

"But what?" she asked.

"Inflated bladders of animal skins or hollow, sealed gourds," he replied. Annia was disturbed by the man's fear. Should she be worried?

Why hadn't she thought of making these flotation devices for her children?

But she had to use her reason. She could see the shore from where they were. Even if a storm came upon them now, she could swim to shore.

But what of her baby? Maelia was tied close to her chest in the baby sling. But would she be able to keep her head above the water? Annia felt sweat bead on her forehead.

She thought maybe discussing it with Lucia would help her make a plan and calm her panic.

Lucia stood with a rope tied to her waist. On the other end was Julius. When he wanted to play with Cato and Flavius, the rope was tied around Cato.

Lucia had been afraid he would jump overboard when they first got on the boat and he had pointed to the water and asked if he could swim.

When the dolphins followed the boat, Lucia had to shorten the rope, as they proved too great a temptation to her small sailor. He rebelled, screaming and kicking, and it took Cato and Flavius together to convince him that he needed to stay in the boat with them rather than jumping overboard and swimming with the dolphins.

Right now they sat in the little coracle Marcus brought from Rome and tied to the side of the ship. They were pretending they were sailors, afloat on the high seas. They allowed Julius to sit in the tiny, round boat with them.

The coracle was of no use in Rome. The currents weren't strong enough in the rivers. But the coracle was perfect for Britain where the currents flowed with the tides.

"I had this coracle when I was a boy in Britain," Marcus told Annia when she asked him why he was bringing it, "and it gave me so much joy. I wanted to share that joy with the boys. I'm hoping they can find a nearby river and fish and swim as I did."

He'd kept the little boat in perfect shape, replacing the old skins that had covered the exterior of the boat with a perfectly carved and fitted wooden exterior. The wood made the boat safer, much more difficult to puncture and sink.

"Did you ever fear drowning?" Annia asked.

"Yes," Marcus replied. "A few times when we crossed deep rivers. We tied inflated and sealed animal bladders to our arms. I'm not sure how much they helped, but they certainly raised the morale of the men who couldn't swim," he said.

"Could you make some for the children?" she asked.

"I'll do my best," he said, and strode away, looking, she was certain, for animal bladders.

As soon as he walked away, she realized she had given him a nearly impossible task.

Where on this boat would he find animal bladders?

Or skins? The only thing this boat was full of was wine and military supplies for the soldiers stationed in Britain.

On her next journey, she would be better prepared.

The tide pushed the boat out to sea on this, the first day they attempted to make landfall. They decided to try for safe harbor the next morning.

Late in the night, the wind began a ghostly howling. Rain fell, first as a delicate mist, and then in long, slashing drops.

Annia awoke when the rain began. She stabilized the portable canvas roof over the boys sleeping peacefully in the coracle. Then, she made certain there was a roof over Lucia and Julius. They all slept so peacefully. She wished she could do the same.

She heeded the sailor's earlier advice and kept watch over her boys.

When the wind whistled over the waves and the boat began rocking, then climbing, higher and higher on waves that grew larger and larger, then falling down what felt like a valley without a bottom, Annia grew scared.

She made certain once again that all were sleeping peacefully, and went looking for Marcus.

In the rainy darkness, she found him.

"You scared me," she said. "Why aren't you on the men's side?"

"I was worried," he said. "This storm is like many others I've seen. It's going to get worse before it gets better."

He strode hurriedly over, looking over the sleeping passengers.

"Where are the boys?" he asked.

"Sleeping in the coracle. It's their favorite place. I've put a canvas over them."

"Good," he said. "Stay close by." He pulled twine from around his waist.

"Hear me," he said. "Listen well."

"I am," she said, trying not to tremble at the warning he carried between his words.

"I was unable to find bladders or gourds," he said. "I'm sorry."

"I thank you for trying," Annia said.

But he stopped her before she could continue. "You must listen to me, as we haven't much time."

She moved closer to him. The wind whipped his words away from her.

"This storm is serious, Annia," he said, his hands working with the twine. "I'm going to attach the boys to the coracle by twine. If my plan works, it may save them."

"How can I help?" Annia asked.

"Tied to the coracle, if they go overboard, they will be able to find the boat, right it and climb in. It's light enough that you can flip it when you are in the water.

"You will have to hold it steady for them, do you understand? First, you get Maelia in. Then hold the boat steady for the boys to climb in. I've done it, Annia, when I was a boy. You can do it, too. Promise me?"

"I promise," Annia said. "What of the others?"

"I'm going to look for Virginia and Titus as soon as I finish securing you and the boys. Here," he said, tying the twine around her waist and securing her to the boat.

"Stay steady, Annia. You can do this. You are a strong swimmer and a survivor."

He touched the bear charm at her neck, his fingers brushing her cheek.

Her voice shut down on the words she wanted to say. Before she could speak again, he was gone.

The ship gave a sickening lurch, and Lucia sat up.

Already the sailors were running across the boat, pulling down the sails and hoisting the anchor.

Lucia called for Annia. "I'm here," Annia said.

Lucia came over to her, a wide-awake Julius in her arms.

"Water," he said, pointing delightedly at the sheets of rain falling in torrents from the sky.

"What is it?" she asked.

"Marcus is concerned about the storm."

Marcus worked quickly, and in just a moment the sleeping boys were secured to the coracle.

"Now you," he said, and reached for Julius to tie him. But the child thought it was a game and darted from his hands and ran to the other side of the boat, Lucia following closely behind.

How had the boy come untied from Lucia? Annia suspected he had untied himself.

"Stay tied, Annia," Marcus called back to her when he saw that she was going to go after the child. "I'll get Julius."

He ran into the pounding rain, the boat tipping from one side to the next. If the child went overboard, Lucia and Marcus would follow.

Annia cradled Maelia's head with her hand and climbed between her two boys and held on to them.

Cato woke, but Flavius slept soundly.

"What is it, Mother?" Julius asked, his voice sleepy. He sat up and the boat lurched. Annia caught him to keep him from sliding to his doom.

"Are we going to sink?" Cato asked.

"I hope not," Annia said, and prayed.

The ship lurched again, and this time, took on water.

The deck was awash, and all of them slid, the coracle breaking its safety rope and nearly cracking on the other side of the boat.

The wind blew harder, and it was difficult to be heard above the wind and the rain.

"Hold tight, boys," Annia said. "We are all attached to the coracle. When we get in the water, help me keep it afloat. I am going to put your baby sister in first and then hold the boat for you to get in one at a time. Can you do that?"

"Yes, Mother," Cato said, but his lip trembled.

"Are we going to die?" Flavius asked.

"No," Annia said. "We are not going to die."

She prayed for protection, and in the next moment, the merchant ship pitched high on a wave, but, instead of sliding smoothly down, it hit the bottom of the watery canyon with a heart-wrenching crash, and the ship's hull cracked.

"Hold on, boys," Annia said, gripping the side of the coracle with all her strength.

The boys grabbed on, too. The water rushed over the deck, pushing them into the storm-tossed sea. They landed in the wild surf and were tossed to and fro upon the waves. The pounding waves pulled them away from the safety of the coracle, but their ropes pulled them back.

The coracle spun madly around, pulling them with it. It turned upside down, but it did not sink.

Annia was blinded, her head beneath the water, she kicked as hard as she could, and pushed Maelia's head above the water.

The baby coughed and sputtered.

Cato surfaced near her.

"Son," she said to Cato, "we must flip the boat back over."

She was struggling to right the coracle in the wild sea.

Cato did not hear her calling, but he could see what needed doing, and together they heaved the coracle on its side and then righted it.

Flavius surfaced, coughing and gagging, on the opposite side of the little boat.

"In, Flavius. Get in," Cato ordered. He worked his way around to the side Flavius was on and boosted Flavius into the coracle just before a wave crashed over them.

The coracle righted itself, and Annia lifted the baby out of the water once again.

"I'm going to hand you the baby," she said to Flavius. "Hold her," Annia yelled over the raging sea.

She pulled the sling over her head with one hand while Cato steadied the coracle.

A wave rolled ever closer, and she feared she would not be able to get the baby in before it crashed.

She heaved the baby over the side of the boat with all of her strength, and she landed on the hard bottom of the coracle. Flavius grabbed the baby and she cried angrily, letting them know she was alive.

"Tie it over your neck," Annia called to Flavius, "the sling…tie it over your neck."

Flavius understood, and holding the baby securely, he crossed the sling over his head, then tied the baby as tight as he could against his chest.

"In," Annia ordered Cato, who was waiting for her to get in first.

"No, Mother," he shouted over the waves, "you first."

"You are lighter," she said. "Get in. Now."

The tone of her voice allowed for no argument, and the boy slipped in while Annia fought to hold the boat steady.

"Now," she said, "hold on tight. If I try to get in, I will tip you all over, but I will hold to the back and kick like mad until we are headed in the direction of the shore. We are going to make it to the shore. Do you hear me?" she yelled.

"Yes, Mother," they said in unison, though their voices were weak with fear.

The waves had pitched them far away from anyone else, and they were alone in the storm.

Annia could see nothing but the waves.

She thanked God that the coracle was small enough to keep afloat in the sea's fury.

Then, just as quickly as the storm had risen, it abated.

The rain stopped falling down, and the waves turned from raging mountains, to peaceful hills, to glass.

The sea had lost its fury.

Annia tried to see land to know where she wanted to steer the boat.

The sky grew brighter, and she was able to see far beyond the boat. Was it moonlight or dawn? She didn't know, had lost all track of time.

Then, like a vision from God, she saw them. Rising on her left, white cliffs. The white cliffs of Porte Dubris, shining in the soft light.

She had pushed them closer to shore as she had prayed, rather than pulling them farther out to sea.

She kicked toward the shore with all her might.

"We're going to live, Mother," Cato said. "We are going to live."

Soon, she felt the flinty pebbles beneath her feet.

They had made it.

When they reached the beach, she pulled the coracle up. "Jump out," she said to the boys. "Let me get it safely wedged, and then you can snuggle up and sleep until the sun comes up and dries your clothes."

The boys eagerly obeyed her, Flavius being careful with Maelia.

Annia and Cato pushed the little boat far from the waves' reach and nestled it against a dune.

The boys jumped back in, and Annia, sitting with her back leaning against the boat, gave thanks.

Inside, her children slept, huddled on the floor of the coracle.

The summer night was warm enough that they would not catch their death, and she let them sleep, warming each other.

She could not sleep.

The moon's light was bright now, and she walked back down the beach, searching the shore for her friends, for Lucia, for Julius, Titus and Virginia.

And Marcus.

Surely they had not gotten this close to freedom, to joy, only to lose it all.

The beach was deserted but for their coracle and her three children. She wandered as far as she dared, keeping the coracle in her line of vision.

Exhausted, she returned to the coracle. As soon as dawn cast its first healing light, she would renew her search.

She lay down and slept.

Chapter Sixteen

The baby woke just as the sun peeked over the horizon. Annia stood and raked the ocean with her eyes, desperate for sight of Marcus, Virginia, Titus, Lucia and little Julius. *Please, Lord,* she prayed, *please let them be found.*

She wanted Marcus to be alive so badly it hurt.

For now, she had to be practical. Annia needed water, and she prayed that there was a town close by with a public fountain.

She roused her boys. "We must go and find water."

In the distance, beyond the pebbly dunes and over the gentle lapping of the waves on the shore, she could hear the sound of pounding mallets against stone. Workmen must be in the area.

When they cleared the dunes, the boys cried, "Look! Roman soldiers building something, Mother. It looks like a fort."

They ran over the hill as fast as their legs could carry them.

It was the first time they had been on solid ground in weeks. She was proud of her boys, how well they had done on the sea journey and their courage in the previous night's storm.

The sight of the Roman soldiers filled her with joy. Where there was a fort, there was water, and she and her children desperately needed water.

A woman carrying a clay amphora walked beside the busy soldiers. She hurried along, and Annia followed her. She guessed her to be going to the local water supply.

Annia pulled the boys away from the exciting sights and sounds of the tower being built by Roman soldiers, and herded them along in front of her.

The woman, who looked to be in her middle years, stopped and dipped her amphora beneath something they couldn't see. She was graceful and attractive. She looked back at them and smiled.

They had found their water, and perhaps a friend.

The woman had only filled her amphora halfway, when she turned to Annia and said, "You are very thirsty?"

Annia nodded, and Maelia wailed.

"Here," the woman said, "you go ahead. Your baby, I believe, is thirsty, too."

Annia looked around for something to use to get water. The boys had found bits of broken amphorae in the grass behind the fountain.

"You drink first, Mother," Cato said. He knew that Annia had to drink so that their baby sister could eat.

She thanked him and drank greedily.

When she had finished drinking, and settled in to feed Maeila, the boys drank their fill.

"Can we go play now?" Cato asked, wiping the cool moisture from his lips.

"Yes, but stay close," Annia said.

The boys ran behind the fountain and played on the green.

"You have good boys," the woman said. "You've raised them well."

"Thank you," Annia said. "I have been blessed, and I pray this little one will be as strong and kind as her brothers."

The nice woman had waited patiently while Annia's little family drank, and now she finished filling her amphora. When the jug was full, she sat beside Annia.

"You and your boys look as though you washed up on the shore in last night's storm."

"We did," Annia said.

The woman was beautiful, and obviously wealthy. Her *palla* was a richly embroidered light wool, and it lay in graceful folds over her bright white *stola*.

What was she doing out in the morning sun filling her own amphora? Shouldn't her slaves be doing that for her?

The woman smiled. "You are wondering why I—instead of my slaves—am filling my amphora," she said.

Annia blushed. "I was," she said, embarrassed.

"I gave them a holiday," the woman said, and laughed.

Annia tilted her head to one side. "Really?" she asked. "Is it a holiday?"

"No, not officially," the woman said, and gave her a pained smile.

"My husband has gone to Rome on one of his extended stays. He thinks I don't know why he stays so long—the last time he was gone it was five years before he came back."

"That's horrible," Annia said. "Is he serving?"

"No, not serving," the woman said. "I believe that he prefers the company of the women there."

"I'm sorry," Annia said. She understood only too well.

"So I give the slaves one day off per week, a day of rest," the woman said.

Annia nodded. "I like that."

"Our scripture is very clear on this teaching," the woman said.

"You're Jewish, then?" Annia asked.

"Partially," the woman said.

Annia furrowed her brow. Could she ask the woman the question she wanted to ask? She took a deep breath and plunged forward

"Are you a follower of the Master, then?" Annia asked almost too quietly to be heard.

"Why, yes, I am. And you?" she asked.

"Yes," Annia said. And breathed a sigh of relief. The question was dangerous, but hadn't the woman admitted she was Jewish?

"I had a feeling you were when I first saw you," the woman said.

"What made you think that?" Annia asked, somewhat alarmed. In Rome, to be recognized as a Jew or Christ follower could now get you exiled.

"Nothing in particular. Just a feeling I had."

Annia nodded and smiled. There was something very calming about being in the presence of this woman.

"Can you talk about what happened last night?" the woman asked.

Maelia, happy and satisfied after being fed, now began squirming and whimpering.

"But first things first. It looks like your baby may be happier in dryer garments," the woman said. "Why don't you come to my house and let me feed you and give you some clothes?"

"That would be so kind," Annia said. She felt safe with this woman. She did not think she would harm her, or her children, and they all needed to eat. "I haven't had a chance to even think. My name is Annia."

"I'm so pleased to meet a fellow believer," the woman said. "I'm Theodora. My house is just over the hill."

Theodora's house was very close. Her back garden overlooked the very beach on which Annia and her children had landed.

The villa sat close to the road, and was obviously very new, in the Roman style. At the front of the villa was a grand entrance with an open veranda held up with pillars. The entrance door was a massive oak structure, and when Theodora pulled it open, there was an atrium, a lovely pool and an inner garden.

Theodora led them into the house, where the walls were painted in muted greens, oranges and yellows. Inside the house, the painted columns and garden scenes made it appear that the entire house was actually outside rather than in.

"Would you like to eat or go to the baths first?"

"I think we will have to eat first," Annia said. "I know the boys will. They have not had a morsel since last night, and I'm sure they're famished after their struggle. I know I am," she added.

Theodora smiled and nodded. "That's what I would have guessed. We still have a few hours before the baths close for women and open for the men."

And she led them into the back garden where there was a well-oiled shale table. The woman directed the boys to the folding benches leaning against the garden walls. The boys carried the benches to the table, unfolded them and waited for their mother to be seated, then sat on either side of her.

Theodora disappeared inside.

"Who is she, Mother?" Cato asked.

When she brought out bread and three kinds of cheeses, apples and pears, Flavius looked at her adoringly.

"Oh, thank you!" he said.

The woman looked somewhat surprised at his enthusiasm. "You are most welcome," she said.

Looking at the food, Annia felt her mouth watering, but she had to laugh at her son.

"Please feel free to eat your fill," Theodora said. "I know what it's like to endure that long sea voyage. Now introduce yourselves," she said to the boys.

"Oh, I'm afraid I was so busy thinking of food that I've been quite rude," Annia said.

She motioned Cato and Flavius forward. "Tell her your names," she whispered.

"I'm Cato, and this is my brother, Flavius, and we are very pleased to meet you." Cato gave a formal little bow and pulled his brother down with him.

"And you, too," Theodora said.

"Stop," Flavius said, jerking himself away from his brother and making a very formal, much exaggerated bow on his own.

Theodora laughed. "I am delighted to meet the two of you," she said, and it was obvious that she meant it. "It has been many years since the house was filled with children's voices, and I miss it very much."

"And this is Maelia," Annia said.

"What excellent manners your sons have," Theodora said. "You must be proud."

"They are good boys," Annia said when the boys had excused themselves from the table and gone to explore the garden.

"Can you tell me about your night?" Theodora asked. "I know it will be hard, but I would like to help you find those you were traveling with."

Annia related the story of the fast-approaching storm, of Marcus's quick thinking that probably saved their lives.

Annia talked about Lucia and Julius, Titus and Virginia, as well.

"We will pray they are found," Theodora said. "Let's get you to the baths. There we will begin making inquiries. There is no better place to pick up the latest news or gossip. Perhaps others were still floating and were picked up by early morning sailors."

"Yes," Annia said, happy at this hopeful thought, "maybe." Would she see Marcus again? She prayed that he and the rest of her friends had indeed survived the storm.

Chapter Seventeen

Still a mile or so from shore, Marcus and Lucia clung to a long plank, formerly part of the ship's keel. Sitting atop the plank was Julius, acting as though he were beside the bathing pool on a warm summer's day.

Marcus had to laugh at the child.

"Does nothing frighten him?" he asked.

"Nothing," Lucia said. "He is beyond my reckoning. Thank you for snagging him when you did and tying us together. You saved us."

Marcus nodded. "I've gone down with two ships in this very water. It is treacherous, though who would believe that now?" he said, gazing out across the sleek gray channel.

They bobbed gently as they floated toward the shore, their legs working with the current to carry them in.

"I don't recognize the land," Marcus said. "I fear we've been blown a few miles down the shore from the Porte Dubris for which we were headed."

"I pray the shore will be friendly," Lucia said. "And that we are not met by wild animals or wilder natives. Not everyone welcomes the Romans, you know," she said.

"Yes, I do know that," he said. He continued scanning the gray expanse.

"You'll find Annia," Lucia said. "You saved her and her children. I saw them in the little boat."

"Did you? I never saw them. I was certain the coracle had flipped, and Annia and the boys drowned. Are you sure it was them you saw? The seas pitched high, it was dark and nearly impossible to see even a few paces away."

"It was them," she said.

He had to believe her.

He was thankful for Julius's happy disposition. It could be very different. He could be a whining, clinging child.

If Julius had clung to Lucia rather than running, Marcus would not have had to chase him, and they could have all stayed together on the ship, and, perhaps, found each other more easily when it broke up.

But Lucia's sighting gave him hope.

They made it to shore as the sun reached its zenith.

Marcus was cold, though it was midsummer, thirsty and hungry.

"I'm hungry," little Julius said, shivering and echoing Marcus's thoughts.

"We will eat soon," Lucia said, then looked to Marcus for confirmation.

"Yes," he agreed, "soon."

Marcus scanned the water one last time before searching the shore for something with which to build a fire.

He walked down the shore, and what looked like a purple sea creature fanning out in the water caught his eye. He watched it for a moment, then walked into the water and touched it.

It was cloth. He pulled it out of the water, and gold threads glinted in the sun. He squeezed out the water from the cloth and saw the familiar line of leaves, flowers and birds and realized he was holding Maelia's toga band filled with Annia's handiwork.

He was a seasoned soldier, and still, his throat felt swollen, and his nose stung. He had to squeeze his eyes to keep the tears at bay.

He would trust Lucia's sighting and believe they were alive. He would find Annia and the children. He searched the water again, hoping to see the coracle bobbing along.

Something glinted out in the gray expanse. His heart leaped.

He waved madly, and in a few minutes, he made out two figures clinging to a long piece of wood.

The figures came closer; the tide was coming rapidly in now.

It wasn't Annia. He could see that.

But it *was* Virginia and Titus.

Marcus rushed to pull them in to the shore.

"God be praised," Lucia said, helping Virginia in. "I was afraid you two were gone. I never saw you on the ship last night."

"It was a terrifying night," Virginia agreed. "Where is Annia? Where are her children?"

"We don't know," Lucia said.

"But I found this," Marcus said, and held up the embroidered purple band.

Lucia ran her finger over the gold threads gingerly, and held it up for Virginia to see. Virginia took it and buried her face in the wet wool.

"I saw them," Lucia said. "I'm sure they are alive. They were all in the little boat."

Virginia could not speak, but she nodded. "I hope," she was finally able to get out. "I pray."

Marcus and Titus headed off together into the wooded

area just beyond the beach. They left the women and Julius to rest on the pebbly shore.

"I don't know this area well," Titus said, "but I have people who live near. We are, I think, a few miles west of Dubris. I saw the chalk-white cliffs gleaming in the moonlight last night before the storm."

"I hope you are right," Marcus said. "I hope we are only a few miles away. Lucia feels fairly certain that Annia and the boys made it safely to shore. I fear from there things might have gotten tricky if she landed at a place as desolate as this."

"She's a survivor," Titus said, "a bear, like the bear she wears around her neck."

"That she is," Marcus agreed.

A few hundred yards up from the water, Titus came upon a stream. "Water. Fresh, too," he said after tasting it.

Marcus hurried back to the beach to get the women and Julius.

But before he had gone even a few yards, he nearly ran over Julius, who had, apparently, been following him since he left. Lucia puffed behind, chasing him, followed by Virginia.

"The child just doesn't stop," Lucia said, smiling in wonder.

"No," Virginia said, sardonic, "he doesn't."

"I have good news," Marcus said. "Titus found water."

They followed him, excited by the prospect.

After drinking their fill, they went in search of food.

It was summer, and the women found wild blueberries growing in the woods while Marcus found and whittled a stick to pierce the fat fish swimming in the stream.

Titus found the necessary flint—abundant in the area—to strike against the iron knob he had salvaged from his door-raft. Titus was ready to make a cooking fire.

Marcus thanked his heavenly Father for Titus's resourcefulness.

"You would have made a good soldier," he said to Titus.

Titus smiled and worked the fire patiently and blew it a bit until soon the sparks caught and a small fire burned.

Virginia helped him, gathering twigs and sticks and feeding it until it was big enough to cook the fish. Then she fashioned a spit and held the fish over the fire, toasting it evenly on each side.

Marcus tried his hand at cooking, but his fish landed with a sizzle and a plop in the fire.

"Not much of a cook are you?" Virginia said, rescuing his fish for him.

"You never rest, do you?" Marcus asked shaking his head. "Could I ever do anything that would please you?"

He had been joking, but Virginia became suddenly serious.

"Find Annia and her boys," she said. "Take her home. Reunite her with her mother and father. Then," she continued, her gaze penetrating, "marry her. She can stand no more pain in her life, so you will spend your life protecting her from any further pain. And if you don't, if you cause her any further pain, any at all, I will hunt you relentlessly, and make certain that you never—"

"Stop," Titus interjected. "You've said enough, Virginia. Marcus saved her life once. Why would you think he wouldn't do it again?"

He motioned Marcus to the fire. Marcus was relieved. Virginia's anger at him was very real. What, exactly, had he done to deserve her ire?

"Did they pay you to come after her baby?" Virginia asked, following them to the fire, her eyes flashing.

Marcus had to be honest with her and with himself.

"Yes," he said, "Janius did."

He felt the tension increase.

"I've heard as much," Virginia said. "Rome is very large, but Rome is very small."

"Familiar words," Marcus said.

"I can tell you who said it."

"Nona?" Marcus said. "How do you know Nona?"

"She is my mother's sister," Virginia said.

"Nona came and stayed at your house? It was you who kept her and Flavius safe while she waited to take him home to her mother?"

"Yes," Virginia said, "it was."

Titus's mouth was set in a grim line.

Marcus sat heavily down beside Virginia.

"I wasn't sure I believed in my mother's mission," he said. "I did it—I saved the babies, but it didn't make sense to me. How could saving a few babies make even a small dent in the thousands of babies lost to slavery every year?

"And then I met Annia. She went after her baby and fought like a bear. And I realized that even one was worth fighting for. I realized then that some things were more important than valor on the battlefield, that loving someone so hard that you were willing to give your life for that person was worth more than any power or position I might be able to gain as a prefect, or general, or commander.

"Annia saved my life, and she doesn't even know it. Before I saw her that night, I was willing to believe Galerius Janius. I accepted pay to take the baby from an adulteress. I knew that I would actually be delivering the baby to my mother's household. But I felt somewhat justified in taking the baby away from its mother. I'm ashamed to say that now, but it's true. But when I saw Annia—when I remembered who she was—when I spent only a few hours with her, I realized what a fool I had been. I was able to see Galerius Janius for what he was. And I was able to see the path down which I headed with alarming clarity."

"You are not, then, the hero Annia thinks you to be," Virginia said.

"No," Marcus said, his head down, "I'm not."

"Well," Virginia said, "you're more brave than I thought. At least you admitted your shortcomings. To me, at least. And will you admit them to Annia?"

"I will lose her if I do," Marcus said. "I don't want to lose her."

"Yes," Virginia said, "you probably will lose her if you tell her. But I guarantee you something else. You will definitely lose her if you don't."

Marcus cooked his fish in silence.

He didn't want to think about it.

Why did things have to be so complicated?

When he came home from the army after having served twenty years, he was not ready to retire.

Retirement meant managing a villa, but without a family of his own, why would he want to do that? His father had wanted Marcus to stay in Britain and manage the family estate.

But Marcus had been stubborn. "I'm not finished with my career yet," he'd told his father, hinting to him that power and position were his in Rome if he were patient.

So, upon his return to Rome, he planned to serve as a commander of the *Vigiles* until he reached his goal: to be made a prefect of the *Vigiles* and then the highest office, the Praetorian Guard.

It was true. That had been his goal.

Until he met Annia.

When he first met Galerius Janius, he believed the man could help him gain the position he wanted.

Janius had hinted at such. He had, after all, married the emperor's cousin.

"My wife cheated on me. She spawned a child, and is trying to pass it off as mine," Galerius Janius had told him.

When Marcus was introduced to the new wife of Galerius Janius, Marcus believed her to be a good choice. She was beautiful, she was wealthy and she was nearly ready to bear his child.

Galerius Janius convinced him he deserved this new wife.

He convinced Marcus that he did not deserve to have the child born of his new wife lose any of the dowry she brought into the marriage.

What did it matter that his new wife was six months gone when the marriage was made legal and that a mere three months later his adulteress former wife had given birth?

Did that make the child any less unworthy?

The child could, at any time, come back and claim that the father was Janius. Janius would then be forced to divide his wife's fortune with a child that was not even his.

No. The child must be exposed.

It was the only fair thing to be done for Galerius Janius.

And in return?

Janius would whisper into the ear of the emperor, and Marcus would be made head of the Praetorian Guard.

The deal was sealed with gold coins. And then Marcus met Annia.

In one night. Everything changed.

Marcus believed Annia to be innocent.

The fact that Galerius Janius fell out of favor with the emperor had not changed things for him. At all. He made his decision for Annia before he discovered that.

And, to complicate matters further, the senator had stepped in at just that time, spoken to the emperor Claudius on his behalf and had seen to it that he was made prefect of the *Vigiles*.

It appeared, then, that loyalty to Annia had nothing to do with his change of heart about his decision to help Janius. It appeared to be a decision made based on the fact that he was getting help to advance his career elsewhere.

Who would believe him?

Did Virginia believe him?

If Virginia didn't believe him, Annia would never believe him.

He had to clear his name before Annia would accept him. But how? His mission for now was this: he would find Annia, take her to her parents and make sure she was safe.

Virginia stood watching him, waiting for an answer, for a full confession.

"I'm interested in Annia," he said.

"Then take her safely home," Virginia said.

"I must return to Rome. I must fulfill my duty. I have a position. Will she wait for me?" Marcus said, though the words were hard to push from his mouth. Was he willing to give up his position to stay in Britain with Annia.

"I don't know."

Titus watched him.

Marcus met his gaze.

Titus walked away from the fire. Marcus followed.

"Can you?" Titus asked him. "Can you give up the office you've just been granted?"

Marcus looked away. He had gained the position in spite of Galerius Janius. He had help from the senator, but he wanted to believe that he'd gotten it because he was good at what he did. Doing a good job as prefect would prove it. For history.

"I don't know," Marcus said, his honesty peeling away the grim wrinkles on Titus's face.

"What is it that you want, then?"

"Whatever do you mean?" Marcus said.

"Nothing more than that," Titus said. "What do you want?"

Titus turned and walked back to the fire.

Chapter Eighteen

Theodora was right. At the baths, people knew about the shipwreck, and there had been several sightings of survivors all up and down the beaches.

Fishermen had reported seeing survivors as far away as the next town.

How would Annia know if her friends had made it?

"I'll keep asking," Theodora said. "I've lived in this town my entire life. I know many people."

The next morning, Theodora sent some of her slaves out to find out what they could.

Annia and the children slept late, their bodies recovering from the long sea voyage and subsequent storm.

Maelia woke Annia for her morning feeding. Flavius played quietly beside Annia's bed. Cato slept.

"I've been very quiet," Flavius said. "I didn't wake you, did I, Mother?"

"No, sweet child, you didn't wake me," Annia said.

"What are we going to do today, Mother?" Flavius asked.

"I don't know," Annia said. "We are waiting to hear good news about our friends."

"But we must do something while we wait," Flavius

said. "Doing nothing makes the time pass very slowly. I know. Cato and I tried sitting and waiting for you to come back to Father's house. It took a very long time and made us sad."

Annia's throat caught and she felt the pressure of tears behind her eyes. "Come up here and sit with me," she said and hugged him.

"I'm never leaving you again," she said.

"I know, Mother," Flavius said. "It was Father. He was very confused. And Marcus. He and Father talked in the garden many times. Marcus is no longer confused, but I think Father is still confused."

This time, the feeling in Annia's stomach was cold, hard fear. "What did you say?" she asked Flavius.

"About what?" he asked. When he saw Annia's face, he looked worried. Very worried.

"About Marcus talking with your father in the garden," she said.

"Oh, Father and Marcus were friends. And I would sit in my jungle and pretend to be a slithering snake. Sometimes I would be a sleeping snake. It was then I could hear them talking."

"And what did they say?" Annia asked, trying hard to keep her voice calm.

"Oh, many things," Flavius said. "Marcus talked a lot about being a soldier."

Perhaps it wasn't as it seemed, Annia thought. Perhaps in order to do his job as a *Vigile*, he needed to talk with the people in his neighborhood and get to know them.

"I'm sure he had good stories," Annia said, imagining how much fun it must have been for Flavius to lie in his hiding place and listen to soldiering stories.

"Yes, he did," Flavius said. "But mostly he talked about prefect."

"Prefect?" Annia asked.

"Yes," Flavius continued eagerly. "He talked about that. I think it was something he wanted to be. And Father said he could help him get it."

Annia tensed, and Maelia looked up at her, startled and began wailing.

"Oh, Mother, she's crying," Flavius said.

Annia calmed the baby and herself.

"Now," Annia said, hoping Flavius would not be put off by the false brightness of her voice, "how was Father to help him?"

Flavius's face grew red. "Mother, could we go and get the coracle? I think Cato and I would have a great deal of fun playing storm on the beach."

Annia knew better than to press her son. He had said everything he had to say about the matter. He was a perfect little clam when he wished to be.

Annia was left with emotions swirling in her heart. Had she been fooled? Was Marcus not what he seemed?

She didn't want to believe it.

Besides, trusting the words of a boy of six years was not wise. Perhaps she needed to hear from his elder brother.

She recalled the vicious attack Cato had made on Marcus. She remembered his wariness when Marcus was near and how hard she'd had to talk to convince him that Marcus had actually saved her.

"No, Mother," he'd said. "Father wanted you gone. And Maelia fed to the dogs."

What if her son was telling the truth? What if Marcus was in league with Janius?

She tried to think clearly, but her thoughts were a tangled mess. She was exhausted and confused, still recovering from the harrowing sea journey.

She would spend more time thinking, and then question Cato further later.

She looked over at her sleeping son. He was breathing evenly, his curly brown lashes so long, so thick, nearly brushing his cheek. He jerked in his sleep and then sighed.

Flavius played happily while she decided what to do next.

Later that morning, she knew her path.

"Theodora, my parents live in Londinium, and I would like to get there and see them as soon as possible."

Theodora looked a bit surprised. Earlier Annia had wanted nothing more than to see her friends safe and whole.

"I understand," Theodora said.

"I would like to borrow a wagon and horse and one of your slaves who knows the roads and can get me home," Annia said. "I've not seen my parents in many years, and I'm eager to see them."

Annia could see that her friend did not entirely believe her.

"I will help you in any way I can," Theodora said, but her brow was creased with worry. "But what about searching for your friends?"

"I know it seems that I have changed my mind, and it is true, I have. I've learned some things from my son that have helped me see a little differently. I feel it imperative to get to my parents as soon as possible." Her words sounded cold and ungrateful. She did not mean to offend Theodora.

"Have I done something to offend you?" Theodora asked.

"No, no, my friend," Annia said, reaching forward and taking Theodora's hand in hers. "You've been nothing but generous and kind. I ask you this favor because being here has made me long for my parents and my home"

Theodora looked deeply into Annia's eyes. "Then I will do what I can to get you there with haste," she said. "Would you like for me to continue my search for your friends?"

"I don't think so," Annia said. "Virginia knows exactly where my home is, as does Titus."

"And the other two, Lucia and Marcus, and the boy, Julius?"

Annia was amazed at Theodora's ability to remember the names of each friend.

"They know where they are going. Marcus has a family villa close to the port on the Thames. Lucia has a home there with Marcus and his family."

Theodora's eyebrows lifted at this. "I thought Marcus was special to you."

Annia could not bring herself to respond to this. What could she say? How could she explain what she didn't understand herself?

Was Marcus still under the pay of Galerius Janius?

"I will pay you, or at least my father will pay you," Annia said.

"I'm not worried about coin," Theodora said. "My husband has left me with plenty of time and money."

Theodora studied Annia for a moment. "What if I ride with you?" she suggested. "I could help with the children," she added.

Annia looked at Theodora. Why would this woman want to travel with her?

"I need to go to Londinium anyway," Theodora said. "There are things you can buy there that you can't find anywhere else. I need some new glass for the windows in these upstairs rooms."

Annia looked at the blue-glass window, and it was true, the window was dotted with holes and in sore need of repair.

"And your slave can't get it for you?" Annia said.

"No," Theodora said, "truly. I've wanted to make the trip to Londinium for a while now but have put it off because I hate traveling alone. If you will allow me to go, it would be very kind of you."

"Allow you to go?" Annia said, laughing with Theodora. "It is your horse, your cart and your coin. Of course I will 'allow' you to go. I will be happy for the company."

"I would like that," Theodora said. "I don't have many friends here. The minute they discover my faith, they back away from me as if I had the plague."

"I understand," Annia said. "It was the same in Rome."

"I think we can be prepared to leave by the morning. I will make certain."

"I can be ready at a moment's notice. As you can see, we have brought very little with us," Annia said.

"The boat," Flavius said. "We must take the boat. Marcus will be sad if we leave it."

Annia was tempted to leave it for that reason. She felt enraged just thinking about him. Before she could rearrange her face to calm, Theodora glanced at her, her brow wrinkled.

Annia shook the anger away and went back up into the room where Cato was sleeping. Flavius was playing quietly beside him.

She took Flavius's hand.

"Come, son," she said. "Let's go get that boat."

At these words, Cato woke. "I want to go get the boat, too," he said.

"We must eat first," Annia said, "and then we will go on our morning adventure."

Annia met Theodora in the kitchen, busily preparing breakfast. "You are so kind to take such good care of me and my boys," she said. "Thank you. Now, what can I do to help?"

"Nothing other than following me to the storehouse to tell me what the boys like to eat so we can pack meals for the next two days."

Annia's face was a question.

"It will take us that long to reach Londinium," Theodora said in response.

"Only two days?" Annia asked.

"Ah, yes," Theodora said. "You've not lived here since we've had the new roads. For the past five years, the pounding of iron against stone has been constant. The roads are well laid and safe for easy passage from here to many other towns. I don't think the road is complete all the way in to Londinium, but it was close the last time I was there."

Annia was amazed. When she was a girl, it was a three-week trip from Londinium to the white cliffs to the south. "I wonder what else has changed," she said.

"Much, I assure you," Theodora said, "and not all for the good."

Chapter Nineteen

Annia trudged reluctantly along to help her boys fetch the little boat. She did not want to go anywhere near the beach. The possibility of seeing Marcus was great.

She wasn't worried about missing Virginia, Titus and Lucia. Virginia knew the way to her home, and she was certain that Lucia would want to come home with her, and not go with Marcus. Lucia did not know anyone currently living at Marcus's villa other than Marcus.

Women needed other women, especially when there were small children to raise. Lucia would choose the support of her friends over Marcus, Annia was certain.

The fisherman had said just this morning that it would take her friends a day or so to get to Porte Dubris from where he had seen them beached.

Her chance of running into Marcus was slim.

Her chance of getting more information from her son, Cato, was excellent.

She hastened her steps and caught up with her boys.

"Mother, can we stop for a moment and watch the soldiers build?" Cato asked.

Theodora had explained this structure was to double as a watchtower and lighthouse.

When it was complete, it would be three stories high. Ships could see it in fog and storm and use the light to guide them safely to port.

Cato and Flavius had already planned to build one on her father's villa, which sat on the bank of the river Thames. The boys watched the construction carefully so that they could copy it on a much smaller scale.

When the boys finally grew tired of watching, Annia urged them to the beach. "Let's get the boat and take it to Theodora's in time for our midday meal."

The boys liked this plan.

Annia wasn't certain how to broach the subject of Marcus with Cato.

They walked along in silence for a while, Flavius rattling on about the lighthouse.

"And when we get there, maybe Grandfather can find us a small lantern, very small, so that we can hang it up in the top of our lighthouse. And we can make it burn forever and ever so that no one will ever get lost on our river."

"No one gets lost on a river," Cato scoffed. "People get lost on the sea."

"Oh," Flavius said, kicking pebbles out of his way.

"Well," Annia said, "that's not always true. In Londinium, sometimes the mist can be so thick that you lose track of which way you are headed. I believe a lighthouse on the riverbank might be a very useful thing," she said.

Cato absorbed this information. "Are there bogs near the river, Mother?" he asked. "I've heard there were. I've heard of soldiers being so weighted down by their gear and armor that they drowned in a few inches of water in the bogs beside rivers in Britain."

"That is probably very true," Annia said.

Caton smiled. "It is. I heard Marcus tell Father the

story of how he lost ten men one day in the bogs beside the Thames River."

Flavius picked up the story. "I heard that, too. That was the day he and Father had lunch in the yard, and Father's baby boy was born."

"I remember that," Cato added. "The midwife brought the baby down, and Father was so engrossed in Marcus's story that when he picked the baby up, he nearly dropped him." Cato laughed.

"Yes, I saw that, too," Flavius added.

Annia was burning to ask more questions, but she knew that if she did, she might hear nothing more from her boys. Best for her to be silent and see how much they might share.

"That was the day Father gave Marcus a gold piece," Flavius said.

"Yes," Cato said, and then looked at his mother and was silent.

Flavius took Cato's cue and was silent, as well.

"Why did your father pay Marcus, Cato?" Annia asked.

"I don't know," Cato said and shrugged.

"I do," Flavius added, eager as a puppy. "He paid him to expose Maelia. Father said it was a gift to his new wife. He'd promised to give it to her as soon as her baby was born, but only if it was a boy."

"Shut your mouth," Cato said. His face was red with anger. "I told you never to speak of that again. Ever."

Flavius looked at his brother, and then his bottom lip began to tremble. Soon he was crying. "I'm sorry, Cato. I forgot," he said.

The feeling in the pit of Annia's stomach was stone. Her entire body felt heavy.

The remaining journey to the coracle was silent. Flavius eventually dried his tears and soldiered forward.

They pulled the coracle from its hiding place in the sand dune. They dusted it off as best they could and hoisted it on their shoulders. The burden wasn't heavy.

It was the other burden that made Annia's shoulders sag and her heart hurt.

"Mother," Cato said, breaking the silence. "Look."

He pointed down the beach.

In the distance were four figures coming toward them.

They were too far away to see whether they were fisherman or picnickers.

"Yes," Annia said, "I see them. Come along, now. We don't want to be late for lunch."

"But they might be Marcus and Julius," Flavius said.

He made absolutely no connection between the information he had just shared with Annia and the pain she felt in her stomach. He was just a little boy. He couldn't begin to understand.

Flavius only knew that his family was happy when Marcus was with them.

Cato looked up at his mother. She was relieved that she was able to keep her face impassive.

"Come on, Flavius," Cato urged taking his cue from Annia's mood. "Turn around and let's take the boat to Theodora's."

"Yes," Annia encouraged, "we'll load it on the wagon this afternoon so that in the morning, it will be ready. Perhaps the two of you can sit in it on the way to Londinium."

"We're going to Londinium tomorrow?" Cato asked. "Aren't we waiting for the others?"

"No, but do not worry, they will be able to find us," Annia said, her voice, once again, falsely bright.

The sun was warm, though not hot. It was a lovely clear summer day. She should be the happiest woman on earth. She had her children, her friends. She was home and would soon see her parents.

But she was miserable. Every hope she had allowed to resurface in her heart was gone. And not only was she miserable; she was angry.

Marcus had deceived her.

She needed to understand why.

She understood enough to know that all of his attentions to her had been false. He was under the pay of Galerius Janius.

She was a fool.

"Mother," Flavius said and dropped his corner of the boat. The boat fell to the ground, and Annia and Cato were forced to stop.

Cato looked at his mother for guidance. "Rest a minute, son," she said.

"I'm not tired," Cato said.

Her sweet, brave firstborn. His loyalty warmed her heart. She smiled her appreciation.

"Thank you, son," she said. He hefted the boat and waited for her to get the other side. He didn't even look back.

Before she could get the boat on her shoulder, Flavius ran in the opposite direction.

"Marcus. Julius. Virginia. Titus. Lucia. I see you!" the little boy called joyfully.

He ran into Marcus's open arms. Marcus picked him up and swung him round and round until they collapsed in laughter on the sandy beach.

"We've been looking for you," Flavius said. "We were worried that you all had drowned."

"Here we are," Lucia said, "safe and sound." Julius had already tumbled from her arms, running and leaping into the pile on the pebbly sand that was Marcus and

Flavius. Flavius hugged him hard. Julius wriggled away like a little puppy.

"Swim," Julius said, and ran for the water.

Marcus caught him around the waist. "Oh, no, you don't, young friend. We've had all the swimming any of us want for a good long while."

"Flavius," Annia said, her voice harsh, "you and Julius may swim as long as you wish."

Marcus was taken aback. He turned to Annia and moved forward, ready to embrace her and swing her in his arms as he had done with Flavius.

"Marcus," she said, coldly, nodding.

"Annia," Lucia effused, and ran to her, hugging her.

"Move over," Virginia said to Lucia, but she was smiling. "Give me a chance to hug my oldest and dearest friend."

Annia and Virginia embraced. "What is it, my friend?" Virginia said. "You look like you ate a sour pear."

"I almost did," Annia said, indicating Marcus with a nod.

Annia fought an inner battle between tears of joy at seeing her friends again and fury that Marcus was there, spoiling her joy.

Marcus moved toward her again, opened his arms and said, "Annia. I was afraid you had drowned and the babies. But Lucia said she saw you. She saw you and the boys floating away, the boys in the boat. And Maelia." He touched the baby's cheek.

Annia jerked away and threw her *palla* over Maelia's face. "Don't you ever touch my baby again," she said, her voice a threatening hiss.

"Mother," Flavius said, "what's wrong? Why are you so angry at Marcus? He saved us."

"Yes, he did, son, and I thank you for reminding me."

Annia stood as tall as she could and turned from her son to Marcus.

"I thank you in the name of my father for saving the lives of my precious children and mine that I might live to old age and see them grow, mature and have babes of their own."

Her tone was cold as an icy Londinium winter.

Lucia stared in astonishment.

Titus looked away.

Cato held his head high and stepped beside his mother, placing his hand in hers.

Annia was trembling.

Virginia looked from Marcus to Annia.

"Well," she said, "it appears you have lost your status as the conquering hero. I mourn with you, Marcus. I really do."

Annia looked at Virginia. She knew something. What was it?

Annia didn't much care what she knew. Had Marcus told Virginia the same lies he had told her? Virginia had been with Marcus for almost two days, and no one knew better than Annia how persuasive he could be.

Flavius and Julius stood between Marcus and Annia, not sure which way to move.

Julius put his little hand in Flavius's.

"Go, swim," she said to the children. "For a few minutes. The weather is lovely, and the sun is warm. You will be dry by the time we get home."

Happy to do so, the two little boys ran for the sparkling gray water, their attention completely diverted from the tension around them.

"Swim with them, Cato," Annia said. "The water is a lovely place to be. Sometimes a much better place to be than land."

Chapter Twenty

The dull thud in Marcus's head reminded him of night watch. He backed away from Annia and tried to collect his thoughts. On night duty, staying awake had been simple. The challenge had been to hear anything because of the tension induced throbbing in his head.

What had happened? Why was Annia being so cold? What had she heard?

He was afraid he knew.

Now was the time to prepare for a battle of the heart that Marcus intended to win.

Annia and her children were the symbol of everything important to him.

This battle would be the most important of his life.

He forced himself to back away and allow Annia her space.

Annia might read his backing away as giving up. He would never give up.

Sometimes fighting meant waiting. Hadn't she told her son these very same words?

He must order his thoughts. He must be rational.

He needed to talk to her best friend. Wasn't that the best way to find out information about women?

Virginia. He would start there.

He doubted he would get a moment alone with her any time soon. She was sticking as close to Annia as mud to *caligae* in a British bog.

He watched Titus, Virginia and Lucia close in around Annia, eager to share their adventures following the shipwreck.

"Fish were plentiful in the brook we found," Lucia said. "And I've never tasted anything so sweet as the wild blueberries we found."

"We were so blessed!" he heard Annia exclaim. "We landed very close to Porte Dubris, and met a lovely woman, Theodora, at the town fountain."

"Fountain?" Titus said. "We've been scooping water with our hands for days. I look forward to drinking water out of a clay cup."

"And eating something other than fish and berries sounds good, too," Virginia said.

Marcus walked over to the water where the boys swam.

"Come along," Julius said to Marcus. "Swim with us!"

"No, I don't think so," Marcus said. "I was quite serious when I said I have had all the swimming I want for many, many days."

The boys took this as a direct challenge. First they sprayed him with water from water windmills they made of their arms.

When he ran into the shallows away from them, the three laughing children tackled him, hanging from all of his limbs like seaweed on a ship's anchor.

"Come swim, old man," Flavius said gleefully.

"I am an old man—too old to swim with you young stallions," Marcus teased. It felt good to be wanted.

"Come on, then." Even Cato joined in the fun, the water protecting him from his mother's vision.

Marcus finally dove in and pretended to be a sea creature gobbling the boys' legs.

The boys squealed in delight, and Marcus glanced over
as his friends on the beach moved closer to Porte Dubris.

In her anger at Marcus, would Annia allow him to stay
near her children?

She looked back to check on them, acknowledged Marcus with a curt nod and walked on.

He felt vastly relieved.

The fact that she trusted him with her children had to
count for something.

Annia and her friends chatted in the makeshift shade
Titus created by propping the boat on its side against the
dune. They weren't in any hurry to get back.

He and the boys were free to swim until they were
exhausted.

An hour or so later, Annia turned back and waved
them from the water. The boys pretended to ignore her
for a while, but then Marcus intervened.

"You know you see her," he said to Cato.

Cato smiled. "I know," he admitted. He looked back
at his mother, caught her attention and then waved at her
to let her know he'd seen her and was on his way.

She watched until they made their way out of the water
and then turned and walked with the rest of the party
back to Porte Dubris.

"Pretend you're a dog," Flavius said, and shook himself all over.

Julius copied him, and it looked like so much fun that
Cato shook, as well. Marcus joined in, jumping up and
down.

Now it was a contest. Who could get dry fastest?

Like a group of drenched puppies, they shook so hard

and so long that the party disappeared over the sand dune, leaving them far behind.

"Oh," Marcus said, looking up from their fun, "I think it's time to go."

"Who won?" Cato asked. "First you have to say who won."

Marcus felt each head carefully, and inspected each one for stray water droplets.

"I think that in all the jumping and shaking, you all are as dry as clothes hanging out on a line."

They were a jolly group heading back down the beach.

Marcus was in no hurry. He would like to prolong this moment as long as possible. It could be the precious last moments he was allowed to be with Annia's children.

"Mother is very angry with you," Flavius said. He shot his brother a quick glance to see if he was going to make him cease talking.

But Cato walked along, expressionless, his eyes on the pebbled beach.

"Yes, I agree. She is angry with me."

"Do you know why?" Flavius asked, shooting another nervous glance at his brother.

Cato kept his eyes forward.

"No," Marcus said.

"It's because Father paid you gold coins to take baby Maelia to be exposed."

Flavius quoted exactly what he must have overheard them discussing in the garden on that cloudy June day when Janius's third son was born.

Flavius waited for Marcus to respond. Again, Marcus composed himself so as to show neither surprise nor any other emotion.

"So your mother is angry because your father paid me gold coins to take the baby to be exposed?" Marcus asked.

"Yes," said Flavius. "What does all that mean?" he asked.

The child was innocent.

Marcus guessed that Flavius had related the conversation to Annia having no idea what the repercussions might be. How frightened the boy must have been to Annia's reaction. The boy needed to be told his mother's pain and anger was not the boy's fault.

Marcus groaned inwardly, but kept his face placid. And then he prayed. *God, forgive my foolishness. Give me wisdom to follow Your precepts and trust in You. Bless these boys. In Your divine power, please give me the words that will help these boys.*

Marcus took a deep breath, but before he had a chance to speak, Cato broke in, his face red, his voice choked with emotion.

"It means Marcus took our baby to die."

There. It was out there. It was exactly what Janius had paid him to do.

"No," Flavius said, "it's not true, is it, Marcus?"

It wasn't true. But how could he explain it?

Marcus had known the baby would never be exposed, and would instead be restored to her mother.

What he didn't agree to, what Cato and Flavius had not overheard, was the rest of the conversation.

"I'm not a killer," Marcus had told Janius on that June day.

"But you're willing to expose the baby?" Janius had replied.

"I will lay the baby at the place of exposure, and it's up to the gods from there," Marcus had said.

Janius had laughed, a deep-throated laugh. "Ah, equivocation at its finest. If I didn't know better, I would accuse you of being a Greek."

Marcus had said nothing in reply.

"But," Janius said, "you've pleased me. I will speak to the emperor in your favor. It just won't be quite as good as it might be were you to take care of *all* my business for me. There are plenty of brutes on the street who will do the deed for far less money and favor than you require."

And Marcus had taken the gold coin, turned on his heel and left the lush garden of Galerius Janius.

It was the first time he had been paid to expose an infant.

Cato and Flavius stood waiting for his answer.

"This is a very long story. But I am going to tell you because you asked."

"I think we better sit down," Cato said, his anger spent. He looked nervously ahead, seeking his mother. "I don't think Mother needs to overhear this."

"That will be for you to decide after I tell you my story," Marcus said.

Cato nodded.

"When I was a boy, there was a job I wanted to do. I wanted to be the commander of the Praetorian Guard. I wanted nothing more than to protect my emperor."

"I've seen them," Flavius said. "I like their uniforms." He looked to Cato for agreement. Cato nodded.

"A very bad man named Sejanus became prefect just as I entered young manhood," Marcus continued.

"I've heard of him," Cato said. "He was killed."

"Yes, he was killed," Marcus said. "Do you know why?"

"Yes. Because he planned to kill the emperor," Cato replied.

"That's right," Marcus said. "From that day, through each of my twenty years of military service, I could think of no higher calling than being the man who guarded the life of the emperor with his own life. I wanted to be the one in charge of protecting the most important man in the world."

"And did you?" Flavius asked.

"No," Marcus said. "I finished my foreign service and came home to Rome. My plan was to first become commander of the *Vigiles*."

"The fire brigade, right?" Flavius. "I want to be a *Vigile* when I grow up."

"Stop interrupting him," Cato said. "I want to hear the rest of his story."

"Sorry," Flavius said, and sat back down again.

"Someone had told me that if I became the commander of the *Vigiles* and then came into favor with the emperor, I could be a prefect for the *Vigiles* and maybe one day a prefect for the Guard."

"Sort of like practice?" Cato said.

"Yes, like practice."

"Your father needed my help, and I needed his help all at the same time," Marcus said.

This was where it was going to get very hard. How could he tell this story without further implicating their father? Without calling their father a murderer?

"In Rome, people like to kill one another. I heard that the emperor's grandmother killed seven people so that her son could be emperor. I heard that the emperor Claudius was not her choice," Cato said.

"You may say that while we are here in Britain," Marcus warned Cato, "but never speak of that in Rome. It could get you killed."

Cato looked around to make certain no one else had heard him speak. They were alone, and he looked relieved.

"So," Cato said, "my father wanted to kill my mother

so that she was out of the way, and my brother and I would not get our new baby brother's money."

"Yes, I believe that was what he was thinking. But how did you know that?" Marcus asked.

"I figured it out when I was reading Sallust."

"Sallust?" Marcus said, his eyebrows raised. "Whatever made you interested in reading Sallust?" As a historian, Sallust was well known, but still, it was heavy reading for a ten-year-old boy.

"I grew bored when Mother left. My tutor didn't care what I read, and so I read everything I could."

"He did," Flavius said. "Sometimes he liked reading better than playing with me."

"Anyway," Cato continued, "According to Sallust, the Roman aristocracy is so degenerate that it might not last another hundred years. My father, you see, is part of that degenerate Roman Aristocracy. He can't help himself. He loves money above all else."

Marcus wasn't quite certain how to respond to the boy's acuity.

"What happened next?" Cato said.

Marcus decided plain words were best.

"He asked me to expose your baby sister," Marcus said. "I agreed to expose your sister. However, I never planned to follow through. Instead, I knew my mother would take her in and save her."

He remembered that night not so long ago when he became equally intent on saving Annia. He remembered nearly losing her on the road in Rome. It had been one of the most frightening moments of his life. She had not made it easy for him to save her.

"But you are a soldier," Cato said. "Don't you kill for pay in the army?"

"Yes," Marcus said, "but in the army, I kill to keep

the empire safe, not to allow someone to gain money and power."

"I heard that the reason the empire has expanded into Britain, and the reason we've killed people here, is so that the emperor can have more money and more power."

Marcus could not respond to this. He was saved by Flavius.

"But you wouldn't kill our baby," he said. "And now you love our mother."

There was a tense silence. Should Marcus admit this?

But it was the truth, and he had decided at the very beginning of this conversation that he needed to tell the plain truth.

"You are right, Flavius. I would not kill your mother because I love her."

He should never have entered into the contract with Galerius Janius.

When you play in the dirt, you get dirty. That's what his father had told him as a young boy.

He had played in the dirt, and he had gotten dirty.

He thought he had pulled out in time to stay clean.

It turned out he had not.

Chapter Twenty-One

"You've found your friends," Theodora said, looking down at Annia and the others as they made their way down the street to her house.

"Yes," Annia said looking up at the open window from which Theodora spoke.

"Just a minute, I'll be right down," Theodora said, and they could hear her pounding through the upstairs hallway, down the stairs, and into the atrium.

Inside the columned portico she stopped, breathless and smiling.

Theodora held her arms out to Virginia and Lucia, greeting them as if she had known them all their lives. She shook Titus's hand and ushered them all inside.

"I know you must be famished and longing for proper baths. But is this all of you?" she asked, looking behind the group and down the street. "Aren't there more children?"

"Yes," Annia said, "the boys stayed back to swim with Julius."

"You let them swim alone?" Theodora asked.

"They are very good swimmers," Annia said, "like fish. They've been swimming their entire lives."

"And there were no adults left with them? Wasn't there another person in your party? Marcus? Wasn't that his name?"

Annia's face burned a bright red.

She didn't want to think about him. She didn't want to see him; she certainly didn't want to speak of him.

Virginia and Lucia exchanged glances.

Titus studied the ground.

Theodora looked confused. "You know, the man you told me about, the one who saved your life and those of your boys."

Annia looked down at the floor mosaic with its bright picture made with thousands of tiny broken colored stones. The mosaic showed a cat having just caught a pigeon, and it seemed somehow appropriate.

"Yes," Annia said.

Theodora waited for her to say more.

"Yes," Annia said, "Marcus is with us. He is with the boys, swimming." She said this as if Marcus had been worthy of no more notice than a servant or a slave.

Theodora looked as if she had no idea why Annia would want to discount the man she had praised two days earlier.

Annia could not bear to tell Theodora what she had learned about Marcus.

He was a liar of the most despicable sort.

How had she ever trusted the man?

"You were right about Marcus," she said quietly to Virginia.

"Well, then," Theodora said. "It looks like we shall have a feast tonight. I will tell my kitchen staff. It has been a long time since we've had a party."

She bustled inside.

"Why do you say he is not your friend?" Lucia asked, her eyes wide and innocent.

Titus and Virginia waited for Annia to answer.

She felt pressed and confused. What could she say? Annia began second-guessing herself.

Maybe, it had all been a misunderstanding.

But Annia knew better. Cato and Flavius had no reason to lie about what they had heard Marcus say to their father. Flavius had innocently reported a conversation he didn't understand. Cato had filled in with his own memory of what Marcus had said, though it obviously pained him. Neither would lie to her.

Not about something so important.

"The boys overheard him speaking with Janius," Annia said.

"Who is Janius?" Lucia asked.

"Her former husband," Virginia answered for her. "And a more vile man you've never seen. It's not enough that he sent her away, he has to poison her name to everyone he comes in contact with. He is spreading it all over Rome that Annia is an adulteress."

"He says these things in front of her boys?" Lucia asked. "Why?"

"To make himself appear to be the victim," Virginia said.

Annia wondered if there was a purpose behind this painful reminder of Janius.

"Janius hates Annia more than he loves his own children," Titus said. "He hates her because looking at her reminds him of all of his failures—how he married her for her money and then squandered it on women and chariot races. When he sees her face, he is reminded that she put up with his foolishness, loved him anyway and loved her children as a good mother should. He had no good reason to banish her and had to fabricate one. He has come to believe the story he has fabricated."

"And what does all of this have to do with Marcus?" Lucia asked.

Virginia was silent.

"The boys said…" Annia began, but just as she started to speak, she heard Flavius's voice followed by Cato's laughter and the deep, gravelly response that told her Marcus was with them.

"And inside is a tiny pool," Flavius was saying. "It isn't big enough for swimming, just big enough for the rainwater to fall in and look pretty. I don't know what the water is used for, but beside the pool it feels nice and cool, even though we can't get in."

"You'll like Theodora. She is very kind," Cato finished for him.

"I'm hungry," Julius chimed in

"We are all hungry," Marcus replied.

Annia could feel the tension growing in her belly. Hearing his voice still made her heart leap. There was something disturbing about being thrilled by the voice of the man who was paid to harm her child, and yet she couldn't help wishing it were a week ago when she had been so happy and Marcus had been innocent. At least in her mind.

But he was not innocent.

The door stood open to the street, and the three boys and Marcus walked in. Julius peeked from behind him and saw the pool. He went running for the *impluvium* to make it his own personal swimming pool, in spite of what he had heard Flavius say just moments before.

Marcus caught Julius by his tunic and yanked him back. "That is a water supply," Marcus said, "not your personal swimming pool. We passed the baths a block back, remember?"

"Yes, I remember," Julius said, solemnly. "But I really like swimming."

Marcus ruffled his head, "I know you do, little friend. I know. And we will swim again. Just not in this pool."

Julius nodded solemnly.

When Julius looked up and saw his mother, his smile filled his face. "Mother," he said, and catapulted himself into her arms as if he hadn't seen her for days. She covered him with kisses and hugged him tight.

"We swam and then we pretended to be dogs," Julius said.

"Dogs?" Lucia asked, and looked up at Marcus for an explanation.

"We were drying off," Flavius explained, "and pretending we were dogs shaking the water off our coats."

"Oh," Lucia said. "What fun. Thank you, Marcus, for watching after them." She shot an apprehensive look at Annia.

It was clear that Lucia was nervous for Marcus. Annia looked away.

"Mother," Flavius said. "Guess what?"

"What?" Annia asked, smiling at her sweet boy.

"Marcus found something, something that will make you very happy."

"Oh?" Annia said.

"You have to guess what it is," Flavius said, jumping up and down in his excitement.

"It is something very important to you, Mother," Cato said, as if to reassure her that this was not some silly joke. "Something very important to you and equally important to Maelia."

Annia thought hard. What could it be? Maelia's blanket? But there was no special significance to the blue silk blanket.

"Would you like a hint?" Flavius asked.

Annia had to laugh at his enthusiasm.

"Yes," she said, "go ahead, give me a hint."

"It's the same color as this." He pointed to his own tunic with its embroidered purple band.

On Flavius's band, Annia had embroidered the sun and palm branches, symbols of hope and victory. She remembered the joy with which she had made the band for his *toga praetexta*.

"I think I know what it is," Annia said, her eyes wide.

"Say it, Mother," Flavius said. "Say it, and then Marcus can give it to you."

At the mention of Marcus's name, Annia's face fell.

"It's the purple band for Maelia's toga," she said, working hard at keeping her voice cheerful for her son's sake.

"Yes," Flavius said. He searched her face. "You are happy about it, aren't you, Mother?"

"Very happy, sweet child," Annia said, and forced herself to smile and accept the soggy offering with grace.

She was happy to have it, there was no doubt. The band, with its intricately embroidered series of leaves intertwined with birds and flowers, finally completed on the merchant ship, had taken hundreds of hours of careful work. She just wished that one of the boys could have found it rather than Marcus.

After handing it to her as quickly as he could, Marcus addressed Lucia and Annia. "Well," he said, "I just wanted to see the boys home."

"Are you leaving?" Titus asked.

"Yes, I've arranged for a room at the garrison for the night. Then I will look tomorrow for passage to Londinium."

"I've already found passage," Annia said curtly, "so you needn't worry about me and the boys."

"That's good, Annia. I'm glad for you," Marcus said evenly.

"I'm sure you are 'glad for me.' Good day," she said as imperiously as an empress dismissing a disloyal subject.

Marcus turned to leave, but before he could get out of the door, Theodora returned.

"Well," she said, overjoyed to see the boys, "Flavius, Cato. I see you are back and brown as berries. Did you have fun swimming?"

"Yes," they said together.

"Marcus was the sea monster, and gobbled us up," Flavius added.

"And, Mother, he took us to the garrison, and we met some real soldiers. They showed us how they set up their tents for camp, and then they showed us how they made the concrete they are using to build the tower." Cato's face was flushed with excitement.

"And," said Flavius, "Marcus helped them plan how to have their own fire patrol."

"That sounds like fun. Would you like to introduce me to your sea monster and your other little friend?" Theodora said, indicating Julius.

"I'm not little," Julius said, leaping from his mother's lap and standing, his brow furrowed and his hands on his hips.

"Oh, yes, now that you are standing, I see you are quite right. You are not little. You are big. Nearly as big as Flavius here." Theodora knelt down and offered Julius her hand. "It is very nice to meet you, Julius."

Julius, having recovered his dignity, could afford to be gracious. "Nice to meet you," he said, taking her hand and giving Theodora a little bow.

Theodora turned to Marcus and held out both hands, taking his in hers. She looked up at him, and gave him a smiling assessment. "I've heard so much about you already," she said, beaming at Annia. "She told me you saved her and her children's lives with your quick thinking. A hero in our midst," she said.

"Hardly," Annia muttered under her breath.

Virginia's fierce look silenced her.

"Well," Theodora said, her enthusiasm contagious, "since we are all here, and I'm certain you are all hungry, come join me at the dinner table, and we will eat a quick supper. Then to the baths."

They all followed her except Marcus.

Theodora noticed him standing back. "You are joining us, aren't you, Marcus?"

"I have already arranged for a room at the garrison," he said, "and I feel certain they will be serving dinner there."

"Oh?" Theodora said. "I suppose that means you haven't heard about the food at the garrison. I hear it's not fit for human consumption." She laughed.

"Marcus," Flavius and Julius said, "eat with us."

"Yes," Theodora said. "I insist."

Did no one understand? This man they were all fawning over had taken money from her former husband to expose her baby to the slave traders.

"I must go feed Maelia. She's hungry," Annia said. Turning on her heel, she headed for the safety of the stairs and her upstairs room.

Away from Marcus seemed the safest place to be.

Chapter Twenty-Two

When Annia left the inner garden and went upstairs, everyone was silent.

"Such a good mother," Theodora said. "Do you know some mothers hire wet nurses because they can't be bothered nursing their own infants? Not our Annia." A look of worry crossed her brow. "I hope she doesn't fall asleep while she is feeding little Maelia. I would hate for her to miss our party."

"I'm sure she is very tired," Virginia said. "Shepherding an infant and two boys through a raging storm would exhaust anyone, even two days later. I'm sure she hasn't completely recovered. After she rests she will be right back down with us." But the brightness in her voice went down two pitches when she added the last sentence. Virginia knew Annia would not be back.

As did Marcus.

"I don't think so," Marcus said.

"It might do her good to sleep, as much as I would love to talk with her. Having a child of three is exhausting, too. I understand how she feels," Lucia said.

Titus stood, walked over to Virginia and put his arm around her. "Theodora has invited us to eat. We should go in and eat. It would be rude to allow the flies to eat the food." He patted Virginia's shoulder. Virginia looked up at him, gave him an apologetic half smile and followed him into the dining room.

The silent exchange between the couple pained Marcus more than he could have imagined. The way Virginia looked up at Titus, trusting him, and then following him was the way Annia used to look at him.

How would he ever regain her trust?

Lucia and the boys followed Titus and Virginia.

Julius stopped and held his hand out for Marcus.

The little boy had no idea how much that extended hand meant to him in that moment. Marcus took it with gladness and walked in.

The food was beyond Marcus's imagining. The glossy red Samian pottery held grapes, olives garnished with a sprig of rosemary and a large platter of bread. A plate of cheeses of many textures and varieties finished off the course.

The next course was a round platter filled with a dozen or more quail arranged in a circle. Between the roasted quail were asparagus tips, and in the middle of the arrangement were several quails' eggs.

The delicious scent took him back to Rome and feasts given by friends of his father's.

Theodora must be wealthy, and she must have a constant supply of goods from Rome.

"My husband is stationed in Rome," Theodora said. "He sends me delicacies as often as he can. It is not often I have a group of people to share them with."

"Thank you so much," Marcus said. "I can't remember the last time I've had such good food. Your servants must keep the oven hot all day long to be able to produce such food on such short notice."

"No, not always. Just today. I was expecting Annia and her children back at any moment. I hoped that she might bring more survivors with her, but I wasn't certain."

"We are all very thankful for your high hopes," Virginia said. "You are very kind."

"It is not often than I am able to break bread with fellow believers," Theodora said.

The others at the table smiled their gratitude.

Marcus wanted to enjoy the bounty but found himself watching the door throughout the entire meal. He was nervous, worried that Annia would come in and equally worried that she would not.

What could he do to make her understand that he had made a mistake? And that the mistake he had made might not be as terrifying as she seemed to think. He regretted it. He would like to correct it. But how?

Virginia had told him to get Annia home to her parents. But Annia had made it clear that she could get her own self home, that Theodora was offering her own personal wagon and horses, that she could take care of herself and did not need him.

She didn't need him. That stung.

Still, he would make certain she got home. He would see her safely to her parents' home, even if he had to follow her without her knowledge in order to do so.

After she was safely home, he would go and visit the *Vigiles* in Londinium. As of yet, the fort was small, so that should not take long. However, there was no telling how long it would take him to make certain his villa was running properly.

From what he gathered, his family villa was not so far from Annia's.

And then, after he got the affairs in order there, he would return to Rome and leave Annia alone. He would help prepare his mother and all the babies for their journey to Britain.

It was clear that Annia despised him. He would accept the prefect position and stay in Rome. It was best for all of them. He would send the letter tomorrow. He wasn't sure why he hadn't done it already. If he could get a moment alone with her, he could explain his decision.

If he came back to Britain to visit his mother and father, Annia would have found someone else.

Annia had made up her mind. He was the enemy. She was the victim. He had been in the pay of the man who had divorced her and tried to kill her baby. Marcus had also been the one ordered by Janius to discard her youngest son as if he were trash.

And though Marcus had not agreed to that and only took the boy to save him from a worse fate, Annia did not know that. Marcus was still haunted by the sound of Flavius crying the night his father had him arrested for being a heretic.

"She won't come in," Virginia said, noticing Marcus's nervous and nearly constant watch of the entranceway.

Marcus looked at her as if he didn't know what she was talking about, but he could tell Virginia wasn't fooled.

But she did come in. It would have been rude not to do so. And Annia was anything but rude. She had taken time to put her hair up in an elaborately severe bun. And she'd changed her clothes. Instead of the *palla* and *stola*, fastened by a broach at the shoulder, she wore a long, brightly colored wool skirt and belted overtunic in the style of the locals.

He regarded her and wondered if these were the clothes

of her youth, the clothes in which she found herself most comfortable.

They suited her slim figure.

She must have felt the eyes of the entire room turn to her when she walked in. "I'm sorry," she said with a gracious little bow. "I had to put Maelia to sleep. She was particularly fussy tonight."

"I'm sure she was," Virginia said. "The baby's mood is a reflection of the mother's."

Annia shot Virginia a look Marcus was quite certain was meant to quiet her.

It had quite the opposite effect. "Well, that is what you always tell me," Virginia responded.

"My mother says you can't blame the mother for the mood of the baby," Marcus said. Having stood for Annia to enter, he found himself between the two women.

"It seems you still have a champion, Annia," Virginia said.

Annia reddened.

Theodora directed her to the seat beside Marcus.

Annia spent the remaining hours of the dinner carrying on polite conversation with everyone around her except Marcus.

Marcus was thankful when Theodora signaled that the dinner was ended. It had not gone well. He hoped tomorrow would be better.

The following morning, Marcus needed to secure a wagon and horse for his own journey home.

"I appreciate your kindness," he said to Theodora as he was taking his leave.

"So happy to have met you. You are everything Annia said, and more," Theodora said.

If she only knew.

"Thank you," he said.

"If you are heading north, we have plenty of room in my wagon," she said. "It was a former military supply wagon that my husband managed to snag in a horse race gone bad," she laughed. "He is a fortunate man. Always has been."

"He is a blessed man to have you for a wife," Marcus said.

Theodora smiled, but there was something hidden in that smile that Marcus could not read.

"Thank you for the offer," he said. "I will be going north, as well, but I'm going to secure my own wagon."

"Well, if you have trouble finding a wagon, please know we could use your help with the team. If you will come along, then I won't need to bring a slave." Her smile crinkled the corners of her eyes.

"You've only known me for a few hours, and already you plan to use me for my brawn," Marcus said, grinning.

"I would like you with us so that whatever is amiss between the two of you can be worked out." Theodora smiled, but there was seriousness to her tone.

"I can only pray for that," Marcus said humbly.

It cheered him to know that Theodora wanted him close.

The thought made him so happy he whistled as he walked. He headed to the garrison, planning to stop first thing in the morning at the forum to find a military scribe. He wanted to write and send his letter to the emperor, and another to Annia's parents apprising them of her arrival. His next task would be to see if any of the shopkeepers or street vendors could lead him in the right direction for a horse and cart.

In the light of a new morning, Porte Dubris proved itself a thriving military community. Roman soldiers were busy building the town up and providing it with all the necessities and some of the frivolities of a typical Roman town. There was the marvelous bathhouse, which he decided to stop by before going to the garrison. There was also a theater and a forum where he hoped to find someone who was knowledgeable about the best place to rent traveling gear.

Marcus was especially impressed with the public fountain, its water tank rising like a tall tower behind it and the public toilets already available.

It had been less than a decade since Claudius had conquered Britain, but already, Rome had made its presence known here in Britain.

He wondered about the changes up north. Londiniun was primarily a merchants' town—both his father and Annia's had grown wealthy as merchant traders, and bought sprawling estates in the area.

His father's land was rich in pastureland, so their herds of sheep were healthy and plentiful.

Their wool was some of the finest in the area, and they exported it to Rome for good money.

Annia's father raised and exported hunting dogs.

He wondered if Annia's father had ever met his own father. Perhaps when his parents were living here, in Britain, they had even eaten dinner together. It was possible that Marcus and Annia had known each other when they were very small. He wondered if their paths had ever crossed. Londinium was, after all, a small town, and had barely even existed when he was a boy.

He stopped at the columned portico on his end of the forum. He was pointed to the temple of Jupiter to locate his scribe.

He looked straight to the other side and could see through matching columns the temple to Jupiter rising two stories above the rest of the forum. He headed in that direction, found his scribe, dictated his letters, one to Annia's parents alerting them to her imminent arrival, and paid him. He then set off on his mission to secure a cart and horse.

The rest of the marketplace was composed primarily of shops, offices and a triumphal arch on the Porte side, a reminder that Claudius had come through this very street on his victory march through Britain.

At this early hour, most of the merchants were just putting out their wares.

"Where might I find a reliable horse and cart?" he asked a man on the street.

The man laughed uncomfortably. "Well, that depends on when you need it. If you can wait until December, you might be able to reserve one."

"I need it for tomorrow," Marcus said. "Where could I go to get a horse and cart for tomorrow?"

"Nowhere in this town," the man said. "Every horse and cart here is promised until the dead of winter to the Romans. They are throwing all of their efforts right now into the tower. Do you see it?" The man pointed to the structure that was now simply a wooden frame, but would soon guard the garrison from invaders and shine a light to ships lost at sea.

"Horses and carts are bringing in stone and the materials for *caementum*. Others are bringing in supplies to feed the soldiers. I don't imagine you will have much luck in this town getting what you are asking for. Not for several months."

"Are you certain?" Marcus asked.

"Certain as the soldiers you see building the tower to defend us from ourselves," the man said, his voice heavy with the accent of the local area.

Marcus had not expected this. Nor had he expected the thinly veiled resentment of the local man for the Roman improvements in his city.

"Thank you," Marcus said.

What were his options?

He went to the baths and asked the same question. The men there laughed at him.

He was trying to determine his course of action when he heard small footsteps running behind him.

"Wait, Marcus." It was Cato. "I want to come with you," he said.

"Cato!" Marcus said, taking the child by the hand and turning to lead him back home. He was flattered that the child wanted to be with him but afraid of how long he had been following him.

"I want you to come with us. I don't want to travel without you," the child said, imploring him to stop.

"I understand," Marcus said, kneeling down eye level, "but your mother has made a different decision. We'll travel together again one day, don't worry. Let's head back. Does your mother know where you are?"

The boy looked down at the ground and shook his head.

Annia would be crazed with worry.

"Come with me, and we will tell her you are safe," Marcus said.

Cato nodded. "I will come with you. But know it is not because I want to do so but because it is my duty to do so."

Marcus's heart swelled with affection for this child.

They began making their way through the now busy marketplace in the direction of Theodora's villa.

From the corner of his eye, he saw a disturbance in the street ahead of him. He heard a woman's voice that sounded very much like Annia's. He pushed Cato into the baker's shop beside them. "Stay here," he said. "Don't leave until I come for you."

Street fights in the garrison towns were common. The Roman ideal was to let the locals fight it out. Disturbances were to be quelled only if there was the threat of the loss of Roman property or persons.

Marcus squared his shoulders and walked casually in the direction of the disturbance.

Mistaken for a local by her clothes, Annia was being harassed by a band of soldiers.

"Get your hands off of me," she cried. "I am a Roman matron."

"So they all say, *domina*." The shortest of the soldiers jeered. He reached in and took hold of her face, her chin cupped in his dirty hand.

Marcus felt anger pour fire into his veins.

"Soldier," he said. His gravelly voice, deep and loud, boomed off the columns of the forum and bounced against the shop walls.

The soldier let go of Annia and turned to see what authority spoiled his fun.

Annia's eyes fixed on Marcus. They were liquid with angry tears.

His hand wrapped around the soldier's neck, and he squeezed until the soldier was down on his knees, begging for mercy.

"Laying hands on a Roman matron. Your superior will hear of this, that I promise you."

"No harm intended, sir. We were just having a little fun."

Marcus turned sharply on the man speaking and cut him off in midsentence. "If you value that tongue you will seal your lips." The authority in Marcus's voice scattered the idle soldiers.

"Come on," he said to Annia, wrapping his arm securely around her waist and guiding her out of harm's way.

Cato stood at the baker's shop door, eyes wide. He had not been able to see everything, but Marcus suspected he had seen enough to be afraid.

Annia clung to Marcus. Marcus wondered if she realized it. Cato hugged her, and she grasped him with her free arm.

The three of them moved without speaking toward Theodora's villa.

Chapter Twenty-Three

Titus climbed out of the wagon to make a final check on the horses, the wagon and the wheels. He made certain the hardware was well fitted and everything tight and ready.

"How does it look?" Theodora asked.

"It couldn't have looked better if I'd done it myself," Titus answered. He swung himself back up on the seat beside Virginia and Theodora.

Eager to see her mother and father, frightened by the day's experience of losing Cato and being rescued from ruffian soldiers by Marcus, Annia had packed late into the night with Theodora, hoping her help would enable them to leave this place and Marcus before the sun rose.

Annia had not allowed herself to miss home in all the years she lived in Rome. She hadn't expected to ever see Britain again, and wanted to protect her heart. But, in less than two days, she would be home. The closer they came to her childhood home, the more eager Annia was to be there.

Her parents would see their grandchildren for the first time. Her children would live in a place where the grass was soft and summer days were long. She was so excited that there were butterflies in her stomach.

Annia, Lucia and the children sat in the wagon bed. They had loaded the supplies on top of the wooden-framed wagon, replete with a sturdy roof and heavy canvas sides. There was an opening in the front so that they could see where the wagon headed, and another in the back. The half door in the back latched securely so that Julius was not in danger of falling out.

The predawn was cool, but not cold, and the day promised to be clear and beautiful.

"We can walk alongside when we grow tired of riding," Annia said brightly. She was headed to see her family, her mother and her father. She was going to start a new life and leave all the hurt and pain of the past behind her.

Marcus.

It didn't matter that he had come to her rescue yesterday. She tried to forget how she had felt when she heard his voice. She had gone weak-kneed with relief. Her eyes had filled with tears of joy. Her rescuer.

Paid to expose her baby.

She had to put him out of her mind. She would stay as far away as possible from him throughout this journey. He only confused her.

She focused on the children: Cato sleeping peacefully and Flavius and Julius playing a sort of ball game with walnuts and a wooden cup. They sat cross-legged with the cup between them and took turns trying to ring it. Flavius was winning, but he kept moving the cup closer and closer to Julius so that Julius would have a chance.

It was going to be a good day. She couldn't imagine a better one. Nothing was going to ruin it for her.

Just then she heard the sound of a familiar, gravelly voice.

Her stomach felt suddenly light, and she put her hand on her chest, trying to calm herself. She could feel Titus pulling the horse's reins, stopping them. The wagon rocked backward and forward a bit before growing completely still.

Annia could hear Titus talking. She listened. It was Marcus. What was he doing here? Why was he stopping their progress? She could not hear what it was they were saying.

"That's Marcus," Flavius said. "He's coming with us."

"No," Annia said. "Marcus is not coming with us."

Flavius and Julius jumped up and down, making the wagon bounce with their excitement.

"Enough!" Annia said, more harshly than she intended. The boys shot her a look of hurt surprise.

"Annia," Lucia said, a gentle reprimand. She turned to the boys. "Annia is right, boys. You can't jump up and down in the wagon. It will frighten the horses."

"I'm sorry, Mother," Julius said, and sat down.

"Sorry, Mother." Flavius sat.

"You are forgiven," Annia said. "And now you must forgive me. You didn't deserve my anger."

"Of course, Mother," Flavius said, his voice contrite, "I don't want to scare the horses. Why, they could run us into a river or a bog if they spooked."

"That is true," Annia said, "but I think jumping just that one time is fine, and the horses will recover."

Annia sat, tense, avoiding Lucia's gaze and trying to hear the conversation taking place outside the wagon.

"What do you think Marcus is doing?" Lucia asked, though Annia could sense that it made her nervous to mention Marcus's name around Annia.

"How could I possibly know?" Annia asked. "Here," she said, handing Maeila to Lucia. "Could you please hold her while I go see the cause of the commotion?"

"Of course," Lucia said, and took the sleeping baby.

"Why are you so nervous, Mother?" Cato asked sleepily. "Where are you going?"

"Just checking on things," Annia said.

"Can we get out of the wagon, Mother?" Flavius asked.

"Yes," Annia said. She opened the back door to let the squirming children file out in front of her. They were going to be confined to this wagon for a very long time. There was no reason to keep them in any longer than necessary when they could be out enjoying the sunshine.

And Annia was determined to find out what was going on.

She climbed from the shady wagon and squinted in the bright sunlight. She walked behind and around the wagon looking for Titus and Marcus. She spotted them, standing beside the horses.

Marcus had his hand on the horse's neck, calming her while he leaned in close to talk with Titus. The conversation was obviously private.

Annia turned back and walked behind the wagon. Even though she had discovered nothing further about why Marcus was there, the exercise would do her good. It would also calm her jittery nerves. She began walking back down the road in the direction from which they had just come.

They had traveled just a little way from Porte Dubris. She could still see the gray water of the channel sparkling in the distance.

The road on which they had stopped was newly paved with irregular gray stone, and yet the road was even and its line straight both before and after the wagon. The Romans had done much work in the seven short years since Claudius had conquered the island.

Beside the road on either side were ancient stone walls

enclosing a deep and wide green pasture, dotted with some farmer's sheep.

She didn't want to stray far. Annia was careful to stay on the opposite side of the road from Marcus and Titus when she circled back around the wagon.

Marcus and Titus moved away from the horses and stood speaking beside the stone wall. Had they moved because they saw Annia drawing near?

Annia approached the upraised front seat of the wagon where Virginia and Theodora sat talking quietly.

Theodora startled when she saw Annia.

"Whatever is the matter?" Annia asked, startling both women.

"You are quite pale," Theodora said.

"I'm not surprised," Annia replied. "What is he doing here?"

"Do you mean Marcus?" Virginia asked, one eyebrow raised.

"Yes," Annia said, looking away.

"What happened?" Virginia asked, getting right to the point. "You've not told me. You seemed in love, but now you can't stand the sight of him."

"You tell me," Annia shot back, her voice low. "You doubted him when you first saw him at my house the day I gave you the manumission papers. Why?"

"I had heard some things," Virginia said. "My aunt hinted at some things that were not entirely favorable."

Annia looked over at Marcus and Titus. They remained engrossed in their own conversation and were too far away to hear Annia and Virginia.

"And what were the things she hinted at?" Annia asked, the blood pounding in her ears. She suddenly realized she did not want her worst fears confirmed.

She wanted to believe that her sons were wrong, that

Marcus was the man she thought she was, the man she had believed him to be when she fell in love with him.

Virginia looked at Annia, then looked over at Marcus.

They couldn't see Marcus's face, but they could see Titus's. And it was clear, Titus was talking to a dear friend, not an enemy.

Virginia studied Titus listening so carefully to his friend. She watched his easy smile, the laughter the two of them shared. They chatted like the comrades they were.

"I found later that I was mistaken," Virginia said. "My aunt holds Marcus in high regard. What she heard was idle gossip, not worthy of being repeated. Before I understood that, I wanted to protect you."

Anger coursed through Annia. She recalled Virginia's complete disdain when she met Marcus. "You are hiding something," she said.

"Be careful, my friend," Virginia warned, "that you do not falsely accuse those who love you."

Annia's eyes narrowed, but Virginia held her gaze steady.

And now all Annia wanted to do was cry. She was so confused and so frustrated that if she had been able, she would have left them all and headed out into the open field and run far, far away. Her heart hurt.

Marcus and Titus walked toward them.

"Might you ride in the wagon?" Titus said to Virginia. "Marcus will be traveling with us."

"Hooray!" the boys shouted. "Marcus is traveling with us!"

"He was unable to secure a horse and cart. It seems there is not a single one available in the city. The army has requisitioned them all for the building of the defense tower," Titus said.

The tone of his voice invited no argument.

Annia walked around to the back of the cart, climbed in, snuggled into the blankets, still warm from the boys, and tried to sleep. It was her favorite way of avoiding having to think.

But today it didn't work. It did, however, keep her from having to talk to Virginia.

She was not going to have any further conversations with Virginia about Marcus. It was clear Virginia was on his side. Annia simply could not understand how her dearest friend could side with her nearest enemy.

The boys babbled away, planning the things they would do with Marcus. They settled into another game with the walnuts. This time, the walnuts were armies. It took them forever to set up their men and clarify the rules.

"If your men get on this side of this line, they are dead, and if my men get on that side of the line, they are dead," Cato said.

"Okay," Flavius agreed.

Annia listened to them setting up their complicated wars and was happy they could be so unfettered with worry and concern. She prayed this would be so for the rest of their childhood.

Lucia held the sleeping Maelia in her arms. Lucia had situated herself in the corner of the wagon so that she could hold the baby safely and rest comfortably herself. She was asleep.

Annia's eyes grew heavy. When she opened them again, the sun had warmed the wagon. She sat up, and Flavius said, "You woke up just in time, Mother. We're stopping soon to eat the picnic you and Theodora packed."

"A meal shared with Marcus," Annia said, her voice bitter with sarcasm. How could she avoid it?

She couldn't.

"This must cease," Virginia said. Before Annia could

think, Virginia had jumped from the moving wagon and pulled Annia down with her. The sun's light was camouflaged by the dense forest they entered.

"I do not want to talk about Marcus Sergius," Annia said, breathless from the effort of regaining her footing on the solid ground.

"You are acting like a child, and it sickens me," Virginia said walking briskly so as to keep up with the wagon. "You must let him tell you his story. It's the least you can do. Have you forgotten he saved your life? He saved Maelia and Flavius. Who cares why he did it? Does it really matter? Does anything actually matter other than the fact that you are alive and have reunited with your children, and soon you will be united with your entire family? What I would give to be so blessed." Virginia's words were punctuated by her pounding strides.

Annia was silenced at the truth her friend spoke.

"I want you to give Marcus Sergius a chance to explain himself," Virginia continued.

"He already did. He explained that it was true what the boys said. He was paid to expose Maelia. Isn't that enough?"

"That," Virginia said, "is only the beginning of the story. You must wait and listen for Marcus to tell you the rest."

In the gloom of the forest shade, Annia felt her heart lighten the tiniest bit.

There was more to the story? She hadn't thought of that. She had smarted at the stark confession Marcus had made to her. She had burned to discover that her worst fear was a truth.

But if there was more to the tale, if Virginia trusted him, maybe Annia should let Marcus tell it.

Soon they reached an agreeable grove, sunny and clear,

with a babbling brook nearby. The walk had done her good. Virginia tended to the boys, and Annia helped Theodora get ready for lunch.

"Where did we put the olives?" Theodora asked.

"In the gray bag, just in front of the water jugs," Annia said. "Here, let me grab them."

"We'll be needing to refill the water jugs, too," Theodora said pointing to the bubbling brook.

When Annia climbed up the wagon and reached for a jug, a well-muscled, sun-browned arm reached from the other side and pulled it down.

Annia groaned.

Marcus.

Annia climbed to the top of the wagon and leaned down as close to his face as she dared.

"I don't need your help," she said.

"You've made that clear," Marcus said. "I'm sorry, but the jug is heavy."

"And you don't think I can manage it?" she asked, grabbing hold of the jug and pulling it toward her. "You underestimate me."

"No," Marcus said, wresting the jug from her arms as easily as he might pull a ripe apple from a tree, "I absolutely do not underestimate you. Perhaps it is you who underestimate me."

He jumped to the ground. Annia nearly toppled after him.

Infuriated, she steadied herself. She made the decision to end this once and for all. She jumped down on his side, and came so close to him that she felt his breath on her face.

"No," she said. "I overestimated you for a while." Her words dripped with venom.

"How is that?" he asked, his voice calm, his tone infuriatingly conversational.

"I thought you actually cared about my baby, about me. I thought you had saved us because you were good. But now I understand. You saved us because someone paid you to do so. Nothing more."

He flinched. His face lost its calm. She had struck a stinging blow.

"You don't know everything," he said through gritted teeth.

He stepped closer to her, and she could see he wanted to explain himself, clear his name, make it all right.

"Do not come near me," she said, holding her ground.

He backed away.

"I don't need to know the whole story to understand exactly who you are and what you are about," she said.

"What do you know?" he asked.

She looked up at him. She couldn't help herself. She wanted to look away, but the plaintive note in his voice forced her to look. There was something raw, something vulnerable in his eyes.

She had been fooled before.

"I've heard what you did," she said. "Will you deny it?"

"I will be honest about what I did," Marcus said, "if you will hear me out."

"I suspect I have little choice," she said.

"It is true what your boys said," he admitted. "But—"

Before he could finish, the sound of horse hooves on cobbled stone forced their attention away from each other.

Four horses but only two riders appeared down the road.

As the horses came closer, Annia could see that the riders were leading the two extra horses. One rider wore what appeared to be a red traveling cloak, the other a plain tunic.

The closer the riders came, the more familiar they looked.

Annia moved forward, shielding her eyes from the sun so she could see more clearly.

The one man had gray hair and looked to be in his early fifties. He was smiling broadly. He held up his hand in greeting. The other was a younger man, his tunic indicating his slave status.

Annia moved still closer toward the riders. Were her eyes deceiving her? Annia's heart began beating wildly. She jumped up and ran toward them as fast her legs would carry her.

"Father," she yelled. "Father."

The man leaped from his horse and ran toward the daughter he had not seen in thirteen years.

"Annia," he called, and picked her up in his arms, swinging her round and round, "you've come home. My child has come home."

Chapter Twenty-Four

"Oh, Father," she said, "you look exactly as I remember you. Only your hair has grayed, but your face and your eyes—the same." She hugged him again, burying her face in the familiar wool scent of his cloak.

He pulled her close and hugged her tight.

"And Mother?" Annia asked. "How does she fare?"

"Your mother is well," her father said. "I nearly had to tie her to the door to keep her from coming. I told her I would bring you home, safe and sound."

"But how did you know where to find me?" Annia asked.

"I received a message from a Marcus Sergius Peregrinus. A soldier who had ridden hard delivered it. It said you would be coming on this road in the next two days. I knew if I traveled immediately, I was sure to catch you." Her father looked around. "And which one is Marcus?"

Annia's heart sank. So soon. Her father would not take kindly to the man who was in the pay of her scurrilous former husband.

"I am, sir," Marcus said, so close behind Annia she could feel his breath on the back of her head.

Marcus, ever the gentleman, offered her father his

hand. "I'm very happy to meet you," he said, his handshake firm, his eyes calm.

"And you, too, my son," her father said. "You are a fine man for letting me know the whereabouts of my daughter. You, my man, are responsible for reuniting a family separated for thirteen long years. I never thought to see her again." Her father's eyes filled with tears, and his voice was choked.

Annia looked in surprise at her father. She'd never heard even a hint of tears in her father's voice. Had age done this to him?

"Will you be our guest when we arrive home?" her father asked Marcus.

"Thank you, I would love to, but I must check on my father's villa and return to Rome as soon as possible. I've been appointed prefect of the *Vigiles,* and I'm due to meet with the emperor as soon as I return."

"Well, then, I am happy for you. As prefect, you will have duties in Rome?" Her father looked questioningly at Annia.

The letter she had sent her parents from Rome made it clear that she believed Marcus was more than a friend. She felt embarrassed at this. Her father would think she had misjudged Marcus's feelings for her. He would be quite correct.

Theodora approached the group.

"Father," Annia said, happy to take his attention off Marcus, "I would like for you to meet my new friend, Theodora. It is she who has made this trip possible."

"Domina, it is very nice to meet you," he said, taking her hand.

"You must be very proud of your daughter and grandchildren," she said. "I look forward to meeting your wife." Theodora spoke with the grace befitting her station.

Her father beamed.

"Father, Theodora found us when we washed up on the shore, and were hungry and thirsty. She made a place for us in her home, and she is a believer."

The words tumbled out of her mouth one after the other.

"Ah, yes," her father said. "So happy to meet you, and thank you for taking care of my daughter. My name, by the way, is Tertius Maelius Secundus."

"A noble name," Theodora said. "I am pleased to make your acquaintance. Please, come join us for a midday meal. Both of you." She indicated her father's servant.

Her father motioned to him, and he tied the horses to a tree. They all sat down on the wool blanket Theodora had spread on the shady green grass and began eating the picnic lunch.

A chestnut tree shaded them from the noonday sun, and a cool breeze blew through its green leaves.

Cato, Flavius and little Julius crowded close to Annia, who was sitting beside her father.

Flavius scooted close to his grandfather and studied him with wide brown eyes.

"This is Flavius," Annia said to her father. "My second born."

"What a fine-looking young man," her father said.

Flavius's face crinkled into a smile, displaying his missing front tooth.

"Perhaps we should look around for that missing tooth," her father teased.

Flavius laughed at his silliness. "No, it's not missing. It's just gone until a new one grows in its place. It means I'm becoming a man," he said, quite seriously.

"And a fine one at that," her father agreed.

"This is my brother, Cato," Flavius said, pointing to Cato. "And our friend Julius."

Annia pushed Cato forward a bit, and he blushed and held his hand out to shake his grandfather's.

His grandfather smiled, bypassed the outstretched hand and pulled all three boys into a giant hug.

"I am so happy to finally meet you boys," he said.

"It's nice to meet you, too," the boys said in unison.

"You've done a good job with their raising, Annia," her father said, beaming. "But I always knew you would make a wonderful mother one day. Do you remember how you would line your dolls up in little beds and sing them to sleep?"

Annia smiled and nodded. Her busy father. She thought he never noticed her when she was a girl.

She remembered his laughter and his kindness, but she also remembered how rarely she saw him. He always seemed to be away on business, but he never forgot to bring her presents when he came home. She remembered that with special pleasure.

"Do you remember the pup you brought me on my tenth name day?" she asked.

"Yes, I do," he said. "You named her Thistle because her teeth were so sharp, and she slept in your room at your side until you left to be married."

"What happened to her?" Annia asked.

"She lived to be fifteen years old," her father said. "Ancient for a hunting dog, but just the right age for a sheepdog."

"Did she whelp?" Annia asked hopefully.

"Yes, she did," her father said. "We have her great-grandchildren running around the barn today. They are good dogs, the best herders we've ever bred."

"I can't wait to see them," Annia said.

"Pups?" Flavius asked.

"Pups?" Julius piped in.

"Yes," Annia said. "Didn't I tell you? There are always pups at my father's house. All of my friends loved visiting me because they knew that there were sure to be pups in our barn."

"I used to have to wait until Annia was sleeping before I could send the pups to new owners," he said.

He looked around. "And Virginia," he said, beaming, "she was just as bad. She stayed up late at night, so it was very hard to sneak the pups. She would always see and cry, and her crying would wake up Annia.

"Never a good time for me," he concluded.

"I remember that," Virginia said. "I thought you were mean for taking our pups away."

"I hope not," he said. "I might have seemed mean, but I hope that you didn't really think me so."

"May I hold the pups when we get home to your villa?" Flavius asked.

"Of course. And would you like to learn how to train them?" her father said, his eyes twinkling.

"Yes," Flavius said. "I like dogs very much. I had to leave mine behind."

"I'm sorry to hear that," her father said, kindly. "A dog is a good friend. It's hard to say goodbye."

"Yes, it is. But Marcus promised that when he goes back to Rome, he will bring my dog back to me."

"Did he, now?" her father said. "He sounds like a nice man."

"He is," Flavius said, "only Mother is very angry at him."

"Oh," Annia's father said, "is that so? And why is that?"

Flavius opened his mouth to tell the tale.

Annia interrupted him. "That's enough, son. Finish your food so that you and Cato and Julius will have a few minutes to run and play."

Flavius flashed her a big smile. "We would like that very much, Mother."

The boys set in on their food like ravenous animals. Soon the three of them had eaten everything put before them, and cleaned up their leavings.

"May we go play now, Mother?" Cato asked.

"Yes, son."

Cato nodded and ran.

"I've brought two horses," her father said. "One for you and one for Marcus. I understand, he needs to get to his father's villa, which is very close to ours, only half a day's ride away."

"That was thoughtful," Annia said, though her face and tone showed that it was anything but.

Chapter Twenty-Five

"You will accept my offer, Marcus?" her father said.

"I will, but I must caution you against separating our party."

"Why?" Tertius Maelius asked.

"While it is true Claudius secured Britain for Rome, there are still pockets of rebels, especially in this area, who would like nothing more than to see Rome suffer."

Tertius Maelius looked disappointed. Marcus hated to upset the kind man, but what he said was true. Britain was not safe, and their only real safety was in numbers.

"You are right, lad," Tertius said. "I like to believe we are safe. Perhaps it is good you are here to keep me from becoming a foolish, old dead man."

Marcus nodded. He understood Tertius's desire to believe all was safe. More, perhaps, than Tertius knew. In order to sleep at night, a man had to believe in the relative safety of his camp. Sometimes he even had to fool himself into a false security. Marcus imagined that to live in Britain, a man had to believe he was safe, even though he knew he was not.

Marcus felt Annia's eyes upon him. He looked at her, but she looked quickly away.

Was it longing he read in that look? Sadness? Regret?

It wasn't anger. She seemed to be searching his face for understanding. Yes, that was it. She seemed to seek to understand.

He'd had a few moments alone with Virginia and Titus after dinner the previous night. They had helped him understand what it was going to take to win Annia's affection back.

"It won't be easy," Virginia had said. "But it's not impossible. The way she looks at you tells me everything I need to know about how she feels. Her heart is broken, but she wants, desperately, to believe in you. It may take you a while to earn her trust. First, she has to hear the truth from you. Then you have to prove yourself."

"What does that mean?" Marcus had asked. He understood very well that he had to tell her the truth, but then, how was he to prove himself? "How do I need to prove myself to her?"

"You will figure it out," Virginia had assured him.

He had not felt assured.

"But first, you have to decide what is important to you. Annia or being prefect."

Virginia's words felt like a kick in the gut.

Was he prepared to give up his dream of becoming prefect of the Praetorian Guard? Was he prepared to become a farmer in this country he detested, a country with so many horrible memories of death and destruction?

Duty in Britain had meant consistent assaults by rebel armies. He preferred the peace of Rome. But what life did he have to look forward to in Rome? He could marry Cassia, but he had no desire to do so. It would be a marriage smiled upon by each respective family and would, most likely, gain him the trust of the emperor, eventually leading to his promotion from prefect of the *Vigiles* to prefect of the Guard.

But Annia. If she would have him, which seemed highly unlikely at this point, she would not be moving to Rome. She was in Britain to stay. He knew this to be true.

He needed wisdom. He needed guidance. He needed someone to talk to.

Heavenly Father, guide me, he prayed. *Show me what You would have me do.*

He would have to make her understand that he had never, ever intended to harm her baby.

If she forgave him, he would trust God to show him what to do next.

He walked around the wagon to where everyone sat eating. He would talk with her. Now.

"Annia?" he said.

The look she gave him was confusing.

A host of eyes were on him. Virginia's eyes were appraising, Theodora's were full of pity. His mouth stuffed with cheese, Annia's father simply nodded his greeting. Marcus was uncertain whether the man liked him or not. Did he consider him good enough for his daughter?

It didn't matter. Marcus was probably going back to Rome. After he made Annia understand. But what, exactly, did he want her to understand? Only that he never intended to harm her baby. Marcus hated the way his mind was jumping back and forth. Under normal circumstances, decisions were simple for him. He was a man of action, a leader, someone his men trusted with their lives. So why was he so confused?

"Could we take a walk?" Marcus asked.

"I'm eating," Annia replied.

This was going to take some work.

"I'll wait," Marcus said, and to do something with his

hands that made him feel he had control over at least one thing, he busied himself currying the horse, who waited patiently, munching the sweet grasses growing beside the road.

Marcus watched Annia out of the corner of his eye. She was beautiful. Even when she was so angry. She finished her olives, cheese and fruit from Theodora's stores and delicately brushed crumbs from her mouth, then swept her tunic clean. She checked the boys, who had long since finished eating and were making leaf ships on the little brook.

"Be careful, boys," she said.

They smiled up at her. "Don't worry, Mother," Cato said, "we won't get wet."

Marcus smiled. Separating a boy from any body of water was next to impossible. He guessed that before they continued their journey to Londinium again, at least one of the boys, if not both, would need a dry tunic.

Annia walked reluctantly toward Marcus.

"I am listening," she said as soon as she reached the horse he combed. "What did you want to talk about?"

He noticed her face had turned a bright shade of red. He wasn't certain if anger made that happen, or if it was simply the same awareness that gave his own face a matching flush.

"Will you walk with me?" he asked.

"Yes," she said, "but not far. We have a long journey."

"We do," he said, "but from the looks of our companions we have some leisure before we begin our travel."

Annia's eyes followed his to her father, who had nodded beneath the shade of an ancient oak, his back against the trunk, his chin sunken into his chest. The rest of the caravan, except for the boys and Theodora, dozed, as well.

Theodora held baby Maelia and walked up and down

the banks of the brook soothing the baby and keeping a watchful eye on the boys.

Marcus secured the horse's comb in the saddlebag and looked down at her to see if Annia would follow him.

She did. It was a small victory, but it gave him the confidence he needed.

They walked along the road, never straying far from the company, circling around the field opposite the brook. The soldier in him, alert to the dangers posed by the thick woods on either side of the fields, would not let them stray farther.

"What did you want to say?" she asked. Was it his imagination, or was that softness he detected in her tone. But, abruptly, she became impatient, almost as if her own soft tone had angered her.

"How far do you plan to walk before you are able to form the words you plan to say to me?"

He couldn't help smiling at the accuracy of her assessment. It was true. Now that she was standing with him, he was confused about what he wanted. And what he wanted to say.

When he looked at her standing beside him, he doubted he would find as prefect of the Guard, the kind of joy he felt in her presence, even when she was angry.

"I need to explain something to you," he said. "I fear you believe the worst about me."

"I probably do," she said, "though at the moment my feeling is that it is the worst that is in fact the truth."

"Yes," he said. "That may be so, but please give me a chance to explain."

"I'm listening," she said.

She stumbled a bit on a branch that was hidden in the verdant grassy knoll in which they walked. He caught her about her waist and kept her from tumbling to the ground.

He found that he didn't want to let go of her. He held her until she pulled away.

"Thank you," she said crisply. "I'm quite capable of walking on my own now."

He nodded, took a deep breath, let her go and began speaking.

"To protect the emperor was my boyhood dream, only I wasn't sure how to achieve that goal. When I returned home after having served my twenty years with the legions, my mother sent me the perfect opportunity, unknowingly."

"Your mother?" Annia asked, drawn in, it seemed, by the urgency of his words.

"Yes," he said. "I had already helped her save many babies by the time you gave birth to your child, so she knew I could do it."

"Do what?" Annia asked. "Take gold?"

The comment stung, but Marcus chose to ignore it. "When Mother laid Maelia at Galerius Janius's feet, he refused to pick her up. Mother was ordered to expose her.

"Instead, she took Maelia back to the villa where you had been sent to live when Janius divorced you. Mother thought that Janius simply wanted to rid himself of the responsibility of a girl baby. She thought him too stingy to raise her, care for her and eventually pay her dowry. And mother knew that you were no longer in his household, so it should not have mattered to him that the baby went there rather than to the place of exposure. But, Mother did not expect his new wife would insist the baby be killed."

"When Mother found out, she knew Janius would order the baby exposed.

"Mother finagled an invitation for me to a dinner thrown by Janius. He had no clue I was the midwife's son sent on a mission to earn his trust.

"I let it slip that I worked as commander of the *Vigiles* and would sometimes be sent on a mission by private individuals that had nothing to do with fires.

"Janius understood. We talked for a while over dinner. He let it be known he was now married to the emperor's soon-to-be cousin and would then have special favor with the emperor himself. He invited me back for the next week.

"I returned and asked for him to put a word in for me to the emperor. I wanted to be prefect of the Guard. Janius understood I was making a deal with him, and he told me about you and Maelia.

"We agreed that I would expose his baby—which meant I would give it to my mother, though he didn't know that—and he would pay me and put a word in with the emperor.

"And then I met you, Annia. I felt soiled to have made a deal with the man who discarded you, and your daughter and then your son.

"I saw Janius for what he was, and I wanted no further dealings with him.

"I never intended to harm Maelia. I knew from the beginning I was taking her to safety."

"But you used her," Annia said bitterly, "to press forward in your ambitious desire to become prefect of the Guard. You used my daughter, my baby, to move closer to your own selfish goal."

"I did," Marcus said humbly, "and I am bitterly sorry. I brought danger not only to you and your children, but also to my mother and all of the women and babies at her villa. It was a foolish plan." He uttered these final words with a guttural groan. "Can you forgive me?"

Just then, a splash, followed by laughter. "I told you not

to step out any farther," Cato's little voice broke through. Marcus hurried toward the sound.

"But my boat," his brother said, "it was going away."

"Yes," Cato said, "but it was also winning!"

Marcus pulled the sopping-wet child from the middle of the brook. Flavius clutched a leaf and twig boat in his hands. "Did I win?" he asked.

"Yes," Cato said. "You still won."

Annia looked up at Marcus. Her brown eyes were filled with something confusing. Was it admiration? Gratitude? Joy?

Marcus wondered if *he* had won.

"Marcus seems a good man," Annia's father said to Annia as they continued their journey northward.

The conversation with Marcus had only confused Annia's feelings. She was no longer angry at him for putting her baby in harm's way for money. She understood his desire to become prefect of the Guard. She also understood that Janius had fallen out of favor with the emperor.

This made Marcus's marriage to Cassia all the more necessary. Cassia came from a very old senatorial family. Her family name would be all he needed to guarantee being prefect of the *Vigiles,* as had now happened, and prefect of the Guard for the future.

When Annia didn't reply to her father's comment, Virginia broke in. "He is a good man. Like all of us, he has made his share of errors, but unlike many of us, he is able to admit his mistakes. He is not a prideful man."

"I admire such a man," her father said.

Annia kicked her horse forward. She had to shake away her foolishness. Marcus had reiterated the fact that being made prefect of the Guard was his lifelong dream. There was no hope of any sort of future for the two of them whether she forgave him or not. He would have to go back to Rome. She must remain in Britain.

"Let me be clear," Annia said, slowing her horse to speak to her father. "Marcus Sergius has done some very kind things for me and for my family. I will be happy to smile at him if I should happen to pass him on the street, and invite him over for supper to thank him. Saving lives is no small thing. But I feel nothing more for him. I do not view him as a woman views a potential mate."

Her father studied her face.

"Why are you smiling?" she said, her anger burning to her ears.

"I'm not," he said, though he was. "I detect something more," he said. "You seem to have more feeling for him than you admit."

"I am not interested in anything other than friendship with any man. If you will agree, I would like for my boys and Maelia to live in peace with you and Mother for the rest of our lives."

"You named her for me, did you not?" her father asked, beaming.

"If you are trying to move our conversation to a new subject, you needn't. I am finished with that one. And to answer your question, yes, I did," Annia said.

"Well, then," he said, "if you insist, we will not speak of Marcus Sergius again."

"Good," Annia said, glancing back to assure herself that Marcus had not by chance overheard any of the conversation. He was watching her. She hated herself for blushing and turned quickly so he couldn't see.

"I wish you could have seen your mother's face when she received your letter announcing you were coming home," her father said. "She has read it over and over again and keeps it in a special place in her clothes chest.

I told her that if she read it any more, it was going to turn to dust in her hands."

Annia laughed, relieved to think of her mother and not Marcus. "I can't wait to see her. I hope she has not exhausted herself preparing."

"You know your mother," her father said. "She has prepared a feast beyond anything I've ever experienced. All of the animals for miles around are holding their necks, fearing that they will be next on the chopping block. She has prepared enough meat for roasting to feed the entire village."

Annia laughed again.

When they made camp that night, Marcus approached Annia.

"What?" she asked. "What more have you to say?"

"Please understand, Annia," he said, his voice pleading.

"I understand. You've made it clear. You want to be prefect."

"Yes, I do, but do you know why? It is to keep all of us safe. The emperor, the empire, you, my mother and the babies, your father in this tumultuous country of Britain."

The taste in Annia's mouth was bitter. "Tumultuous country?" she said. "You will remember, sir, that this country is my home. The place of my birth. My mother's people have lived here since nearly the beginning of time. Be mindful of what you say." She was furious. She wanted to kick him. But her frustration and anger was less at his feelings about Britain than the complete confusion of her emotions about him.

"I'm sorry," Marcus said. He was silent.

His silence shamed her. It would have been much easier if he had fought her, defended his words. The look in his eyes spoke of the unmentionable horrors he had witnessed on this very soil.

"The Iceni," Marcus said. "They are a strong, valiant people. Their home is deep in the forest. Their warriors come unexpectedly, slaughter and leave without a trace. I fear one day they will gather their forces and wreak havoc on the Roman peace."

Annia was silent. Her mother believed the same. Though she was not of the Iceni tribe, her people had traded with them. They were feared.

"So that is why you wish to return to the safety of Rome?" she asked. "And is Rome safe? We are all here, are we not, because the emperor has banned all Jews. Does he know that you yourself believe in the one God?" She wanted to hurt him.

"The emperor does not concern himself with such mundane matters," Marcus said. "He signed the papers making me the prefect of the *Vigiles,* but would not recognize me on the street."

"I hear Claudius is a wise man."

"Yes, but even the wisest emperor couldn't possibly know all of his men."

"But it is Rome that you love," Annia said. Was she looking for him to deny this fact? Would that make things easier for her?

"I feel I can protect you in Rome," Marcus said, appealing to her. "I can't here."

Though his words pierced her heart—she longed for his protection—she couldn't admit it. She was not his to protect. "And why would I want or need your protection? Isn't protection something you would more logically supply for Cassia?"

"You are correct in your assessment," Marcus said. "I am under family obligation to protect Cassia and her family. They have done me a very generous turn, and I owe them the same."

"I see," Annia said, her words clipped. She didn't need to hear any more.

"But, Annia, I am not marrying Cassia."

She searched his eyes. This was not a declaration of love to her. This was a declaration of fact.

She said nothing. She kicked her horse's side and rode away from yet another man who threatened to break her heart.

Chapter Twenty-Six

Marcus spent the last day of the journey praying. He prayed for grace. He prayed for understanding. More than anything else, he prayed for wisdom to know what exactly it was he should do next. Was it fair to Annia to declare his love for her and beg her to take her children and follow him back to Rome?

Rome wasn't safe for them. But neither was Britain. Could he depend on the protection of her mother's people to keep Annia's family safe from the attacks that continued against Roman citizens throughout the island?

Was his place in Rome? It was a once in a lifetime position, he knew that. To give it up to live in Britain would mean to never be offered such a prestigious position again. How could he best protect and provide for Annia and her children?

That was it. If he was honest with himself, he knew that was what he wanted more than anything. Assurance that he could keep them safe.

"You're quiet," Titus said after several hours of silence. "The quietest you've been. What's on your mind?"

"Annia," Marcus said, cutting right to the truth.

"Yes," Titus said. "I imagine so."

"What I want seems simple enough until I am actually in her presence. Then, it seems, my words become as muddled as my brain."

"Not easy for a man accustomed to giving orders."

Marcus laughed. "You are correct."

Titus chuckled. "I've found the thing that works with Virginia is listening to her. Really listening and not letting my mind wander while she talks."

"That, my friend, is not easy," Marcus said. "Women, they talk in circles."

"So the first thing you have to do is listen to her words. Maybe even say a few of them back to her, a few things that she's just said to be sure you get it, and to show her you're listening."

"That is ridiculous," Marcus said. "Why would I say back to her what she just said to me?"

"Trust me," Titus said. "You do that and watch what happens to her eyes. They'll open wide like this." Titus demonstrated.

Now it was Marcus's turn to hold tight to the wagon seat so he wouldn't fall off from laughing.

"And then, she'll say, 'Why, yes, that is it,' and you will feel as though you just won a very important battle."

Marcus heard soft giggling in the wagon behind him. He slid open the half door and sure enough, Lucia and Theodora had their ears up to the door and were both laughing, the tears rolling down their faces.

"What do you find so amusing?" Titus asked.

"Nothing," Theodora said, "nothing at all."

Lucia poked her head through the door. "We are laughing because what you are saying really is true. It's enlightening to hear how difficult it is for you two to understand women."

"Well, maybe you could give us some insight?" Marcus asked.

"My advice is this," Theodora said, "declare your love for her. It's all women want—to know they are loved and loved deeply."

Marcus felt his heart give a little jump when Theodora said that word *love*. Was it possible that Annia loved him?

Marcus heard horses approaching from behind. Annia's father, Tertius, appeared, a bright smile on his face.

"We're almost there. This is Londinium," Tertius called, almost as proudly as if he had built it himself.

Annia followed close behind. "I am amazed," she said, looking with wide-eyed wonder at the busy little town. "Where there were thick woods, now there are round houses."

Marcus followed her gaze. Children played in the grassy front yards, and stone fences enclosed small farms. As they grew closer to the settlement, he heard a pig squeal.

Farther down the road they passed shops that had sprung up since he was last here two short years before. There was a baker, a fish house and a wine shop. It was a Roman town right here in Britain. There was new construction up and down the freshly paved streets. One especially large building promised to be a bathhouse.

Annia laughed. "Leave it to the Romans to make cleanliness as important as security." She pointed to the garrison tower close to the banks of the Thames and the soldiers who stood atop the tower watching the arrivals and departures of merchant ships. Londinium even had its own inn.

Her joy was infectious. This was the Annia he knew before she started hating him.

A few short miles past Londinium, Marcus hardly recognized the new road leading to the countryside villas. Two years before, the road had been dirt.

They drew near the pasture Tertius identified as his.

It reached over two hills, and the rambling stone wall reached farther than he could see. Sheep dotted the rolling green hills.

Watching Annia's face flush with pleasure as she drew near her home gave him joy.

But would he have a moment alone with her to share everything that was in his heart?

As they approached her parent's villa, the dogs began barking, first one, then another, and then, it seemed, hundreds joined the chorus from a building beyond the villa. Annia looked back at Marcus. In spite of her confusing emotions about him, she wanted him to love this villa. She wasn't certain why this was important to her, but it was.

He flashed her a smile that was warm and engaging, and she couldn't help smiling back.

Several dogs circled her father's horse, tails wagging furiously. One whined and pushed his way until he was the closest to her father. The dog looked very much like the beloved hound, Thistle, she had left behind. She knew it was not her dog, but, perhaps, a descendant.

Annia's heart pounded, tears rose in her eyes. She was home.

She looked up to see her mother running toward her. She engulfed Annia and baby Maelia in her arms, and Annia felt her mother's tears against her face.

As a mother comforts her child, so will I comfort you; and you will be comforted over Jerusalem.

The verse came to her each time her mother hugged her.

"She is just beautiful!" her mother said, hugging Maelia close. "She looks just like you when you were a baby."

Annia found her voice choked with tears, and she couldn't respond.

Her mother filled in. "I've arranged a dinner for tomorrow night with a friend eager to see you again. But, your father spoke of things that make me believe your heart belongs to another. I don't want to make a fool of the young man we've invited, so you must let me know the truth."

Annia's eyes widened. She stole a quick glance at Marcus, but he hadn't heard her mother's words. The wagon rolled to a stop, and the boys tumbled out followed by Lucia.

Theodora climbed down from the seat and looked around her, surveying the villa grounds.

Annia's mother held her hand out to first Lucia and then Theodora. She led them through the ivy-covered entryway and into the house where they were greeted by two female servants and taken up to their rooms.

Annia led her sons to their grandmother.

She knelt down and hugged them one by one, holding them out in front of her and examined them like precious jewels, running her hands gently over their hair, and cupping their chins in her hands.

"You are both handsome," she said. "You will make big and strong warriors someday. I will feel safe knowing you are guarding me."

The boys' smiles nearly reached their ears.

"Grandmother, may I see the pups?" Flavius asked.

"Why, yes," she said. "As soon as you bathe and we eat, I'll get Rufus to take you out to see them. He is in charge of all the dogs."

"Do you have so many?" Cato asked.

"We have over a hundred," his grandmother said. "We raise them and sell them. Many go across the ocean to

Rome. You may even have seen some of our dogs in the villas of your friends."

"Amazing," Flavius said. "So many and so far."

"My grandsons make me proud," her mother said to Annia. "I'm so happy to have children in the house. What joy they bring."

Marcus stood quietly back watching the exchange. When the children had run inside with Annia to wash up for dinner, he stepped forward.

"Ah," Annia's mother said, "you must be Marcus,"

"Yes, *domina,* and I am so pleased to meet you." He bowed respectfully, but she pulled him out of the bow and hugged him tightly.

"I am Flavia Domitilla, and I am so happy to make your acquaintance. You saved my child."

Marcus shook his head. "In truth, your child saved herself. She fought like a bear to stay afloat and keep her children safe. You can be proud of her, very proud indeed."

"You are kind as well as brave. It is an honor to have you in our home. We hope you will stay and eat," she said.

"Thank you, I look forward to it."

Titus stepped forward, and Flavia met him with the same generous hug with which she had greeted Marcus. "Titus, old friend. You've brought my child safely home."

"That I have, *domina,* but not without the help of this man without whom two of your grandchildren would not be with us."

"So I've heard, Titus, so I've heard. I look forward to hearing the whole story when you have had time to bathe and eat. You know where the baths are. That has not changed. I'm sure you are hungry after your long trip. I am eager to feed you."

Titus smiled his thanks and led Marcus to the private baths.

The home was grand indeed.

There was both a hot and a cold room in their private bathhouse, and Marcus was happy to bathe in the warm waters of the hot bath, where soap was available. This custom of soap, borrowed from the Gauls, had not caught on yet in Rome, and he had missed it while he was there. He scrubbed himself down and then went directly to the cold baths.

The boys splashed happily in the cold baths, and Marcus floated beside them.

"I hope Mother is no longer angry at you," Cato said.

"So do I," Marcus replied.

Cato shook his head with Marcus. "Sometimes it takes a long time for her anger to disappear. But then, it is like it never happened," Cato finished with a triumphant smile.

"Well," Marcus said, "I'll look forward to that day."

Cato patted Marcus's back. "Don't worry. It will come."

Marcus wished he could be half as optimistic as the boy. He did, however, appreciate the encouragement.

"All will be well," Titus said, and patted his back also.

Marcus got the strange feeling he was going into battle, and he wasn't sure he was prepared.

Nor was he sure what he would do even if Annia did forgive him. Would he go back to Rome? To do so would mean making more money than he could ever make by staying here. If Annia forgave him, as prefect, he could save his silver to buy her the villa of her dreams.

But how long would that take? And did Annia even care?

He did feel better after the baths, and he looked forward to the dinner.

He had a mission now. He needed to get her alone so that he could declare his love.

All afternoon, the smell of grilled venison, rabbit and beef filled the gardens and spilled out into the surrounding field. Savory roasted vegetables and berry pies, oatcakes and wheat and barley loaves were being prepared, and the heavily laden table would feed everyone gathered here already, and more besides.

Annia busied herself with the bread, making certain it baked an even golden brown. When it was done, she heard the boys returning from the bath house. She knew Marcus was with them.

She ran upstairs and arranged her hair. She held the bronze looking glass in front of her, pinched her cheeks and wet her lips.

Virginia caught sight of her as she was hurrying down the hall, having tidied the upstairs rooms for sleeping.

"You caught me trying to look beautiful," Annia admitted.

Titus led Marcus to the dining room, and he was relieved to see that Annia's mother did not believe in the Roman habit of lying down to eat and, instead, had a very sensible long table with benches rather than couches.

Annia and the children did not appear at first, only the men were in the room. They chatted amiably, the room calm.

Marcus watched the door, trying not to make it obvious. But he looked forward to seeing Annia, despite the fact that she wasn't talking to him.

Theodora, Lucia and Virginia all came in, dressed in their best *stolas* and *pallas*.

Flavia came in next, her black hair piled on top of her

head in a beautifully twisted braid, the white streaks only highlighting the beauty of her face.

Marcus waited and still Annia did not appear.

He tried joining into the conversation with Flavia and Theodora, who sat on either side of him. They sipped their drink and talked of the local governor and the horrendous taxes they were forced to pay to Rome.

Idle chatter to pass the time.

When Annia finally came through the dining room columns, he heard a sharp intake of breath and realized it was his.

The light from the window shone on her face, and sparkled across her glistening gown. Her *stola* was a soft gauzy blue, her *palla* yellow silk that rustled behind her as she walked. Her hair was caught up in a golden band that wound around her head like a crown. Soft, curly tendrils escaped, softening the beauty of her face. Her arms sparkled with delicate gold bracelets, and dangling earrings shimmered at her neck. Her soft brown eyes glowed, and she stood tall, a gold belt around her gown. The belt dangled at her side, nearly touching the gold sandals outlining her graceful feet, thin gold anklets jingling around her delicate ankles.

Marcus stood with the rest of the men in the room as they had for each woman who had come in.

But Marcus forgot to sit down, so taken away was he by her beauty.

He had always known she was beautiful, but he had never had the opportunity to watch her walk into a room.

A nervous laugh from Theodora and Flavia alerted him to the fact that he was still standing, watching her even though she and everyone else had sat down.

Theodora whispered into his ear, "Hold steady, my friend."

He sat down quickly and gave Theodora a quick nod, thanking her for saving him from further embarrassment.

Chapter Twenty-Seven

The dinner lasted until long past the sunset. Courses were brought in one after the other. Annia sat immediately to Marcus's right, but the room was crowded. Would he ever be able to get her alone? They must talk.

When the dinner was over, musicians were brought in. The harpist from Caledonia sang a song that was so sad it made Lucia cry. The poignant melody made her long for her home. Annia put her arm around Lucia and led her from the room.

Marcus halfway rose, then sat down. It would be selfish of him to follow them.

He needed to be alone with Annia, just for a few moments. She would most likely see to Lucia, feed Maelia and go to bed herself. He tried not to be too terribly disappointed. There would be other days.

"Well," Tertius said, "I know you are eager to see your father's villa."

"Yes." Marcus knew his response was less than enthusiastic. He wasn't certain he was ready to leave. "I thank you for your kindness," he said, collecting his manners and his wits so that he could travel to his family villa. Marcus stood as if to leave.

"Surely you don't mean to leave tonight," Tertius said, "the sun has set, and your father's villa is half a day's journey from here. You won't reach home until dawn. Stay here with us. We have more rooms than people."

Marcus tried to think of a reason to leave but couldn't come up with one. He would stay.

"Thank you, Tertius. You are as kind as you are wise. I would be a fool to begin a journey at this late hour. I would probably fall asleep, topple from off your horse and break my neck."

Marcus smiled, and Tertius laughed heartily. "I hope not, but it would please me for you to stay."

Titus showed Marcus to a room.

His stomach fed and his body clean, Marcus fell into the bed and tried not to think of Annia. He needed sleep.

Instead, he tossed and turned. His mind whirred.

He rose in the dark of the night, and walked to the tiny window of his bedroom. It overlooked the fields beyond, dark now. He looked up to see a black velvet sky filled with twinkling stars. The very stars gave him hope.

He loved her.

This he knew.

But what to do about it?

He knew without a doubt after being here for only a few short hours that this was her home. This was where she felt safe. And here, he believed, with the help of her father and the men in the village—many of them retired legionaries—he could keep them all safe.

Rome was a distant dream. He understood, now, that it was the honor, the respect, the prestige that made him yearn for a position as prefect of the Guard.

While it was true that he wanted to protect his emperor and his country, he wanted to protect Annia and her children more.

He loved her.

He would do what it took to win her over.

He lay down and fell into a second sleep, this one more peaceful than the last.

He was jerked awake near sunrise by a lantern shining in his face. He reached to draw his dagger and realized he didn't have it.

"Arise," a familiar voice whispered. "If I can't sleep, neither will you."

It was Annia. He sat bolt upright in his bed.

"What are you doing in here?" he asked.

"Be silent. You are going to wake the entire household," she hissed. "Get out of the bed. We are going for a walk."

He jumped up more quickly than if there had been an enemy attack.

He saw she was not alone. An elderly servant woman tottered behind her carrying her own oil lamp.

She handed him his cloak, and Annia pulled hers more tightly around her.

He was giddy, and he was uncertain whether it was lack of sleep or excitement about the possibility he saw stretching out before him, nearly within his grasp.

What if she had come to him to bid him farewell?

They tiptoed down the stairs and out into the cool, predawn morning, followed by the swishing sounds of the elderly woman's sandals on cobbled stone.

Annia led him to a bench at the far end of the garden. The woman sat on a bench directly across from them. She sat her oil lamp down, leaned her head against the stone wall the rose behind her and dozed.

"We must talk quietly," Annia said. "It wouldn't be polite to wake her again, nor do we want to awaken all of the dogs. They will howl for hours and wake everyone."

He'd never been very good at whispering, and he was going to have to whisper the most important words of his life? The scene was not playing out as he had imagined.

She looked at him.

"Well?" she said, after a moment of silence. "Talk."

Gathering his thoughts was difficult. He felt he was being questioned by enemy soldiers.

"Do I need to refresh your memory about where we were?" she asked, the irritation in her voice growing by the second.

"No, I can remember," he said, trying to keep the near panic out of his own voice while squeezing his brain to remember what it was that Lucia and Theodora had advised him to do. Listen. That was it. He was supposed to listen carefully to what she said.

He listened, but she wasn't saying anything.

She held her hands out and jerked her palms up in exasperation. "Am I to believe that you have nothing to say?"

Repeat what she says to you, that was what Titus had told him to do. That way she would know he was listening to her.

"You asked me if you were to believe that this is all I have to say." He smiled, waiting for the wide-eyed appreciation Titus had promised.

Instead, she looked at him as if he were a complete idiot. "Are you daft?" she said. "Why on earth are you repeating for me what I just said? I know what I just said. I'm the one who said it." Her volume was rising, and Marcus held his finger to her lips to shush her.

He didn't want the dogs waking the world.

She snatched his finger away as if it were a hot coal against her lips.

"I knew this was a stupid idea," she said, and rose to leave.

"No," he said, "wait. I'm doing my best, Annia, please be patient."

"Your best?" she asked, over her shoulder. "To run me off? Well, you've definitely done that."

"No, wait," he said, and caught hold of her arm and spun her around to him. She landed against his chest. He held his breath, afraid she would run.

But she didn't. He could feel the beating of her heart against his.

She looked up at him, her eyes pleading. "I can't have my heart broken again."

He took her hands and pulled her gently down. They sat on the bench, and the words tumbled from his mouth before he could think or plan.

"I know I've made mistakes, Annia, and I'm sorry. What I've been seeking is not at all what I thought it was. I wanted to be prefect so that I could protect my emperor and my country. I thought that was what I was called to do—something big, something grand, something important. I could think of no better way to prove my loyalty and do my duty to God and my country.

"But something my father told me a while ago has stuck in my mind. God does not necessarily call us to do big things. God calls us to do small things that are big things in His kingdom."

"What do you mean?" Annia asked. Her anger had dissolved replaced by gentle curiosity.

Marcus, relieved, continued. "I am no longer certain that being prefect is my life's calling. Perhaps one day it will be. But right now, I am only certain of one thing. What I feel about you. When I met you, I envied a man so blessed as to have such a perfect family—a beautiful, kind wife, two healthy, happy boys and a sweet baby like Maelia. I did not understand how anyone would throw

such a beautiful thing away. It made me angry that anyone could be so foolish as to let someone so precious go,
and I wanted to fix it, somehow. And I didn't know how.
I am a soldier. I don't know how to fix people. I only
know how to fight."

Annia batted away at the tears that traced a path down
her cheek, glistening in the pink of dawn. He caught a
tear on the tip of his finger and gently caressed her cheek.

"I'm sorry," he said. "I didn't mean to bring you more
pain."

She shook her head.

He took a deep, steadying breath. "I only knew that
if I could ever be so blessed as to have such a beautiful
thing, I would treasure it forever. And last night, I realized what it was I needed to fight for."

Annia looked far, far away. Her gaze was focused on
the thin line of gray light creeping over the horizon.

"Every moment I've spent with you, every laugh we've
shared, everything we have done together has made me
happy in a way I never imagined. I've never felt so understood, I've never felt so right with anyone or anything
in my life.

"I've dreamed someone else's dream for far too long,
Annia. You are my dream. You are the most beautiful
woman I've ever known. You are brave, you are charming, you are strong. You are the mother that all children
dream of having, and the wife that good men long for. I
love you, Annia. I love you more than I have ever loved
in my life."

His words came out in a torrent of feeling, like waves
crashing on the shore. He couldn't stop them, nor could
he wait for her response. "I want to marry you, Annia. I
want to live with you and the children for the rest of our
lives. I want to protect you. I want to take care of you. I

want to keep you safe and make you happy. You deserve happiness. You are the most wonderful woman I know. I love you with all of my heart."

She looked up into his eyes and smiled. His heart swelled.

"Will you?" he asked, holding his breath, fearful of her answer. "Will you marry me?"

"Yes!" she said. "Oh, yes, a million times, yes!"

He stood and pulled her to him. He took her face in his hands and tipped her chin up. His lips sought hers.

But she pulled away.

"You want to marry me even if it means living in Britain?" she asked.

"Even if it means Britain."

"You hate Britain," she said.

"But I love you," he said and laughed.

"Well, then," she said, "I look forward to a lifetime of laughter together. Come on." Before he could respond, she stood, wrapped her cloak around her and said, "Race you to the sunrise!" And she ran full speed in the direction of the pink morning sunrise.

He laughed out loud and followed her.

She looked back and shouted, "Come on, soldier, I'll get there before you."

They ran over the smooth green pastureland, and kept on running.

He gained on her. She threw down her cloak, and he nearly tripped over it when it wrapped around his ankles.

He threw his cloak off, as well, and now they ran together into the sunrise, their white tunics reflecting the soft golden rays of the morning sun.

When she reached the edge of a hill, a hair's breath in front of him, she stood, her arms up in the air in exaltation. "I won," she said. "I won."

He grabbed her from behind, swung her around and kissed her full on the lips.

"No," he said, holding her face between his hands, "I've won."

Epilogue

Maelia toddled over to the cradle where her baby sister lay sleeping.

"My baby," she said. She giggled, then ran and threw her arms around Marcus's strong legs.

He picked her up, swinging her high in the air.

"Five babies and counting," he said pointing to the infant twins.

Annia sat rocking the cradle with one hand and holding the twin boy in her arms.

Marcus put Maelia down gently and kissed Annia on her pretty lips.

There was a clattering up the stairs, and eight-year-old Flavius burst in, his cheeks red. "Father, the south gate is compromised, and the sheep in that pasture are escaping. Bella is doing her best to keep them all rounded up, but I think we need your help."

"How did the fence break?" Marcus asked.

"I don't know," Flavius said, his eyes wide.

Marcus turned to Annia. "Duty calls," he said, and kissed her.

Flavius made a face of mock disgust. "I wish you two wouldn't do that stuff!"

"We'll try not to," Marcus said, "but I'm not making any promises." He ruffled Flavius's hair.

The boy had grown into an excellent dog trainer. He seemed to be following in the footsteps of his grandfather, who had given him a pair of sheepdogs. Flavius had already trained them well.

"Bella is holding them steady?" Marcus asked.

"Yes, she is a good dog," Flavius said. "She can keep them together, but not forever."

"We'll get them," Marcus said. "Where is Cato?"

"He is trying to repair the fence," Flavius said.

"Good," Marcus said. "You are both good men."

"I guess," Flavius said, suddenly studying a rock on the ground.

"What do you mean by that?" Marcus asked.

Flavius shrugged and kicked at the rock.

He was hiding something. Marcus knew the boy well enough to know that it was probably nothing serious.

"No matter what scrapes you two get into, I will always believe that you are good men."

Flavius placed his small hand in Marcus's large one.

"I'm glad you are my father," he said, grinning up at Marcus.

Marcus's heart swelled. Nothing he had ever experienced on the battlefield, no victory in battle, no advancement in rank had filled him with the pride he felt being called *Father*.

For Marcus, Britain was no longer a place of nightmares. For now, a peace had settled upon him, and upon this part of the land. He and Annia's father were able to trade peacefully with merchants from all over the empire from their Thames tributary riverfront homes.

Marcus never imagined that one day he would be a

sheep farmer, but here he was, as happy as he had ever been in his life.

He took care of the sheep, and Annia oversaw the group of women who worked for her. They worked pallets of sheared wool through the long process required to create red waterproof capes, the *birri,* that were worn by soldiers and civilians alike from Caledonia to Corinth.

While the women worked the wool, his mother, Basso and Nona took care of their babies and toddlers.

Claudius's proclamation had made it unsafe for his mother to continue her baby villa. A year after Marcus and Annia married, his mother and father, along with the rescued babies and their mothers, had moved here and settled into the lovely family villa in Britain.

"I'll go back to Rome as soon as I can," Scribonia said to Marcus when she stepped off the boat her first day back in Britain. "I haven't given up. Babies are still being exposed, and I want to encourage other women like me, well-off women who have chosen to follow the Christ, to use their bounty to help the poor babes and mothers who have been forced into that tragedy."

Marcus had shaken his head and laughed. His mother and Annia, two headstrong women living in the same house. How would they make it?

But make it they did, and joyfully so.

The meetings his mother held in her home every Sunday attracted people from all around who came to worship and hear the words of the Master. Mother's friend Priscilla had gone south from Rome to settle in Corinth where the great teacher, Paul, lived, as well. Priscilla sent his mother letters in which she wrote down the teachings of Paul so that his mother could read them aloud to her little flock.

The meetings grew. Soon they would have to find a larger meeting place.

Flavius pulled his attention back to Marcus's own pasture. "Oh, no," Flavius said, pointing. "There's another hole, and they're going out there, too."

He and Marcus ran down the hillside leading away from their villa, and herded the sheep from that hole back into the pasture. Marcus repaired the stone fence while Flavius kept the sheep away.

Bella barked and nipped the heels of the other strays, keeping them in a tight circle just outside the fence where there was another large hole.

Marcus walked to the far side of her circle of sheep and gave Bella the command to herd the sheep back into the pasture through the large gap that still existed in the stone wall.

Once the sheep were in, the two boys and Marcus worked to repair the original hole.

The sheep were now safe. "Any idea what is causing the fence to buckle just here?" Marcus asked.

Flavius kicked a rock, and Cato's face turned a bright red.

Marcus waited.

The boys were silent.

"What?" Marcus asked. "What are you not telling me?"

"Cato, tell him. He's going to find out anyway."

"We found something," Cato said. "You want to see?"

"Yes," Marcus said. What were the boys up to now?

"Come on," Cato said.

The boys climbed over the freshly repaired fence. They led Marcus beside the river tributary of the Thames on which they lived, and back into the woods. They hiked for a while in the cool green twilight until Flavius said, "We're almost there."

A break in the tree cover, and Marcus heard a strange sound, a bubbling, gurgling noise.

The sunlight shone down on a muddy brown circle of water.

"Come on," Flavius said. "Jump in."

The boys stripped down to their underwear and climbed into the muddy water.

Marcus had no choice but to follow.

"Leave it to the two of you to find a new place to swim," Marcus said, shaking his head and smiling.

The swimming hole was not wide. Marcus could toss a stone and easily reach the other side. But the waters were strangely warm. Steam rose from the water, and Marcus felt as if he were in the hot room in the baths in Rome.

"Just like Rome," Cato said, laughing.

"Who says you have to go to Rome to take a proper bath!" Flavius said.

"So this is why the stone fence is broken," Marcus said.

"Yes," the boys said, somewhat sheepishly.

"We can put a gate on that part of the fence," Marcus said as they headed home from their brief swimming excursion. "That way, we won't have a repeat of this afternoon's experience."

"You didn't like the springs?" Flavius asked.

"Not that part of the afternoon. I liked that," Marcus said. "It was the fixing-the-fence part I could do without."

When Marcus related the adventure to Annia as they lay in bed that night, she said, "You are a good man to have such patience with the boys. Not many men would be able to come in and father them as you do. I know it isn't your ideal life. I know what you had planned was beginning a new family with a wife who had never been married."

"Stop," he said, putting a finger to her lips. "I am living my dream," he said. "I love you and my boys and my girls more than you will ever know. Don't you ever forget that."

He rolled her over, and she lay on her back gazing up at him. He kissed her lips.

"I will never forget," she said. "Never."

* * * * *

Dear Reader,

A few years ago, while researching for my dissertation, I came across the alarming fact that in the ancient world, infant exposure was an accepted practice. I had just given birth to my third child, and I was horrified at the thought of carrying a baby for nine months, and then being forced to send it away to die or be sold as a slave.

I knew then that the thousands of women who had been forced to give away their babies deserved to have their stories told. Thus, the idea for *Her Roman Protector* was born.

In Rome, it was the father who determined whether the infant lived or died. After a baby was born, the midwife would lay the child before the father. If the father picked up the child, the child was considered a part of the family. If not, the baby was exposed.

Historians tell us there was a particular place in the city of Athens where unwanted babies were abandoned. The same was true in Rome, where unwanted infants might be left in the vegetable market. If no one picked the child up to be raised as a slave or foster child, the infant would die.

Infants were exposed for a variety of reasons: if the family couldn't afford to raise the child, if the child was deformed or if the family didn't want to share wealth with yet another heir.

Although I have no factual evidence, I feel certain that there were Godly women, like Scribonia, who worked to save these babies and help reunite them with their mothers.

I hope you enjoy reading this novel as much as I enjoyed writing it!

I look forward to hearing from you.
Milinda Jay

Please visit me at my website, www.milindajay.com, or email me at milindajaywriter@gmail.com.

Questions for Discussion

1. When Marcus comes to take baby Maelia in the opening pages of the book, what kind of man does he seem to be?

2. Why is it so hard for Annia to believe that Marcus intends no harm to her baby? When does she begin to believe that he intends no harm? Why?

3. What surprises you about Annia's actions in the first two chapters of the book? Why?

4. The fact that Annia does not have custody of her sons is very painful for her. Do you see any similarities between custody issues in ancient Rome and custody issues today? How so? How have things changed? How have they stayed the same?

5. What does Marcus want for his life in the early chapters of the book? Why?

6. What is Marcus willing to do to get what he wants?

7. What does Annia want in the early chapters of the book? What is she willing to risk to get what she wants?

8. Why is sharing her skills having to do with the care of sheep so important to Annia?

9. Both Annia and Marcus have fears regarding their relationship with one another. What does Marcus fear

about the possibility of a relationship with Annia? Why? What does Annia fear? Why?

10. What function do Gamus and Nona serve in the book?

11. Galerius Janius is the bad guy we love to hate. What makes him particularly odious? Is there anything redeeming about his character? If so, what? Why does he act the way he acts? What does he want, and what is he willing to do to get it? How does his character compare with Marcus's?

12. Virginia is very independent for a slave. What do you know about slavery in the Roman Empire? How does Virginia differ from your concept of slaves in ancient Rome? Do you think she acted differently with Annia before she was given her freedom? Why or why not?

13. Marcus has a very tough decision to make about whether or not to become prefect. What would be the positives of his becoming a prefect? The negatives? What do you think he ultimately decides? Why?

14. In the epilogue, Annia and Marcus's family is living on a country estate. Do you think they are in Britain or Rome? Why?

15. The children play an important role in this novel. Describe each of the children and discuss what they add to the novel's action and emotional content.

REQUEST YOUR FREE BOOKS!

2 FREE INSPIRATIONAL NOVELS
PLUS 2
FREE
MYSTERY GIFTS

Love Inspired
HISTORICAL
INSPIRATIONAL HISTORICAL ROMANCE

YES! Please send me 2 FREE Love Inspired® Historical novels and my 2 FREE mystery gifts (gifts are worth about $10). After receiving them, if I don't wish to receive any more books, I can return the shipping statement marked "cancel." If I don't cancel, I will receive 4 brand-new novels every month and be billed just $4.74 per book in the U.S. or $5.24 per book in Canada. That's a saving of at least 21% off the cover price. It's quite a bargain! Shipping and handling is just 50¢ per book in the U.S. and 75¢ per book in Canada.* I understand that accepting the 2 free books and gifts places me under no obligation to buy anything. I can always return a shipment and cancel at any time. Even if I never buy another book, the two free books and gifts are mine to keep forever.

102/302 IDN F5CN

Name _____ (PLEASE PRINT) _____

Address _____ Apt. # _____

City _____ State/Prov. _____ Zip/Postal Code _____

Signature (if under 18, a parent or guardian must sign) _____

Mail to the Harlequin® Reader Service:
IN U.S.A.: P.O. Box 1867, Buffalo, NY 14240-1867
IN CANADA: P.O. Box 609, Fort Erie, Ontario L2A 5X3

Want to try two free books from another series?
Call 1-800-873-8635 or visit www.ReaderService.com.

* Terms and prices subject to change without notice. Prices do not include applicable taxes. Sales tax applicable in N.Y. Canadian residents will be charged applicable taxes. Offer not valid in Quebec. This offer is limited to one order per household. Not valid for current subscribers to Love Inspired Historical books. All orders subject to credit approval. Credit or debit balances in a customer's account(s) may be offset by any other outstanding balance owed by or to the customer. Please allow 4 to 6 weeks for delivery. Offer available while quantities last.

Your Privacy—The Harlequin® Reader Service is committed to protecting your privacy. Our Privacy Policy is available online at www.ReaderService.com or upon request from the Harlequin Reader Service.

We make a portion of our mailing list available to reputable third parties that offer products we believe may interest you. If you prefer that we not exchange your name with third parties, or if you wish to clarify or modify your communication preferences, please visit us at www.ReaderService.com/consumerchoice or write to us at Harlequin Reader Service Preference Service, P.O. Box 9062, Buffalo, NY 14269. Include your complete name and address.

LIH13R

SPECIAL EXCERPT FROM

Love Inspired

A new job has brought Heath Monroe to Whisper Falls.
Cassie Blackwell might just convince him to stay. Read on
for a preview of THE LAWMAN'S HONOR
by Linda Goodnight, Book #4 in the
WHISPER FALLS series.

As he left the garage and started down Easy Street, a jaywalker caught his attention.

He whipped the car into a U-turn and parked at an angle in front of Evie's Sweets and Eats. He pressed the window button and watched as Cassie stepped up on the curb.

"Morning," he said.

"How are you?"

Better now.

"Healing." He touched the bruise over his left cheekbone. "How's it look?"

"Awful." But her smile softened the word.

Cassie had something that appealed to him. A kind of chic wholesomeness mixed with Southern friendly and a dash of real pretty.

He hitched his chin toward the bakery. "Were you going in there?"

"Lunch. Want to come?"

"Best invitation I've had all day." The ankle screamed at the first step, causing an involuntary hiss that infuriated Heath.

Cassie paused, watching him. "You're still in pain."

"No, I'm fine."

She made a disbelieving noise in the back of her throat. "You remind me so much of my brother."

"Must be a great guy."